LOVE DUST

A whimsical Romance that may or may not be true.

KAY CHANDLER
A MULTI-AWARD-WINNING AUTHOR

i

This full-length novel has been lengthened and revised from the Novella, "Gonna Sit Right Down & Write Myself a Letter. Names, characters, places and incidents are products of the author's imagination or used fictitiously.

Scripture taken from the King James Version of the Holy Bible

Cover Design by Chase Chandler

Dedicated

To all first loves and the unforgettable memories

PROLOGUE

HHS Graduation night
Twenty long years ago

Liz Farley slid into a wooden booth at the Heartsboro Diner, across from her high school sweetheart, Mack Mackenzie. It was *their* booth—the one they always sat in. She ran her fingers over the initials MM + LF carved inside a crude heart, while recalling the night Mack whittled the letters on the tabletop. It was the night she promised to marry him after they finished college.

Her throat tightened when he tilted his head and embraced her with his eyes, in the same tender way he always looked at her. He ordered an ice-cream float with two straws—just as he'd done after each Pep Rally, every Thursday night.

Nothing appeared out of the ordinary, yet Liz sensed nothing would ever be the same. A strange silence dominated their space.

She was a cheerleader. He was the center on the basketball team. He had a scholarship to State—she'd soon be leaving for

Cottonvale Teachers College. Seldom at a loss for words, yet tonight the words stuck in her throat, choking her.

Mack pulled a small box wrapped in shiny white paper from his pocket. "I hope you didn't mind missing the Graduation Party tonight, Liz, but I wanted to be alone with you when you opened your gift."

Her mouth gaped open. "Mack, I'm so sorry. I don't have anything for you."

"Having you close to me is all I want—all I'll ever want." He leaned in and brushed a wisp of hair from her face and winked. "Well, maybe all except for one of your pecan pies every night for the rest of my life."

"One day, I'll have my own bakery, and you can have all the pies you want."

"I'm counting on it."

Liz glanced down at Mack's hands and giggled. "Are you gonna sit there and hold it, or can I see what's in it?"

His lip curled as he placed the tiny box in her hands.

She ripped off the paper and lifted the lid from a jewelry box. Her eyes widened. "Oh, Mack, it's beautiful."

"You really like it?"

"I love it." He slipped the ring on her finger, and she thrust her hand forward to admire the gold band with three sparkly chips. Diamonds or glass, she didn't care. It was a ring from Mack Mackenzie. That's all that mattered.

"It's a promise ring. One day, I'll buy you an engagement ring

3

with a diamond that doesn't require a magnifying glass to see it."

Throwing her arms around his neck, she gushed, "No, Mack. I'll never want another. This is perfect. I love it. I'll wear it until my hair turns gray and my teeth fall out."

Wrapping his arm around her shoulder, he pulled her close. "When that happens, look across the table. I'll be the ol' geezer gumming his oatmeal."

CHAPTER 1

Twenty years later . . .

"You did what?" Liz Blackstone shrieked. "Maggie, please tell me you're joking."

Liz's spry, elderly neighbor Maggie Askew curled her arms over her head. "Oh, honey, don't get your tonsils twisted. *Luvluvluv.com* is a reputable online dating service and trust me, those folks really know their business. They found the perfect match for you. He thinks you're a doll. Humor me, hon, and take a peek at his picture on my computer. Please?"

A sudden rush of nausea sent Liz to the bathroom gagging. Maggie had pulled some real doozies before, but nothing to compare with this latest fiasco. Wiping her face with a wet cloth, Liz thought of the many other outlandish stunts she'd managed to live through, but she had a gut feeling she might not be so lucky this time.

Maggie stood at the door and yelled, "I only did it because I love you, Liz." When there was no answer, she added, "And did I tell you how handsome he is?"

The door popped open, and Liz stormed out. Her voice quaked. "Maggie, how many times do I have to say it? I don't need a man in my life. Why can't you get it through your thick head?"

Wringing her hands, Maggie whined, "Oh, dear. I was afraid you'd take it like this, but—"

"Then why did you do it? Why, Maggie? Besides the fact I have no plans to start dating again, do you know how many predators come out of the woodwork when you put your name on those lists? You could be setting me up with a serial killer. Did the thought ever cross your mind, Miss Matchmaker?" Liz pounded her head with both hands. "This is the most idiotic, harebrained, frightening stunt you've ever pulled, and you've pulled your share."

"Lizzie, if you'll stop ranting long enough for me to explain, you'll see you have nothing to fear. He's not a killer, I promise, and the fact that you're only twenty-nine is why I did this. You're too young to remain a widow."

"I'm thirty-seven and you know it."

"Okay, I'll admit I might've fudged a little—so, you're almost forty, which only serves as a gruesome reminder that your clock is tick, tick, ticking."

Liz grimaced. *Almost forty?*

"Take it from one who knows, sweetie. The older we get, the

faster the clock ticks. I was like you when Robert died. I didn't think I needed anyone, either, but there are times I've regretted not finding someone to share these golden years with."

Though Maggie's meddlesome ways often made Liz want to pull her hair out, she couldn't deny her neighbor had been a Godsend. If only she could keep her out of her personal affairs—or lack thereof.

Maggie's youthful appearance defied her age. She looked fifteen years younger than her seventy-six years, which Liz contributed to three factors: Love, health and wealth. For forty-two years, Maggie had a wonderful husband who loved her dearly and showered her with affection. Liz contended that true love was a known youth potion, although she didn't want a dose of it herself. She'd rather shrivel up and die than take her chances on another man.

Maggie was financially secure, and Liz asserted that with enough money, any woman could look younger than her years. Maggie took care of herself and was in excellent health. Although she often complained about her hearing, and being forgetful, Liz didn't believe either complaint to be valid. Maggie Askew could hear what she wanted to hear and remember what she wanted to remember. She was more like a mother to Liz than a neighbor—an occasional bossy, sometimes nosey and oftentimes overly protective, meddling mother.

Maggie said, "Hon, after that little hissy fit you just threw, I almost forgot what I came here for." Pulling a small manila envelope from her apron pocket, she waved it in the air. "I brought you something and I can hardly wait for you to open it."

"What is it?"

Maggie held it up to the light and squinted. "I can't tell. The postman put it in my box by mistake." She handed it to Liz. "Go ahead and open it, honey. I think it might be from him."

"Him?" Liz shoved it back into Maggie's hands. "If this is an invitation for a date, you can take my place. I've had one man in my life, and I don't need another, thank you very much."

****

Jim MacKenzie missed his sweet Thelma. He now questioned the decision he made four years ago when he moved into the exclusive condo on the Gulf of Mexico with his son, Doyle. Jim's bedroom window overlooked the beautiful white sands and sparkling emerald waters. He couldn't deny there was no grander view than the gorgeous sunsets. But Jim was homesick for the little house in Heartsboro where he and his wife Thelma lived for over fifty years.

Doyle had been insistent on the move and after weeks of badgering, Jim reluctantly agreed. He must've been out of his mind. It wasn't as if he hadn't sincerely tried to adjust to his new surroundings, but he was weary of trying. Not only had he lost his darling wife, but he'd given up his home, his church, the domino club and all his friends. The only thing he had in Point Clear was his son, whom he seldom saw because Doyle was a workaholic. He longed to be back in Heartsboro, his little hometown in Southeast

Alabama, but Doyle wouldn't hear of it.

Jim constantly dreamed of going back to the place where he and Thelma met and fell in love. It was where they raised Doyle, their only child. It was where they went to church as a family. It was where they attended all of Doyle's baseball and basketball games. All the memories worth keeping were made in Heartsboro. Jim didn't know who came up with the slogan, "The Little Town with a Big Heart," but it was fitting, indeed. According to popular folklore, Heartsboro was the birthplace of Cupid and though Jim had never been one to put much confidence in the rumors surrounding the legend, neither could he disprove them. All he knew for sure was that over half the couples in town claimed to have found love at the annual Cupid's Ball held on February 14th, every year.

Though he'd made many friends in Point Clear, it wasn't the same as the friends he'd had forever. He knew his son only wanted what he thought was best for him, but sometimes best is not good enough.

Doyle had pestered him for a year after Thelma died to move in with him before he ever agreed. He wouldn't have given in if it hadn't been for the promise he made to his precious wife before her death. Now, sadly, it seemed he may have made a promise he couldn't keep. On her death bed, Thelma made him promise to "help our boy find a good woman—someone who'll love him as much as we do." Jim gave his word, although he had no idea how difficult the undertaking would prove to be. That is, until George, a

9

friend of his at the Senior Citizens Center introduced him to a dating service called luvluvluv.com.

George encouraged Jim to join, but Jim let him know quickly he was not interested. He still considered himself to be a married man, even though Thelma had been dead almost five years. He couldn't imagine himself with another woman. His son, however, was a different story, he told George. "Now that boy needs a woman in his life, but I'd never in a million years be able to convince Doyle to sign up with a dating service."

"I thought your son's name was Mack."

"No, that's what everybody calls him, but his Mama and I named him Doyle. It was her maiden name. Kids in school started calling him Mack years ago. Now everybody calls him that, but I still call him Doyle."

"If you can't get him to sign up, then why don't you sign up for him?"

Jim scratched his head. "Can I do that?"

"Sure, just use his name, and when you find some sweet looking thing you'd like to have for your daughter-in-law, you pour it on her good."

"Pour what on?"

"You know, Jim . . . those sweet nothings women want to hear. It's simple. You fill out a form, which will ask for hobbies and that sort of thing."

"Why do they want to know what my hobbies are?"

"Not yours, ignoramus. You type in Doyle's hobbies. He

10

doesn't have time to go wife hunting, so you're doing it in his place. It's done all the time. It's what you call role-playing. And who knows him better than his ol' man?"

Jim's cheeks billowed with air. He exhaled slowly. "I'm in trouble if he has to have hobbies. He works all the time. No woman wants to hear that."

"Jim, you've got to use the ol' noggin. Think! What would he do if he didn't work all the time?"

"I don't know. That's all he ever does. What are some good hobbies, George?"

"Read the personal ads in Sunday's paper. You'll get ideas from there. Some of the popular hobbies are 'taking romantic moonlight walks along the beach, candlelight dinners, traveling to exotic places . . . things like that. That wins 'em over every time. That's how I found Myrtle and that woman is the apple of my eye. I just copied some of the stuff I read in the personals. Worked like a charm."

"This sounds interesting enough, George, but what if I get the apple core and not the apple? What do I do?"

"Jim, you have to think of it like using bait when you're fishing. You throw it out and see what you can pull up. If you don't catch what you want the first time, then try a different bait. I caught me some doozies before Myrtle took my bait, but I kept letting 'em off the hook until I found me a real keeper. Women are romantics. They want to hear all that mushy stuff. Just take my advice, Jim, and Doyle will thank you for it later. I wouldn't take a pretty penny for landing Myrtle. She's quite a gal." George clicked his tongue and winked.

Jim took copious notes. He logged on to the site the way George taught him and filled out the application. He typed he was searching for a lady with high morals between the ages of twenty-five and forty, within a 150-mile radius from Point Clear Beach. He went through Thelma's picture album and found the best-looking picture of Doyle he could find.

He figured George knew what he was talking about, because he took his advice and didn't have to look long before he found the perfect girl for Doyle. She was the prettiest apple on the tree—a real looker with long dark hair hanging loosely around her shoulders. All she needed was one of those tiara thingies to make her look like a Princess out of a Fairytale book. Jim could hardly wait to tell his son the good news, but he figured it best to wait until he had her ready to reel in. His lip curled when he looked at Thelma's picture on the mantle. "Oh, Mama, I know you'd approve of Elizabeth. She's a real humdinger."

****

Maggie tapped the unopened manila envelope against her palm several times. "Hmm . . . I wonder what he wants?"

"I can probably answer that for you."

"Tell me, Liz—am I so wrong to want you to know what true love feels like?"

"I do know, Maggie, and it's not for the faint of heart."

"Hon, trust me, I understand why you believe as you do. If I'd been married to Carter Blackstone, I'm sure I'd feel the same way. You went from the frying pan into the fire after getting burned in college by that Mark fellow and then you turned right around and married Carter on the rebound." Rolling her eyes, she mumbled, "May his conniving soul rest in peace."

Liz felt the resentment building. "There you go again. Enough already about Carter, and his name was Mack, not Mark. Please, stop it, Maggie. I'm sick and tired of your meddling." Liz cringed at the snarky tone in her voice. It wasn't as if this was their first conversation about finding her a man, yet as many times as the subject came up, neither were likely to budge on their position.

"I know I shouldn't speak ill of the dead, but I'm just saying all men aren't controlling like Carter Blackstone."

"Maggie!" Liz bit her tongue to keep from blurting what was in her heart. She knew they weren't all like Carter. True, her late husband had been everything Maggie claimed but Liz had learned to love him despite his faults. She admitted she had a few of her own. Undeniably, the love she felt for Carter wasn't the same kind of love she once had for Mack Mackenzie—but Mack was her first love. She fought back the tears. Wasn't first love supposed to be special? Stronger passion, deeper hurts? The familiar ache in the pit of her stomach returned. The passion died sixteen years ago, but the hurt caused from the betrayal would live forever.

Maggie closed her eyes and sniffed. The appetizing aroma of buttery syrup and oven-roasted pecans wafting through the kitchen door brought a smile. "Ah! Is that a pecan pie, I smell? Did you bake it to sell in the kiosk or do you need me to taste-test it for you?"

Without responding, Liz led the way into the kitchen, although there were more important things than pies occupying her thoughts. She could only imagine how much of her private life might be floating around in cyberspace.

CHAPTER 2

Mack Mackenzie and his longtime friend, Luke McGallagher were enjoying a business lunch at the famous Salty Seas Restaurant in Fairhope, Alabama. The beautiful building with its original wood floors, high ceilings and winding staircase leading to a balcony had held many dances among the elites in the late 1800's. White cloths and a vase with a single red rose graced each of the antique oak tables. But it was the magnificent buffet that made it a popular dining spot for business luncheons.

Both men grew up in the same small Alabama town on the Florida line. Owner of Mackenzie Construction Company with offices in Mobile and Fairhope, Mack had recently designed and constructed a large processing plant for Luke in their hometown of Heartsboro. As the men attempted to guess the ingredients in the Mystery Crabmeat Salad from the exotic buffet, the conversation evolved from business to personal.

Luke smacked his lips. "I don't know what I'm eating, but it's delicious."

"I thought you'd like it. I eat here every chance I get. Say, I was surprised to learn the Oyster Bar in Heartsboro is still open. Maybe I'll go back one day to see if the oysters are as good as I remember them."

"You won't be disappointed. The only thing that's changed in the last fifty years is the calendar. Remember Shorty? He's still shucking those suckers faster than you can let 'em slide down your throat. He must be in his eighties, by now. He's been there forever. Speaking of Heartsboro, did you get your invitation to the HHS Homecoming?"

Mack sipped on his coffee, then nodded. "Hard to believe it'll be my twentieth reunion."

"Say, why don't we get together while we're there? We'll let Shorty get a workout shucking oysters. My class will be celebrating our tenth."

"Rub it in, will you, kid?" Mack gave a bleak laugh, then lowered his head. "Actually, I've never been back for an HHS Homecoming, and I won't be attending this one."

"Man, that's a shame. I try not to miss them. Going out of town?"

"No, I don't want to go back and risk seeing her again."

"Her? Who are we talking about?"

Raking his fingers through his hair, Mack said, "I forgot, you wouldn't know since you were barely out of diapers when it

16

happened. Forget I mentioned it. It's not a very interesting story."

"Hey, you can't leave me hanging. Who's the woman?"

Mack wrung his hands under the table. What possessed him to open that can of worms? Now that he had, he might as well finish what he started. "I was once engaged to a classmate. Man, I thought she was straight from heaven, and I felt I was one lucky guy." He took a sip of water to wet his dry throat. "She was a knockout, and I suppose I allowed her looks to deceive me into thinking she was as wholesome and beautiful on the inside as she appeared on the outside."

"Not so, huh?"

"You can say that again. Liz Farley and I dated our last two years of high school and planned to marry after college." He paused. "I think I'll head back to the buffet. I saw pecan pie on the dessert table." If he was lucky, he could change the subject when he returned.

He sat back down with his pie, and the waiter came over and refilled his coffee cup. Mack took a bite of pie and licked his lips. You should try it, Luke. It's delicious. "Almost as good as—" He paused. "As any I've ever tasted."

"You say you were engaged? What happened?"

So much for redirecting the conversation. Why not tell the whole ugly truth. He had no reason to feel ashamed. Besides, after sixteen years, it was water under the bridge, as they say. "A few months before I graduated from State, I got a letter from her boyfriend."

"Her *boyfriend*? Yikes."

Mack's nostrils flared. "Yep. Out of the blue, the guy wrote and said Liz was no longer wearing my ring, and she wanted to know if I'd rather have it mailed to my home address or sent to my dorm. She didn't even have the guts to break up with me to my face."

"Man, that's tough. You had no idea she was seeing someone?"

"Not a clue. But when I went back and reread her letters, I picked up on the hints. She wrote, 'Mack I feel so lucky to have a principal like Carter Blackstone, who is interested in my future plans." He shook his head slowly. "I should've known at that point."

Luke scratched his head.

"Don't you get it? They were planning her future, after she'd led me to believe her future was with me. I didn't even catch on when she called him Carter. That's not common practice, is it? For an intern to call her principal by his first name?"

"Maybe I'm slow, Mack but if that was all you had to go on, it seems to me you've been beating yourself up over something you couldn't have possibly known."

"Well, you haven't heard the clincher yet. When I reread her last letter, it was like a warning light flashing in my brain. She wrote, 'You know it's funny but in high school I had a fear of being sent to the principal's office. Now I go there all the time. Ha Ha!'" Mack's Adam's apple bobbed. "It was the 'ha-ha' part that tore me up. As you can imagine, I felt like a dunce."

Luke's eyes squinted. "I'm trying to imagine, though it's still a little fuzzy. So, after you received the boyfriend's letter, did you write him back?"

"Why should I? I didn't owe him anything. I sent Liz a letter and simply said something to the effect, 'Keep the ring, I don't want anything that reminds me of you. I hope you have a wonderful future, because I plan to. I got along without you before I met you, and I can get along without you now.' That was it. I was through, and I haven't looked back, since."

Luke took a swig of tea and waited for Mack to finish what he started.

Mack picked up his napkin. "Well, I guess I'm lying to myself, huh?" Blotting his lips, he said, "I judge from your expression that you know as well as I, that I've never looked forward since that day, although I've wanted to. I'd give anything if I could find someone to love, the way I loved that girl, if for no other reason but to satisfy my dad."

"Your dad?"

"Yeah, Pop stays on my back constantly to start dating again. But to be honest, Luke, I'm not sure I could ever trust another woman. It's been over sixteen years. You'd think I'd forget."

"Believe me, I understand. Whatever happened to her?"

"She married the guy." Mack shoved his chair back. "Man, how did we ever get on the subject of my sorry love life? I can't think of a more boring subject."

Luke said, "Well, we could talk about mine, if you'd like to compare bad to worse."

"You too?" Mack grimaced. "That's all these Homecomings are good for . . . it's just to get us thinking about all the old heartaches of high school, and I guess everybody's got a story to tell. Why don't they just pour salt in our wounds about every ten years, instead of trying to get us all together to rehash relationships gone awry?"

"So, is the memory of that little girl the only thing that's kept you from attending your Homecomings? If it is, you're crazy, man. She's not worth it. I thought you told her you planned to have a good life. What will she think if you never go back?"

"Who cares what she thinks?"

"I'll tell you what she'll think." Luke upped his voice two octaves and batted his eyes as he facetiously played the part of Mack's old girlfriend. She'll think, "Poor Mack is still so heartsick over losing me, that he can't bear to face me."

"I get your point, but to tell the truth, I don't want her finding out I never married and have her thinking I'm still in love with her."

"Are you?"

"Are you kidding? I've fought daily, just to keep from hating her. I suppose I've spent more time confessing that sin than all the others put together."

"So, you're still in love with her?"

"Sheesh, Luke. You should've been a psychologist. You seem

to know what I'm saying, even when I'm telling you the opposite."

"It's not what's coming out of your mouth that I'm hearing. It's what's coming from your heart. Maybe I understand because I've been there. But please, Mack, you need to go. Don't let that Carter guy take everything away from you. He took your girl. Are you gonna let him take all your high school friends from you, too? You'll be surprised how many people you'll see over the weekend. Believe me, Heartsboro knows how to do a Homecoming. It's terrific."

The guys finished their lunch, and before Luke drove away, he stuck his head out the window and yelled, "I'll look for you Wednesday night, the twelfth, at Shorty's. You'll be glad you came, I promise. Be there!"

****

Mack went to look at a building site after lunch, then met with an engineer at the coffee shop to go over some drawings. Heading back to the office, he mulled over Luke's words, 'Don't let that Carter guy take everything away from you. He took your girl. You gonna let him take your friends from you too?' He dug through the papers on his desk, until he found the Homecoming invitation.

He couldn't count the times in a four-hour period that he changed his mind about going to Heartsboro. One minute he was set to go, and the next, he counted the many reasons why he shouldn't. But Luke's words kept rolling over in his mind like a hamster on a monotonous wheel. Don't let Carter take everything . . . take everything . . . take everything.

Mack couldn't get the conversation out of his head as he drove home. "Luke's right. Why should I let Liz and that creep control my life? Debate's over. I'm going." He called the committee chairman, and told her to count him in.

He walked out on the deck of his condo around dusk, sat down on the glider and stared at the ominous gray clouds shifting and regrouping. The smell of ozone after the afternoon rain had a clean, refreshing smell and it appeared another shower could be on the way. His head throbbed. Why did he make the call, saying he'd go? Did he really want to go back to the place that held painful memories he'd spent years trying to forget? Licking his lips, he could taste the salt coming from off the Gulf. If only he could invent a way to shift and regroup like the clouds—leaving the old behind and coming up with a happy new beginning.

It seemed everything Mack went after in life he had managed to achieve with great success. Everything, except Liz Farley. At thirty-seven-years old, he had a thriving business and owned a strip of exclusive condominiums at Point Clear Beach, near the Grand Hotel. He wouldn't be able to spend all the money he had if he lived to be a hundred. The faster he gave it away to charities, the more he seemed to accumulate. Drinking an ice-cold glass of sweet tea, he watched as the sun set over the beautiful emerald waters, creating a Masterpiece. Why was he so miserable? He had it all. What more could one ask? The answer came quickly—someone to share his good fortune with—someone besides his moody father, who failed to see the beauty outside his window for grieving over what he left behind in Heartsboro.

Jim walked out on the deck. "I opened a can of biscuits and made corned beef hash and for supper, Doyle. You ready to eat a bite?"

"Sounds good, Pop, but I'm not hungry. I met a client at the coffee shop before I came home, so I ate a sandwich there. I should've called to let you know."

"No problem. It came from a can. I just heated it up."

Mack stood and wrapped his arm around his dad's shoulder. They walked inside and Jim had just sat down at the table when Mack popped the question: "Pop, how would you like to go back to Heartsboro?"

Jim's heart pounded so fast he was afraid he'd have a heart attack sitting there at the table. "Do you mean it, Doyle? You're really gonna let me go home?"

"Dad, you *are* home." He waved his arm in a sweeping motion, pointing out the luxurious accommodations. "*This* is your home, but my high school class will be having our Homecoming in a couple of weeks, and I've decided to go. I thought you might like to go back with me. We'll stay at the B&B from Wednesday until Sunday, which will give you an opportunity to visit with some of your pals."

Jim's face lit up. If I remember correctly, Homecoming always takes place the week of Valentine's Day."

Mack picked up the newspaper and nodded. It was obvious he

was through talking, but Jim didn't mind. He was going home, even if only for a few days.

CHAPTER 3

Maggie drew the white starched curtains away from the bay window in Liz's kitchen and stood watching as a few dark clouds moved slowly against a pale gray sky. "Looks like we might get a shower today."

Invoking the silent treatment, Liz clamped her lips together while pulling out a bronze-colored bag of coffee from the cabinet.

Maggie quietly watched her scoop coffee from the bag, dump it into the pot, and fill the carafe with water. "Well, bless your heart, Lizzie. Even though you're miffed and don't want to talk to me, you're brewing my favorite. You know how I love hazelnut. Thank you, honey. That's sweet of you."

Liz shot a glassy stare, unwilling to admit she purposely reached for the flavored coffee, knowing it was Maggie's favorite. *I should make her drink dishwater. Would serve her right.* Opening the cabinet, she took out two mugs and two dessert plates.

Without another word, Maggie took the dishes from Liz and placed them on the table. She opened the silverware drawer, removed two forks and sat them next to the plates, then strategically placed the unopened manila envelope in the center of the table.

Liz strummed her fingers on the granite countertop and watched the coffee drip slowly into the pot.

Maggie took a seat at the small oak table and planted her elbows on the red-and-white checkered oil cloth. She gnawed on her fist and watched Liz wipe off the kitchen counter.

Breaking the awkward silence, Maggie blurted, "Those clouds are forming fast. We could sure use the rain."

Liz snarled. "Seriously?"

Maggie's shoulders lifted. "I gather from your expression you don't agree. Actually, I don't know why I said it. Just seems to be something people say a lot."

Rolling her eyes, Liz said, "Seldom do people say it after it's rained five days straight, leaving the ground water-logged."

Giggling, Maggie lifted her shoulders in a shrug. "Oh. I suppose you're right. I had something else on my mind. I wasn't thinking about what I was saying."

"That's your problem, Maggie. You don't think. If you did, you would never have done something so outlandish. A stupid dating service? Really? I am so angry with you." Liz lifted a slice of pecan pie onto a dessert plate. She shoved it toward Maggie and waited for the coffee to finish brewing. There was only one thing on her mind as she pressed her back against the wall—her picture might be on next week's front page, under the caption 'Missing

Woman.'

Maggie forked a smile slice of pie, then smacked her lips. "Hon, I'm serious when I say there's no one who can bake a better pecan pie than you. What makes yours different?"

"Flour," she answered bluntly. "Memaw always put a tablespoon of flour in her pecan pies, but please don't try to change the subject, Maggie. This stunt you've pulled isn't going to go away by itself and I want to know what you plan to do about it."

"Lizzie, I know you're upset with me, but if you'll take a peek at his picture on my computer, you'll feel much better. Can I just tell you if I were your age, you wouldn't stand a chance with this one? I'd snatch him up myself. You've simply got to see his picture, honey. He's a real cool cat. . . the bomb. . . all that, and a bag of chips, as we used to say in my day."

Liz groaned. "You don't even know which era is yours and I've probably already seen his photo—plastered on the Post Office wall."

Maggie cackled. "You're a card, Lizzie Blackstone."

Liz picked up the coffee carafe and filled their cups, then sat it back on the hot plate. Sliding her chair out, she plopped down across the table from Maggie, took in a deep breath, then let it seep out in a slow whisper of air. She had to get control of her emotions. There was no need in letting her anger ruin a friendship. She supposed Maggie meant well, but how many times could she keep using that lame excuse? Maggie's well-intent could literally be the death of them both. "Maggie, I'm trying hard not to be angry with

27

you. I am. I'm sorry I yelled. But please tell me how you know he's not a creep, trying to con vulnerable women—and trust me, only a vulnerable woman would employ the use of a stupid matchmaking service."

Maggie's face lit up. "That's not entirely true. What about me, honey?"

Liz almost smiled. "Point made. I have to tell you, Maggie, this scares me. Now he knows my name, and he's probably a hardened criminal."

"No, he's not."

"And you know that because—"

"I know, because I've been corresponding with him for three whole weeks—using your name and picture, of course. I can tell you all about him. Just ask me anything. Go ahead."

Liz threw her hands in the air and screamed. "My picture? No! Maggie, please say it isn't so. Tell me this is a horrible nightmare and that you didn't put my picture on the internet."

Maggie's eyes twinkled with excitement. "Oh, I did, alright. He thinks I'm you, and sugar, with my help, your love life is really spicing up." She blushed. "It hasn't been so long ago that I've forgotten what men want to hear. I can't wait to show you the emails and let you read what you said."

Liz couldn't breathe. Her hands shook, sloshing coffee from her cup. "What *I* said? Are you nuts?"

Maggie grabbed a napkin and wiped the spill. "You may feel that way now, but you'll thank me later, honey. You're quite a little flirt, you are—but don't worry, sugar, he adores you." She cupped her hands over her mouth, and whispered, "Psst . . . I think you're in love, Lizzie. I declare, he's so precious, if I could reach inside that monitor, I'd squeeze him for you. I've been simply ecstatic over how well things are going. Oh, my lands, you're gonna die when you see him."

Liz moaned. "You could be right about the dying part, Maggie. Have you never heard of stalkers? They often kill."

"Fiddle-faddle. He's no monster. You're getting riled over nothing. Wait until you meet this guy. He's even made my heart do cartwheels a time or two—and if I wasn't sixty-five—"

With clinched teeth, Liz grumbled. "You're not sixty-five, and probably can't even remember that far back."

Maggie leaned across the table and laid her hand on Liz's forearm, though Liz jerked back. "Now, now, honey, you've got this all wrong. I knew from the beginning he was perfect for you. He enjoys romantic moonlight walks on the beach, trips to exotic places, candlelight dinners and best of all, he's self-employed, which means he can meet with you anytime. Oh, and such a romantic, he is!" Maggie fanned her face and swooned. "Now how does that sound?"

Liz shrieked. "Are you kidding? It sounds like he could be an unemployed serial killer, Maggie. I don't mean to sound ungrateful. I suppose you meant well—just like you meant well when you sent the wacky astrologer and the bike rider brute with a ring in his nose over here, but this time you've really crossed the line."

"I'm sorry, Liz. Well, not particularly sorry for doing what I did, but sorry you're angry at me. I suppose I should've asked your permission before signing you up with the website."

"You suppose?"

"It breaks my heart, though, to see you wasting your years all alone, the way I've done. It's too late for me, but honey, you're still a young woman and very attractive when you want to be. But look at you. You have gorgeous hair but pulling it back in a ponytail with a tacky scrunchy is not very chic. There are other ways to wear it up that would be much more becoming. I wish you'd get Denise to style it for you."

"I'm not trying to be chic, Maggie."

"That's my point. You don't try. You have a lovely complexion, but I'd like to see you wear a little lipstick . . . and those sweatpants—ugh."

Liz looked down at her pants and pulled slightly on one leg. "What's wrong with them?"

"Really? You have to ask? They're sloppy, hon. If I was packaged like you, you can bet I'd choose a prettier wrapping. Granted, you made two bad decisions, but it's no reason to give up on love—not at your age. Use the past as a learning tool to not make the same mistakes again."

Liz crossed her arms over her midsection. "Maggie—"

"Okay, that's it. I won't say another word. But I can't help wanting the best for you. Lizzie, you know I couldn't love you more if you were my own daughter."

Maggie clasped her hands under her chin. "If you aren't gonna open the envelope, do you mind if I peek? I'm dying to see what he wrote you."

Taking Liz's slight shrug to mean permission granted, Maggie tore into it and pulled out two pages. Her eyes widened as she glared at the contents. She held it for several minutes, then chuckled. "Well, what d'ya know. All that frettin' for naught."

****

Jim sat at the computer, talking to himself while staring at the monitor. In the past three wonderful weeks, he'd already said all the sweet nothings he knew. He needed help. "It's been too long since Thelma and I courted. Shucks, I can't remember what I said yesterday, and I sure can't recall what I said fifty years ago. I must've had a mighty good line, though, because she was pretty as a speckled pup. I still don't know how I did it."

After typing several lines, and then deleting them, he finally decided to take George's advice. George had reminded him that King Solomon was the wisest man who ever lived, and he had a whole bevy of women falling at his feet. And how did he do it? George insisted it was in knowing how to compose a good love letter.

Jim reached in the desk drawer and pulled out his Bible. If it worked for Solomon, there was no reason it shouldn't work for Doyle.

He'd read the letters in Solomon's Song before, but reading

them now, caused him to shake his head in wonder. He felt a hot blush rising to his cheeks. He couldn't understand why such strange words would impress any woman—Thelma wouldn't have been impressed. But then Thelma was a very special woman. Jim was sure the women in King Solomon's harem weren't of the same caliber as his darling bride.

Maybe it was time to tell Doyle about Elizabeth and let him do his own writing. One look at her picture would be all the inspiration he'd need.

CHAPTER 4

Maggie ran her finger over the empty dessert plate, swiping the last of the pecan pie filling while staring at the contents of the envelope.

Rolling her eyes, Liz grunted. "You don't have to lick the plate, Maggie. There's plenty." She picked up the knife and cut her another slice.

Maggie snickered. "A second helping? Does this mean I'm forgiven?"

"It most certainly does not mean any such thing." With her hands clasped tightly around the warm mug, Liz sipped slowly, waiting for Maggie to reveal what she found to be so intriguing in the letter that she couldn't bring herself to put it down. What was she waiting for?

"

"Well, this is certainly not what I thought it was, honey." Maggie thrust it toward Liz. "Take a look."

Not wanting to appear curious, Liz pretended it was of no

interest. She pushed her chair back and ambled slowly over to the coffee pot. "Would you like a refill?"

"I've had plenty, thank you. Don't you want to see your mail?"

"Not particularly. I figure if it was very interesting, you would've told me."

Maggie giggled. "Hon, it's an invitation to a Homecoming at Heartsboro High School."

"Homecoming?" Liz swiped a strand of hair away from her eyes and picked up the mail. The muscles in her face relaxed, as she perused the brochure. "Wow, I told you I was getting old . . . twenty years. In some ways, it seems much longer." She tossed the invitation on the table and gazed out the window. A lump formed in her throat.

"Liz, I've heard of Heartsboro all my life, but I've never been there. Didn't you once tell me it was near Florida?"

"As a matter of fact, it's on the Florida line."

Maggie lit up like a giant glow-worm on a dark night. Her hopes soared beyond her wildest expectations. Heartsboro? What an ideal in-between-place for Liz and Doyle to meet. With Liz living in Cottonvale and Doyle in Point Clear, Heartsboro would be doable for them both. The trick would be in talking Liz into attending her Homecoming. She picked up the invitation and gushed. "Isn't this an impressive itinerary? I'm jealous. I wish I'd graduated from HHS."

Without commenting, Liz sipped the last of the cold coffee in her cup.

"Won't it be fun? Did you read the last paragraph? Every class will be responsible for decorating a float with a Valentine theme. Doesn't that sound lovely?" Apparently, Maggie wasn't anticipating a response since she forged ahead without a pause. "I've always wanted to ride on a float."

Liz plunked her fork down and shoved her dessert plate aside. "Fine, Maggie. Why don't you take my place?"

Maggie ignored the remark. "Honey, you and I need to go find you something special to wear. Edna's Boutique in Montgomery is having a huge sale. They'll be opening their doors at eight o'clock in the morning. We need to be there when they open, to get the best deals."

"You aren't hearing me, Maggie. I'm not going to Homecoming, so forget it. I hardly know those people, and I doubt they remember me."

"Sure, they do, sweetie, you went to school together for twelve long years. What about the girls on the cheerleading squad?"

"I know who they were, Maggie. I don't know who they are. There's a big difference."

"You're wrong, honey. Once you get with them, it'll be like old times. And we'll have you looking so gorgeous, that Matt fellow who dumped you will be eating his heart out."

"Mack. His name is Mack," Liz said softly. Mack wasn't her

only reason for not wanting to go. She had no desire to spend a whole weekend listening to strangers swapping stories about their adorable children. Liz could think of nothing more depressing, since she always felt the need to explain why she and Carter chose not to start a family. How could she explain something she never understood, herself? She glared out the window.

Maggie's brow shot up. "What about it, hon? You *will* go, won't you? It'll be good for you."

"No, Maggie. It's out of the question. My high school homecoming is the last place on earth I want to go."

"Will you at least promise to pray about it before making a decision?"

Liz snorted. "Actually, I was under the impression I'd already made a decision. Were you not listening?"

"Lizzie, don't make a snap decision. I have a real strong feeling that going back to your roots could be life-changing for you."

"I didn't realize my life needed changing, Maggie. I'm perfectly happy with things as they are. I can think of nothing else that I need. I have my kiosk, a great place to park it across from the Court House and when court is in session, I can't bake enough to fill all the orders. Being able to bake at home on my off days has made it ideal for me. I have all the business I can handle from such a small operation. Life is good."

Maggie stood, walked back of Liz's chair and placed her hands on her shoulders. She leaned over and whispered, "That was a lot of explaining. I'm not sure if you're trying to convince me or yourself that your life is hunky-dory and there's nothing you wish to change. Frankly, my dear, I think you're afraid."

Her neck stiffened. "That's ridiculous. Why would I be afraid?"

"I'm sure you can answer that better than I. Why don't we put the invitation on your fridge, as a reminder to pray about it?"

"But why would I pray about going, when I'm not the least bit interested?"

"Are you afraid to pray about it? Afraid I'm right and you're wrong?"

"That's ridiculous, and you know it." Liz groaned. She might as well pack her bags and make reservations. Maggie reminded her of the woman in the Bible who pestered the judge until she got what she asked for. Liz sometimes wondered if God didn't say, 'I may as well go ahead and tell Maggie yes whenever she asks for something because she's not gonna hush until I do.' Liz pursed her lips. "If I promise to pray about this, will you promise to refrain from trying to find me a boyfriend in the future?"

"Excuse me dear, I believe I hear my phone ringing. Gotta run. Thanks for the pie and coffee. See ya, later, sugar."

Strange. Maggie claimed to be hard of hearing, yet when a subject arose that she didn't wish to address, she could mysteriously hear her phone ringing next door.

CHAPTER 5

Mack Mackenzie was with a developer and his crew in the Conference Room, discussing plans for a multi-million-dollar shopping complex to be built in Fort Walton, when his secretary tiptoed in.

With her hand cupped over her mouth, she whispered, "Excuse me, Mr. Mackenzie, but you're needed on line three."

"Uh . . . thank you, Debbie, but would you take a message, and hold all my calls?"

"It's your father—he says it's an emergency."

"Thanks, I'll take it in my office." Rising from his chair, he said, "Pardon me gentlemen. I do apologize."

Mack went into his office and closed the door. "Pop, what's wrong?"

"Nothing's wrong with me. It's you I'm worried about," Jim replied.

"What are you talking about? I hope this is important. Debbie said it was urgent?"

"Yep, that's what I told her, all right. It's urgent."

"Pop, please! I'm terribly busy—"

"Son, that's your problem. I've been real concerned about you lately. You're always busy. You never have time for yourself. Before your Mama died, she made me promise I'd take care of you. She worried that you gave up on love after that little girl you were engaged to dumped you. I'm telling you the truth, it broke yo' Mama's heart to think you might go through life all alone. I made Thelma a promise, God bless her, that I would—"

"Pop, I have a conference room full of men, waiting for me to finish a presentation and contrary to what you might think, this conversation you and I are having doesn't fall under the heading of an emergency. We'll talk about this when I get home, okay?"

"But Son, I wanted you to know that I found the perfect—"

"No, Dad! I know where this is going, and I told you we aren't getting another dog. I loved Rusty, but he's gone. End of subject. Forget it."

"Son, I wasn't gonna say nothing about a dog. I simply wanted to tell you that I've done about all I can, and I think now it would be a good idea if you would—"

Mack slammed down the phone.

****

Later that evening, Jim sat at his computer and seeing mail in his inbox, he punched his fist in the air and read:

My Dearest Doyle,

What a lovely letter. I do admire a romantic man. I'd love to meet you face to face. You are such a handsome devil. Since I live in Cottonvale and you live in Point Clear, could we meet somewhere in between? I plan to be in the little town of Heartsboro for several days in mid-February. Would that work for you?

Jim cackled out loud. He couldn't have planned it better.

"Did you finally win at Solitaire, Pop?" Mack muttered, while reading the stock market report.

"Better than that, son, better than that." *She thinks I'm a handsome devil*—but then he remembered it was Mack's picture she'd seen, and not his. *Oh well, he got his looks from me.*

If Jim couldn't get Doyle to write his own love letters, he had no choice but to continue writing them himself. Besides, it was the most fun he'd had since before moving to Point Clear. He could hardly get one email typed, before he'd have a response. He carefully reread Elizabeth's last email, then with his fingers on the keyboard, he pecked out a reply:

My Darling Elizabeth,

I'm so excited that we'll finally meet. Heartsboro is perfect. I know the town well. May I suggest breakfast at seven o'clock, February 16th, at a little restaurant called Heartie's Diner? Any of the locals can tell you where to find it. I hope that isn't too early but I'm eager to spend as much time with you as possible. . .

****

Exhausted from worrying about what type criminal might have access to her picture and personal info, Liz welcomed the night.

What was Maggie thinking? Was the woman becoming senile?

After showering, and putting on pajamas, Liz stuck a cup of left-over coffee in the microwave. Normally, she took her supper on the porch, but tonight she wasn't hungry. She cupped her hands around the warm mug, walked outside, and laid down on the glider. The night was so quiet it felt eerie. She shivered. Where were the sounds? On any given night she could sit in the same spot and hear the plunk, plunk, plunk of a basketball dribbling on the pavement across the street. She could hear voices of neighborhood boys playing horse. She could hear dogs barking in the distance, and frogs croaking in the creek behind her house. An occasional car would pass by. But not tonight. It was quiet. Too quiet.

She longed for noises—distractions to keep her from dwelling on the very thing Maggie encouraged her to think about. 'Think about Homecoming,' Maggie said. Liz could think of nothing else. If things had worked according to plan, she and Mack would be attending their class reunion together. She couldn't bear to go back alone. Why put herself through the agony of seeing him with someone else? Did he still have thick, wavy hair—or no hair at all? Did his dark brown eyes still twinkle when he smiled, or had they dimmed with time? Remembering his broad shoulders, tight abs and thin hips, she pictured him now with a paunchy gut. The handsome square jaw that she remembered so well, was likely replaced by hanging jowls and a double chin. Her lip lifted slightly at the mental picture. There was the chance she wouldn't even recognize him, even if he did show up.

41

Running her hand under the cushion beneath her, her fingers touched the glossy paper. She grasped a photo and lifted it out. Her eyes muddled with tears as she gazed at the happy-looking couple. He wore a tux. She was dressed in a long, flowing gown. Prom night. With tears streaming down her cheeks, she ripped the picture in half. She ripped the halves. And the quarters. She kept ripping, letting the pieces fall to the floor. Her body shook with uncontrollable sobs.

She cried until there were no tears left. When the tears ceased, all the noises returned, as if on cue. She heard laughter and the familiar 'plunk, plunk, plunk. Dogs howled. Crickets chirped. Frogs croaked. Cars passed. Owls hooted. Had the sounds been there all along? Was it possible her thoughts completely drowned them out?

Three years widowed, yet never had she felt so lonely as she felt tonight. She trudged back into the kitchen for a glass of water to soothe her dry throat. With the glass held to the ice dispenser, it was impossible to avoid the obvious. Maggie had strategically attached the brochure at eye level with a large magnet. Liz found it hard not to smile. "Okay, this is for you Maggie," she muttered, as she snatched it from the fridge, and carried it to the bedroom.

She lay in bed carefully scrutinizing every line of the itinerary. An aching knot formed in her stomach as her thoughts dashed from the present to a painful past. Liz recognized all the names signed by the Homecoming Committee. The empty ache worked its way up from the pit of her stomach to her heart and trickled out through her tear ducts. She reached over and pulled a tissue from a box on the bedside table. "This is why I don't need to go back. I don't do well when I start reminiscing."

Not being one to break a promise, Liz closed her eyes and quickly prayed, "Lord, you know how I hate to disappoint Maggie, so please, God, let her get it through her thick skull that I'm not going. I need you to change her mind, because I'm quite sure I won't be able to do it alone."

Having fulfilled her promise to pray about Homecoming, she turned over and pulled the satin comforter up to her chin.

****

"A date?" Mack held the phone with one hand and ran his hand through his thick, wavy hair with the other. "Luke, buddy, I know you mean well, but honestly, I'm not interested in dating. Truthfully, I don't have time. Besides, I thought you and I were gonna let Shorty shuck us some oysters."

"Mack, believe me when I say it wasn't my idea to call you, but my little woman and her cousin, Jo, have been worrying me silly over this, ever since I told them you'd be coming back for Homecoming. Trust me, I'd much rather eat oysters with you, but all I ask is that you see her one time, and if you two don't connect, I won't ever try to set you up again. How 'bout it? Will you do it?"

Mack tried to finagle his way out of it, but Luke had awarded him a huge contract. Didn't he owe him something? If only he could pay him some other way. This was beginning to feel like blackmail. He sucked in and exhaled slowly. "Okay, you win. I'll call, but I hope you'll make her understand that I'm not looking for a relationship. I'm not even for—"

"I get it. You aren't looking. Just do me this one favor to get these women off my back. All I'm asking is for your permission for me to give Trudy's cousin your number so she can call you."

"Wouldn't it be better if you gave me her number and let me call her?"

Luke paused. "Sorry, Mack, but this is per her request. I don't know why she wanted to be the one to make the call, but I'm sure she has her reasons. So, are you saying it's okay for me to give her your number?"

"I guess. Now, how did you say you know her?"

"She's Trudy's cousin." He chuckled. "Sheesh, Mack, aren't you even listening?"

"I'm trying. You say she went to HHS? Maybe I know her. What's her name?"

When Luke was silent, Mack said, "Sorry. I'm guessing you told me already."

"It's okay. Her name is Jo Jenkins and she's a beauty. For real. I wouldn't lie to you about that. I think she graduated a year after you did."

"I don't guess I knew her. I don't recall anyone by that name."

"Really? Because she remembers you. In fact, she claims she had a big crush on you, but from what you told me at the restaurant, I suppose you only had eyes for one, who turned out to be the wrong one."

44

Mack felt a tightness in his jaw. "Luke, I appreciate what you're trying to do, but I can't do this. If I sounded lonely when I told you about the girl who broke my heart in college, trust me, I'm over her. I stay too busy to be lonely. I'm doing just fine without a woman in my life."

"I'm sure you are, but I'm having to bow to the pressure from my wife and cousin, Jo. Hey, all you have to do is buy her dinner, enjoy the conversation, and take her home. After that, it's strictly up to you two whether or not you want a second date."

"Date? Even the word makes me gasp. Do you realize I haven't dated in sixteen years? I don't even know what people do on dates. I was a kid in college the last time I took . . . the last time I took a girl out."

"But you'll do it. Right?"

How could he say no?

CHAPTER 6

Startled out of a deep sleep by the shrill sound of Maggie's voice outside her door, Liz jerked straight up in bed. Her eyes fluttered open. She glanced toward the window and groaned, seeing a faint hint of light just now beginning to peek through the darkness. Falling back on the mattress, she pulled the covers over her head.

"Yoo-hoo . . . you awake, Lizzy? Hello?"

Little good it did to give Maggie a key, since she never used it. She'd much rather stand outside yelling in the wee hours of the morning, since it was a sure way to get Liz out of bed.

She beat on the door. "Lizzie? Open the door, hon."

Liz grabbed her robe and stomped through the house to keep her from waking the whole neighborhood. She jerked open the door. "Maggie, do you know what time it is?

Pushing past Liz, she stepped inside. "Go dress, hon, and I'll make the coffee. We're going shopping. Edna's Boutique is having a sale and I'm sure there's a line waiting to get inside, already."

Liz groaned. There was nothing she hated more than shopping. However, since Maggie's last two fender-benders were caused from her trying to parallel park in downtown Montgomery, Liz thought it best to drive her there. "I'll drop you off and hang out at the bookstore while you shop."

Liz was halfway to her bedroom when Maggie yelled, "Put on something decent, please. Not that old worn-out gray sweat suit that I hate."

"It's not worn . . . maybe a little faded, but there's still a lot of wear left in that outfit." Liz pulled a pair of navy slacks and a nautical striped shirt from her closet and came out mimicking a run-way model. "How's this, madame?"

"You look nice. The coffee and muffins are ready so why don't we take our breakfast on the sun porch?"

"Great idea. We can watch the sun come up."

"It's too late for that now, dearie, but I can believe you've never seen it before." Maggie picked up two mugs and the coffee pot, and Liz stuck a couple of napkins in the muffin basket and sat it on the wicker table outside.

After being seated, Maggie said, "Did you do what you promised me you'd do?"

"When I promised to strangle you if you ever signed me up with another dating service?"

"No, silly girl, you know what I'm talking about."

Liz crossed her arms over her chest. "If you're asking if I prayed about the Homecoming thingy, the answer is yes."

Maggie reached across the table for Liz's hand and gave a little squeeze. "Bless your heart, darling. I must say I'm surprised, but I can almost guarantee you that you won't be sorry."

Remembering how she prayed for God to change Maggie's mind, Liz could hardly wait to ask the question. "Maggie, I didn't say I was going—only that I prayed about it. But what about you? Do you still feel as strongly about it as you did yesterday?"

Her face lit up. "Oh, m'goodness, yes. Even more so today than yesterday. After praying about this, I know in my heart that something wonderful is about to happen for you, sweetheart, and I can hardly wait. Why would you even ask?"

"Just curious." Liz sighed.

Liz's life had been a series of struggles, so even if Maggie's prediction was absurd, she found herself wanting to believe it. She lost her parents when she was eight. Raised by a doting grandmother and a strict disciplinarian grandfather in Heartsboro, Alabama, she found her passion at the age of six, while standing on a kitchen stool, rolling out cookie dough, next to her Grandmother Farley. She recalled how her Memaw would let her choose from a variety of nuts, chocolates, dried fruits, and flavorings to add to the cookie mix. Memaw was her encourager and often bragged to her neighbors that little Liz had a real talent for baking.

The biggest thing that Liz and her Memaw didn't see eye-to-eye on was the boy down the street. He was a couple of years older and Memaw never approved of him hanging around. Liz was confident if her mother had lived, she would've liked Blake.

Memaw was old and didn't understand kids. Liz snickered, recalling the time her grandmother called the police because Blake was shooting off fireworks in the city limits. She demanded that he be arrested, though the police simply scared him, threatening to put him in jail if he did it again.

Then there was the time he rolled the trees in their yard with toilet tissue and Memaw called the police again. It wasn't that her grandmother didn't like Blake—she just didn't like him for Liz, and she did everything she could to keep them apart. When Liz was a junior in high school, her Memaw died and her dream of going to Culinary School died with her.

She tried to convince her granddaddy that Memaw wanted it for her as much as she wanted it. But her Pawpaw wouldn't hear of it. Said it was a foolish idea: "Your granny didn't have to go to school to learn how to cook and neither do you. You have a scholarship to a good college, Elizabeth, and you're gonna use it, so make up your mind. Either you get a respectable degree or go to work at the mill when you graduate high school. Makes no difference to me. After you get a degree, if you're still insistent on this silly idea of baking cookies and want to invest your own money into something that's destined to fail, then have at it—it'll be your loss, not mine."

That was exactly what she planned to do. She recalled the night she lay across her bed in the college dorm and wrote her fiancé a letter, outlining her dream. They wouldn't be able to afford a bakery at first, but she'd get a cottage license that would allow her to bake at home. Then as the funds became available, she'd buy a kiosk, and eventually they'd be able to invest in a bakery. It was such a beautiful dream.

But that all seemed so long ago. How did things get so turned around? There were times she longed to be young again, rolling out cookies with Memaw.

****

Mack was working on a drawing when his secretary paged him. "There's a woman on line three who says her name is Jo Jenkins. She said you are expecting a call from her. Shall I put her through?"

Without looking up, he shook his head. "No, I need to finish this. I don't know who she is. Tell her to leave her number and I'll call later."

"Yes sir."

"Hold on!" He immediately dropped his head in his hands. "You say her name is Jo?" He didn't wait for a response. "I'll take it. Put her on. But after about five minutes if I'm still on the line, break through and notify me that I'm needed."

He reared back in his swivel chair and picked up the phone. "Mack Mackenzie speaking."

"Hi, Mack. Jo, here. I want to thank you for taking my call."

"Jo? I believe Luke said you were his cousin?"

"No, I'm Trudy's cousin. I was ecstatic when Luke said you asked about me."

He ran his fingers through his hair and tried to think of

something to say. Was Luke joking? He didn't even know the woman. For someone who gave lectures on a regular basis, he suddenly felt mute. It wasn't as if he were a pimply-faced teenager talking on the phone to a girl for the first time. Why was he so nervous?

"Mack? Are you still there?"

"Uh . . . yes, sorry. You're right I'm very busy." He clinched his eyes shut and grimaced at the coldness in his voice.

"Not too busy, I hope."

He breathed easier, realizing she wasn't turned off by his tone.

"I was flattered that you told Luke you'd be interested in taking me to dinner. I'd like that very much."

Mack's brow met in the middle. What kind of joke was this?

"I was thinking we could meet at Andre's Epicurean Grill, on Wednesday."

"Wednesday?" Relieved that he had a good excuse to put an end to this little rendezvous before it got started, he said, "What a bummer. I'll be out of town Wednesday, but it's been a pleasure talking to you, Jo. Maybe another time. Thanks for calling."

It became apparent she wasn't giving up quite so quickly. "Out of town? But Luke said you'd be arriving in town Wednesday."

"Why would he say that?"

"Maybe because you told him your class would be the honored guests at Homecoming and you planned to be there?"

Did he detect a tinge of sarcasm? He plopped his hand to his forehead. "Oh, but you don't live in Point Clear, do you?"

"Point Clear? No, silly. I live in Heartsboro. You scared me for a moment. You aren't trying to weasel out of our date, are you?"

He cringed that he'd been so obvious. It wasn't until she snickered that he realized she was making a joke.

"So, what if we meet, say around seven o'clock the night you arrive? Andre's Epicurean Grill?"

"Never heard of it. Where is it located?"

"In Heartsboro. It's a chain. I ate at the one in New York and it's amazing. You'll love it. Do you remember Mr. Beckham's Pecan Orchard on Highway 167?"

Of course, he remembered. He remembered everything about his old hometown—everything except a girl named Jo. He vividly recalled going to the orchard every fall with his dad to buy twenty pounds of Stewarts for his mother's holiday baking.

"Well, old man Beckham died, and his children sold the orchard. The new owner cut down the trees and built a swanky restaurant there."

"What a shame."

"You won't think so when you see it. Very romantic atmosphere. Trust me, you'll love it."

Mack chewed on the inside of his cheek. Why did Luke tell her it was his idea to take her to dinner? *What if she doesn't want to go on this date any more than I do?*

"Well? Does seven o'clock work for you? Mack?"

"Seven o'clock, you say?"

"Just a suggestion. I know you won't be coming into town until Wednesday, and if that's too early, we can make it a little later. You'll find I'm very flexible."

"I'm sorry, Jo, but I'm afraid seven is out of the question."

"Not a problem. You tell me what time would be best for you. I'm good, anytime."

"Great. Since it's not a problem for you, I'll meet you there at five."

"Five? Mack, it's barely getting dark at five o'clock."

"You know, I believe you're right. I think the sun sets around five-fifteen. Maybe we should try for four-thirty. I'll be bringing my elderly father, so the earlier, the better."

"You're planning to bring your father on our date?"

He sensed the irritation in her voice. "No, of course not. I meant he's coming with me to Heartsboro. I feel okay about leaving him alone, long enough for you and I to enjoy a wonderful meal, but I'd hate to leave him by himself after dark. He's quite elderly, you understand."

"Well, aren't you sweet for taking such wonderful care of your father. You have a big heart, Mack Mackenzie. You always have had."

Gathering from the conversation that he should know her, he rolled her name around in his head. *Jo?* Her voice sounded vaguely familiar, but the name didn't ring a bell.

"Mack, if you like I could search around for a sitter to stay with your father, so you could relax and not feel the need to hurry back."

Mack kept the phone to his ear as he walked into Debbie's office, making hand motions, urging her to help him find a reason to hang up. But when she couldn't talk for giggling, he gave her the evil eye and said, "Oops, my secretary seems to be having a problem. I need to hang up and see what I can do to help her."

"Fine. Four-thirty, then, Wednesday afternoon at Andre's Epicurean Grill. I'll look forward to it, Mack. I only hope the restaurant opens that early. It'll be great to see you again."

Again? Who is this woman? He hung up and glared at his secretary. "Thanks a lot, friend."

"I'm sorry, Mack. I couldn't help it."

"I ought to fire you, you know that?"

"You couldn't do without me."

It was true, and he knew it. He might be the head of Mackenzie Construction Company, but Debbie Dalrymple was the spine that held it all together.

CHAPTER 7

Liz let Maggie off in front of the Boutique and just as predicted, the place was already crowded with women shoving to get inside. She parked, then walked around the corner to the Book Store and bought the last book in her favorite series. After settling down in a quiet corner with a cappuccino, she read the first two chapters of her new novel, then laid it in her lap.

Why was she finding it so hard to concentrate? Was it because the invitation to the Heartsboro High School Homecoming had renewed painful memories that she couldn't get out of her head? Or was it because of the exciting secret that she'd kept from Maggie?

Liz had never kept anything from her before and she felt guilty for doing so now, but Maggie was generous to a fault and if she knew about the bakery, she'd insist on financing it. Liz didn't know how she would've survived the last few years, had it not been for her precious friend. She was there for Liz during the worse period of her life as Carter's health declined, and his relentless demands increased. Maggie had been her rock, lending a shoulder to cry on, washing clothes and cooking nourishing meals when being Carter's caretaker left her too tired to think about eating.

During those grueling days, Liz was thankful for the kiosk, which didn't require her to have set hours, since there were weeks at the time when her husband's demands required her to be at his side. But after his death, she couldn't get the dream of opening a store-front bakery out of her mind.

As far as Maggie knew, Liz was perfectly satisfied to continue selling from the kiosk and perhaps she should be. Not only had it served to scratch that lingering itch of hers to become a bakery chef, but she'd gained valuable experience by starting out small. There were other perks, too, like the extra money she made and all the wonderful people she met. However, it was a part-time job, since she had to balance her time between baking and selling. Weeks ago, Liz decided the time had come to make her dream a reality. That's when she began looking for a piece of property where she could open a shop, hire help and expand. She'd searched the newspapers, but soon discovered commercial property was much more expensive than she'd imagined.

Mr. Allen Albertson was a well-known Realtor in Cottonvale, and a frequent visitor to the Court House. The first time he stopped by the kiosk, he bought a Cranberry-orange-nut muffin. The next time he stopped, he sampled a Pecan Tassie and ordered three dozen more to take to his office. He said they were the best he'd ever tasted. Liz remembered seeing him look at the license posted on the wall of the kiosk, and then calling her Elizabeth, since that's the way her name was written on the license. He took a bite of a Pecan Tassie, closed his eyes and let out a moan to show his satisfaction. That's the day he told her she should open a bakery. Liz took it as a sign, since he had no idea such a thought had been in the back of her mind for years.

She shared with him it was a dream of hers, and that she'd lately begun to check the classifieds, but so far hadn't found anything she could afford.

He seemed surprised that she'd been unable to find what she was looking for and told her he was confident he could help her find exactly what she wanted at a price that would fit her budget.

She assured him it would be a waste of his time, since she'd need to sell a few thousand more apple fritters before she'd be financially ready to purchase a building.

When he nodded, saying he understood and to let him know if she changed her mind, Liz assumed that would be the last of it.

However, three days later, he showed up at the kiosk and told her he'd found a few properties he thought she'd be interested in and asked when he might be able to show them. She recalled feeling embarrassed that he'd wasted his time. She thanked him and explained she hadn't applied for a loan, and she had no idea how much money she could get from mortgaging her house.

His explanation made sense when he suggested she take one step at the time and begin by checking out the properties available and their asking price. Then, she'd have a better idea of how much she could afford. He told her not to worry about refinancing her house. There were other ways, though he didn't elaborate. How fortunate she felt to have a big-time realtor willing to take up so much time, advising her.

But that was last week, and Liz hadn't heard from him since. Now she wasn't sure she ever would. However, she wasn't discouraged. She understood. He had million-dollar clients with money-in-hand, ready to make deals and he'd already given her something to think about.

Liz had never kept secrets from Maggie. Often, she had tried, but they always slipped out. However, opening a bakery was one secret she was determined to keep. Not that Maggie would try to stop her, but for the opposite reason. She would insist on giving her the money. She wished she had asked Mr. Albertson what he meant when he said there were other ways to get the money, besides mortgaging her house. Were there possibly grants she wasn't aware of?

She closed her book on Chapter Three and walked back to the car, where she sat for another hour waiting for Maggie to finish shopping.

****

Later that evening, Maggie emptied her shopping bags and laid out a complete wardrobe on her bed, then called Liz to come over. "Honey, go to my bedroom and see all the wonderful things I bought today. Let me know what you think. I'll be warming up some soup for us."

Liz yelled from the bedroom, "Such gorgeous outfits, Maggie. Where do you plan to wear these fancy duds?"

"I don't plan to wear them."

Walking back into the kitchen, Liz said, "What do you mean, you don't plan to wear them? I suppose you plan to let them hang in your closet?"

"No, silly. I plan to hang them in yours."

Liz jerked back. "Oh, no you don't. They're beautiful, but I don't need them. Besides, they're way too expensive. You can take them right back where they came from."

"Can't. I pulled the tags, and they can't be returned without the tags."

"Well, you wear them."

"Me?" She laughed. "They're a size eight. I do well to squeeze into a twelve."

"But why? You must've spent a fortune, and it wasn't necessary."

"It was necessary. Your wardrobe needs sprucing up. I want you to have something pretty to wear to Homecoming."

Liz groaned. "Maggie, I never said I was going to Homecoming."

"But you promised to pray, right?"

"I did. But we don't have the answer yet."

"Wrong! You don't have the answer yet. I have the answer. Do you think I would've spent that much money on these clothes if

I didn't already have word that you're going?"

Liz threw up her hands. "I give up."

"Fine. It'll save time. There's no need to make reservations. I took the liberty to it for you. I wanted to make sure you didn't miss the deadline."

Liz snorted. "I'll go, but I'll have a miserable time."

"That's not true, hon. You're going to love it."

"What makes you so sure?"

"Faith, child, faith." In a sing-song voice she chirped, "Just remember the Good Book says by faith the walls of Jericho fell down, by faith the harlot Rahab lived after she hid the spies, by faith the mouths of lions were stopped, by faith the dead were raised—" She took a breath. "Young lady, you intend to stand there and tell me that planting a ray of hope inside your pea-size finite mind while stirring a little desire within your cold, cold heart is too big a task for my God?"

"No ma'am, be it far from me to explain God's mysterious ways to you, dear Maggie. But I have an idea—why don't you go with me? If I go alone, I'll wind up spending a lot of time in a motel room by myself. I'd rather spend time with you, showing you where I lived and the places I frequented growing up. It might be fun going back, after all."

It was going as planned. Maggie could see the ice melting from a cold heart before her eyes. "I'd be delighted."

Liz had a feeling, that was the plan all along.

****

After Liz left, Maggie sat down at her computer and drank in every word of Doyle's last email. She couldn't believe how well things were falling into place. Gazing at his picture, she knew Liz couldn't help but fall for such a handsome fellow. Her heart fluttered as her fingers met the keys.

Hi Honey,

It always makes me happy to see an email from you pop up on my computer. I feel as if I've known you for ages. It's unbelievable how much we have in common. We both love to read Dr. Groft in the morning paper, we like crossword puzzles, and we enjoy playing dominoes. You and I are like two peas in a pod. Like you, I hate shuffleboard. As much as I love dominoes, naturally I'd rather be taking moonlight walks on the beach with you. I can't wait to stroll down the beach in our bare feet—our toes squishing in the sand, side by side.

Maggie swallowed hard. Perhaps she should delete the last sentence. She wanted to sound romantic, but not risqué and she wasn't sure if she'd crossed the line by talking about their bare feet being side by side. After all, she didn't want Doyle to get the idea that Elizabeth was a floozy. With a shrug, she decided to leave it. Maybe just a wee touch of risqué might spark his interest. He'd find out soon enough that Liz was a decent and wholesome sort of girl.

CHAPTER 8

Jim had supper fixed and warming on the stove, when Mack walked in the door at eight o'clock.

Mack filled his bowl and sat down at the table. Jim poured himself a cup of coffee and plopped down in a chair across from his son.

"The chili is delicious, Pop. Thanks."

"Son, I'm not much of a cook, and I know it. Opening a can is about the best I can do. What you need is a wife to cook for you."

The veins in Mack's neck protruded. "Pop, enough already. How can I say this in a way you can understand? Sure, I'd like to have a wife to come home to; someone to share things with and love me the way Mama loved you. But it hasn't happened, okay? I can't put my life on hold while I wait for it. I have my work. And speaking of work—"

"I know what you're gonna say, Doyle. You're upset because I told Debbie the call was urgent. I thought it was, but since you didn't have time to talk, I took it on my own to go ahead and do it myself."

"Do it? Do what?"

"Well, a few weeks ago I signed up as your proxy on what they call an online dating service. I thought it was about time for you to start—"

"Whoa. Stop right there. You did what? Nah . . . I don't believe it. You couldn't have. I thought you said—" Mack laughed but the laugh faded. "I thought you said you signed me up with an online dating service."

"That's exactly what I said—as your proxy, of course, and you'll be proud to know I did good, too. She makes Doris Day look homely, and you know what a beautiful woman Doris Day was—or is? Is she still living?"

"Doris who? It doesn't matter . . . just tell me what you're talking about. Pop, you haven't given my address to anyone have you?"

"Of course not, Son, I've got better sense than that. You wanna see her picture?"

"Thanks, but no thanks."

"Well, just take a gander at her picture. I promise when you see her, you'll change your mind."

"I don't want to see her picture." Mack jumped up from the table and threw his napkin down. "Dad, that was a poor idea. I know you didn't come up with this on your own. Who put you up to this?"

"I heard about it from my friend George, but now I wouldn't go so far as to say he put me up to it. After I listened to him tell about finding Myrtle, I figured if it worked for George and Myrtle, there was no reason why it wouldn't work for you."

Mack ran his fingers through his hair. "Dad, I don't even want you using your own name on a stupid online dating website and I surely don't want you using mine, so close the account. Do I make myself clear?"

Jim hadn't seen him this upset since Robbie Gunter stole his bicycle when he was ten—now that had really ticked him off. "I'm sorry you're upset with me, Doyle, but I wish you'd keep an open mind about this. She's as sweet as she is beautiful."

Mack's chest expanded when he sucked in a lungful of air. "Pop. If the woman is as beautiful as you say she is, there's a reason why no one wants her. A good-looking woman with half a brain can find a man without searching the internet."

"Well, you'd think, wouldn't you? But you'd also think a handsome man with a whole brain could find someone without the internet also, but I happen to know one who can't. Now wouldn't you like to see what she looks like, son?"

"No, Daddy, I don't. I don't, I don't." He shouted. "Please don't ask me again. If she's so special, you date her." Why was everyone suddenly so intent on finding him a woman? He'd managed just fine for sixteen years without a wishy-washy female toying with his emotions. He had a business that required his attention 24/7. The last thing he needed was a woman trying to run his life. Especially one his dad picked out.

****

The next day, Mack Mackenzie walked into his secretary's office. "Deb, please call Ted Johnson and let him know I'll need to reschedule our Tuesday appointment and then call Red Albertson to let him know my plans have changed. I will be at the Montgomery Conference if he's still interested in getting together."

After checking her files, she said, "Would that be W. B. Albertson or Allen Albertson?"

"I'm sorry. That would be Allen."

"Sounds familiar. Where have I heard that name?"

Mack grunted. "How about on television, in the newspapers, on the radio and anywhere else he can garner publicity. I've tried to get out of meeting with him, but I really need to be at that Conference and I'm sure I won't be able to avoid him. I might as well bite the bullet and see what he wants."

"Oh, he's that dude who had his picture in the paper last week for buying sacks of valentines to hand out to residents at the Nursing Home."

"I didn't see it, but if he could find a reason to get his picture in the paper, he wouldn't turn down the opportunity."

"You sound like you've had some bad dealings with him before. What's wrong with him?"

"What's not wrong with him would be easier to answer, although if you stopped anyone on the streets of Montgomery or

65

Cottonvale, they'd tell you what a fine, upstanding citizen he is. How he gets by with all the underhanded shenanigans he pulls and is still able to stay out of jail and fool the masses is beyond my understanding. If I did some of the things he's done, I'd be locked up for life."

While waiting for Ted's call to go through, she put her hand over the receiver and whispered, "Mack, I'm proud of you for going back for your Homecoming. You need a break."

"Trust me, I must've been out of my head when I told Pop we'd go. Now, I can't get out of it."

She giggled. "I know. Mr. Jim is so excited. He's like a kid waiting for Christmas." She hung up the phone. "I couldn't get through to Ted's office. I'll try again in a few minutes, then I'll put in the call to Mr. Anderson."

"Deb, I'm sorry that Pop calls you as much as he does. I know it must bug you. I've tried every way I know how to convince him that you're busy and he shouldn't bother you."

"Oh, Mack, please don't scold him. He never talks for long and if I'm really busy, I tell him and he's very apologetic and hangs up immediately."

"Well, he has no business calling as much as he does. You need to do like me and not take his calls. I know it must sound like I'm an ogre who doesn't love his dad, but that's not true. I love him very much, but it doesn't mean he doesn't try me at times."

"Don't you see what the problem is?"

With his tongue in cheek, he said, "He talks too much?"

"No. He's very lonely."

Mack didn't know why he felt insulted. Was Deb blaming him for not spending hours entertaining his father? Pop was a lot of things, but lonely wasn't one of them. Not possible. Just because he reminisced about what he left behind in Heartsboro was no sign he was lonely. Reminiscing was what all old people did, wasn't it? If Mack moved him back to Heartsboro, his dad would likely want to tell everyone he met what a grand time he had living on the beach. Lonely? No way. The man could always find someone to talk to. He walked to the Senior Citizens Club five days a week; he volunteered to be a Greeter at church, and he made a point of introducing himself to every person in the condominium. He knew them all on a first name basis. Deb was wrong. Jim Mackenzie was constantly surrounding himself with people. He didn't have time to get lonely.

"Mack, it's possible for a person to be acquainted with hundreds of people and still feel alone. Your dad misses his friends back home."

"But he's made new friends in Point Clear. If he's not happy, it's his own fault. He's got it made. You should see the little house he and Mama lived in. Nine-hundred-fifty square feet, and that's not an exaggeration. Two tiny bedrooms and one bath. The neighborhood is going down and after Mama died, there was no sense in him having to stay there by himself."

"Not even if it was his wish?"

"You act like I'm cruel for wanting to have him with me,

living in a four-thousand square foot condo on the beach, where he has his own private quarters."

She rubbed her hand over her eyes. "I'm sorry. It's none of my business. I don't know why I went on the way I did. I'm sure you're doing what you feel is best. I'll make that call to Mr. Albertson as soon as Ted gets back with me."

"Thank you. Deb, and if I sounded ungrateful, I apologize. I appreciate that you want what's best for my father. We both do. We just have different ideas about what's best."

CHAPTER 9

For weeks, Liz purposely set up one o'clock appointments with the realtor to keep her sweet but nosey neighbor from being privy to what she was up to, since that's the time Maggie normally napped. She could never leave the house without Maggie wanting to know where she was going and what time she'd be back, but Liz didn't really mind. It felt good knowing there was someone who held her accountable. She felt a little safer, knowing Maggie was watching out for her.

While waiting for the realtor to come, she quickly glanced in the mirror and traced a fine wrinkle on her forehead with her finger. "You're not getting any younger, old girl. If you're ever going to see this dream become a reality, sink or swim, you need to follow through."

At precisely one o'clock, Tuesday, Allen Albertson drove up and Liz hurried out the door to meet him. The sooner she got away, the less likely Maggie would be to wake up from her nap. "I'm ready if you are, Mr. Albertson."

Opening her door, he waited for her to slide in, then said, "I'd be pleased if you'd call me Allen, Elizabeth. Mr. Albertson makes me feel even older than I am."

"Allen, it is. And please call me Liz. The only time I'm ever called Elizabeth is when I go to the doctor's office and my full name is listed on the insurance forms."

He winked. "And when prying eyes find it posted in open sight on your cottage license in the kiosk?"

When he laughed, she laughed with him, although it had nothing to do with his remark about the license. There was something about Allen Albertson that made her feel all giddy inside. Maybe it was the smoothness of his voice, or the scent of his cologne. Or maybe it was simply because it had been such a long time since Liz had been alone with a man. Any man.

He walked around to the driver's side, sat down and shuffled through papers. "Here, take a look at these and tell me what you think. All three have recently come on the market and are in excellent locations."

She took the printed sheets, glanced at them, then placed them in her lap. "Allen, these look wonderful, but they seem terribly expensive. I feel like I'm wasting your time, since we don't know how much money I can borrow. Shouldn't we wait and see if I'll have the money to do this?"

"Trust me, I do this for a living and I'm good at it, if I do say so myself."

He took her to see two of the properties, but the third had a Pending sign out front.

Liz sighed, "I should've known the only one that would be a fit would be unavailable."

"Please don't be discouraged. We'll keep looking. We've only been doing this for a few weeks. Sometimes it takes months to find exactly what you're looking for, but we'll find it."

"You're a good man, Mr. Alberts. . . Allen."

His gaze locked with hers. "Liz, I hope it isn't improper for me to say, but I've never enjoyed showing properties as much as I've enjoyed these past weeks. You're wonderful company and I find myself looking forward to being with you."

"I've enjoyed our appointments, also and trust me, I'm not discouraged. I've spent a lifetime dreaming about one day opening a bakery, so even if it never comes to pass, I'll at least know that I tried. You've been very patient with me, Allen, and I appreciate it."

He parked in her driveway but didn't run around and open her door the way he always did. Instead, he turned toward her and leaned in. "I don't know why I'm finding this so hard to say, Liz, but the truth is, I've grown very fond of you, and I've sensed you may be feeling the same toward me. At least I hope so. I think we both have something to offer the other."

"I'm not sure I understand, Allen. Are you offering to finance the bakery, because if you are, the answer is no. It's important to me that I do this on my own."

He reached across the seat and placed his hand on hers. "It's not about the bakery. Marry me, Liz." He lowered his head. "Well, that came out sooner than I anticipated, but now that it's been said, I'm glad."

Her throat tightened. "Wow. You've caught me by surprise. You want *me* to marry *you*?"

"I realize I'm at least fifteen years your senior, and I know you're probably thinking you haven't known me long enough, but if you'll—"

"Allen, stop! You know nothing about me. How can you say you want to marry me?"

"Liz, I've known you long enough to know that I want you in my life. I've spent a lifetime searching for you—I just didn't know your name or where to find you. Now that I've found you, I don't want to let you go."

She rubbed her hand over her face. "I certainly didn't see this coming."

He reached up and ran his finger over the outline of her lips. "I promise you I'll be good to you and without question, you'll be good for me. I need you, Liz. You'll never want for anything. I'll see to it."

Their gaze locked. "I believe you, Allen. You're one of the kindest men I've ever known."

"Then you'll consider it?"

The shock of his proposal left her weak in the knees. Her mind raced, imagining how different her life would be, married to someone like Allen Albertson. She wouldn't have guessed him to be fifteen years older than her. He didn't look a day over forty-five, but then maybe he was underestimating her age. She glanced down at their hands, now locked together, and felt him gently squeeze. Her heart hammered.

"If you need time to think about it, I understand. I'm flying to DC tomorrow, but I'd like to take you out to dinner, Friday night and discuss what our future together could look like. If there really is such a thing as a soul mate, I know that I've found mine."

She sat quietly gnawing at her lower lip. "You're very sweet, Allen, but I'm leaving Wednesday to go out of town." Was she crazy for considering his proposal? Or would she be crazy not to consider it? Liz didn't like the thought of growing old alone and as insane as it sounded, she couldn't deny that something inside her clicked the moment his hand touched hers. It was as if he'd opened a part of her that she'd never explored before. But Soul mates? She didn't see it, but was it really important? She had no problem recognizing the many advantages of being the wife of Allen Albertson. He was kind, generous, loving and he believed in her. If he didn't, he wouldn't spend so much of his time seeking out possible locations for her bakery.

She looked at her watch and grimaced. "Yikes, it's later than I thought. Maggie will be through napping, and I don't want her to know I've been seeing you. Not yet."

"Are you afraid she won't approve?"

"Just the opposite. She would be ecstatic. She spends twenty-three hours out of twenty-four, searching for me a man."

He chuckled. "Apparently, she hasn't had much success, to which I am grateful."

"No success is correct. But this is a decision I need to make on my own, without her attempting to influence me." When he leaned in, she knew he wanted to kiss her, but she wasn't ready and backed away.

He said, "I think I'm going to like your friend, Maggie. Sounds as if she might be on my side."

"I really need to go. Don't bother getting out."

"How long will you be gone?"

"I'll be back Monday."

"I'll call you." He kissed the tips of his fingers, then gently swiped them across her lips. "Goodbye beautiful lady."

She nodded and ran toward her house, then stopped when she saw Maggie waiting in the yard.

Why did she feel like a teenager who failed to make curfew?

CHAPTER 10

Mack was walking down the hall in the Administrative Building when someone called his name. He turned around and could only hope the disgust wasn't visible on his face when he realized it was Red Albertson. "H'lo, Red."

Allen Albertson stuck his hand out and grasped Mack's in a firm handshake, while resting his other hand on his shoulder. "How ya' doing, ol' Buddy? I was glad to get the message from your secretary. I know the appointment isn't for another thirty-minutes, but I'm tied up with so many projects, how about if we go ahead and get started?"

Mack's first impulse was to hold out until three o'clock as planned, even though the Conference had ended, and he had nothing else to do. It was the principle of the matter. Red never considered that anyone's business could be more pressing than his. But the sooner Mack could find out what he wanted, the sooner he could go home. "Sure, I can do it now. Why don't we meet at that little coffee shop on the corner?"

"Thanks, friend. I'll see you there in a few minutes. I just finished an interview with the local TV station and they're waiting over at the Capitol for a photo op. It won't take ten minutes. Go ahead, get your coffee and I'll come as soon as its finished."

The coffee shop was crowded, and Mack was on his second cup of coffee before Red showed up.

"Sorry, it took a little longer than I expected. I hope you didn't mind waiting."

"Of course not. I have nothing better to do than sit around and wait. I'm not a big dog like you."

"Okay, I get the sarcasm, but I didn't hold you up on purpose. It's hard to get away from the media, sometimes. You know how it is."

"What do I owe this pleasure to, Red?"

"I'll make this as brief as I can. I have a lot to do, and I'm sure you do, too. There's this little widow—a client of mine—who is dead set on opening her own business. For several reasons, which for the sake of time, I won't bore you with, but I think she'd be making a big mistake."

"Why is that?"

"She's insisting on making application for a loan, but I happen to know she won't be able to purchase any of the properties I've shown her."

Mack had never known Allen Albertson to be concerned about

anyone who didn't have the financial means to make a lucrative deal. Had he misjudged him? He seemed genuinely concerned that a little ol' widow could be losing her meager wages on a bad investment. "I know how you feel."

"Do you?"

"Of course. I have people coming to me all the time wanting me to draw up plans and I know before they ever apply for a loan that it won't happen. It's hard to see the disappointment on their faces when they realize their lifelong dreams are being flushed down the toilet."

"That's where you and I are different, Mack."

"How do you mean?"

"You're a sap for a sad story. I don't waste my time on anyone who has to wait to see if their loan will be approved."

"I guess I misunderstood you. I thought you were concerned that the widow wouldn't be able to purchase property. I'm sorry."

"Don't be. I'm not. There is a piece of property she could get, but it wouldn't be in her best interest."

When had Red Albertson ever concerned himself with anyone's best interests, other than his own? "Why don't we get down to the real reason we're here. I'm sure your financially-strapped client is not what we're here to discuss."

"You're wrong. You have a building for sale in Cottonvale that I haven't shown her, but I'm afraid she'll find it on her own."

"I get it. You're asking me to lower the price, so your client feels she can afford it. Sorry. If it's the building I think it is, it's already way below appraisal." Until today, Mack wouldn't have thought Allen Albertson would've gone out of his way to help his own mother. This was a side of him he'd never seen before.

"Red, I'm touched at your compassion for this woman, and I'd love to help. But I'm sorry, I can't afford to give it away."

"That's just it. I think you *are* giving it away. I'm not asking you to lower the price. I want you to raise it as a favor to me."

"Raise it? As a favor?" Mack had no idea where this was going, but out of curiosity, decided to hear him out. "Seems to me you're leaving out something, Red. And remind me why I owe you a favor?"

"You're still sore about that Rodgers deal three years ago. Man, I know it was a little underhanded, but I think you would've done the same thing if you'd been in my shoes."

"I've moved on, Red. I don't hold grudges, but I do try to learn from experiences, and that was quite an experience. I think I learned to think twice before letting you talk me into something. But I can't help being curious. Why would you ask me to raise the price? I don't see how that could benefit you, and we both know you don't do anything that doesn't benefit Allen Albertson."

"Call me what you will. You won't be able to come up with anything I haven't been called before. We both know that property is worth at least thirty-thousand more than your asking price."

"What's wrong with that? Your client wants to buy, I want to sell . . . what's the problem, Red?" Mack scratched his head. "Let me see if I have this straight. You have a client who needs a property, and I have the only one listed that she could possibly get financing for. Yet, you want me to raise the price? Maybe we didn't take the same Economics class, but that doesn't make sense to me."

"It's complicated, but I just need you to raise the price for three months. That's all I ask. Then, if things don't work out as I'm expecting, you can sell it for ten dollars or ten million, for all I care."

"Red, suppose you level with me. What are you trying to pull?"

"Look, man, you and I go way back. You know I wouldn't do anything that wasn't on the up-and-up." He grimaced. "Okay, so maybe I did you wrong on that last deal, but we're all allowed one mistake."

"Sorry, Red, the price stands, unless you want to tell me what's going on."

He crossed his arms over his midsection. "Fine. I'm planning to marry the woman, and I don't want her buying that building because I don't want her to carry out the silly notion of putting a bakery there."

"That's what she wants it for? A bakery? You *are* talking about the building across from the Police Station, aren't you?"

"That's the one."

"It would be perfect. It was a small café, owned by an elderly couple who recently retired. They hired me to build them a retirement home at Orange Beach. I had no business with that piece of property, but I bought it to help them out. Have you looked at it?"

"No, and I'm not interested in seeing it. Just take it off the market until Spring. That's all I'm asking."

"Maybe you should go take a look. It has a nice kitchen and a few tables and chairs and would be perfect for a bakery."

Allen slammed his fist on the table, sloshing coffee from his cup. He grabbed a napkin to wipe up the spill. "Maybe you aren't hearing me or maybe you don't want to hear. I don't want the property, and I sure don't want her to have it. She has no business sweating in a bakery twelve hours a day. She'd be haggard looking in a month's time. I want my future wife to look like the eye-candy she is, and to be free to travel with me without having a dinky business tying her down."

"Why don't you tell her exactly what you're telling me."

"Because she wouldn't understand."

"Sorry, Red. That's your problem. The price stands."

He threw up his hands. "I was afraid of this, but I had to try. You have a reputation of being hard to work with."

"Only when I'm working with known wheeler-dealers, who'll do anything or hurt anyone for the all mighty dollar. Now, I don't want to detain you any longer, knowing what a busy man you are. By the way, I must have missed the announcement in the paper. When's the big day?"

"Soon. I think I shocked her when I asked her to marry me. I told her I wanted to give her time to think about it, but I have no doubt what her answer will be. I feel lucky to have found her. She's a diamond in the rough."

"What do you mean?"

"She doesn't realize it, but she's a natural beauty, even dressed in sweatpants and wearing no make-up. I can only imagine what she'll look like once we're married, and I send her to that spa in Colorado for a make-over. I'll love being able to show her off."

CHAPTER 11

Alabama had enjoyed a mild winter, but February and March normally tended to bring the coldest weather, and this year didn't appear to be a pattern-changer. Already into the first week of February, the temperature was predicted to drop in the night to a chilling low of thirty-four degrees.

Mack hadn't had an opportunity to wear the heavy woolen overcoat he bought eleven years ago while attending a court case in Baltimore. He'd almost given up the search for the coat when he finally found it stuffed in the top of the hall closet. He pulled it out, brushed it off, and though it was a bit wrinkled, he decided the wrinkles would eventually fall out. It had cost him a hefty sum— more than he'd ever paid for a piece of clothing, but he hadn't forgotten why he bought it.

Over twenty years ago, he and Liz watched "While You Were Sleeping," at the Avon Theatre. Mack had never been one to pay attention to clothes and he might not have noticed the overcoat Peter Gallagher wore in the movie, if Liz hadn't gone crazy over it.

He vowed that night that as soon as he could afford it, he'd have one like it. Several years later and a long way from home, he kept that promise. Court was in recess and Baltimore was covered in snow when Mack walked down the street and saw a coat exactly like Peter Gallagher's in the department store window. Whether it was the memory of a night at the movies or the freezing snow that caused him to dart in and have the salesman retrieve it from the mannequin, he couldn't say. But there was no denying his spontaneous action proved to be a wise one that week, since it was much colder in Maryland than it was when he left Alabama only days before. He'd not worn it since.

If he recalled correctly, Peter Gallagher wore his on every date and there was always snow on the ground. Maybe that's why Mack hadn't found an occasion to wear it. In the past ten years, Alabama had only seen one tiny snow flurry and in that same length of time, Mack had not been on a single date. He frowned while looking in the mirror. He didn't remember the padding in the shoulders being so big, or it being quite so long or nearly as heavy.

Why did he let Luke talk him into spending an evening with a woman he'd never met? He hadn't been able to concentrate since the phone call. It wasn't like he hadn't had dinner with lots of women in the past few years, but it was always business contacts, and he knew ahead of time what to expect.

Never had he spent so much time dwelling on clothes, but then it had been sixteen years since he'd had to think about what to wear on a date. He'd not felt this much stress since the day he

83

moved his dad into his condo. Mack decided to wear the coat to work and let Debbie give an honest opinion—something she delighted in doing, even when it wasn't requested.

He put on a pair of navy slacks, and an argyle sweater. Remembering that Peter Gallagher always teamed the coat up with a wool scarf, he dug through an old trunk and found a nice plaid scarf, still in a Christmas gift box with the tags attached. It had been so long ago, he couldn't remember who gave it to him. He wrapped it around his neck, then put on his topcoat. Gazing at his reflection in the mirror, he concluded he was no Peter Gallagher, but on the other hand, he wasn't a bad looking dude.

As was his custom, he stopped by the coffee shop before going to the office. Mack couldn't help noticing the way people turned to glance his way. The looks on their faces made him wonder why he hadn't worn the coat before now, until he remembered the thermometer in Alabama seldom had digits low enough to warrant a topcoat. It seemed a shame to have such an expensive coat and not be able to get his money's worth out of it.

Stopping by the cleaners, he picked up two suits and hung them in his office, then rang for Debbie.

He stood in front of his desk so she could get a good look.

When she walked in, she stopped short and blinked several times. "What is that you are wearing and how long has it been deceased?"

Mack hung his thumbs in the pockets. "Like it?"

"It reminds me of an old movie."

He smiled, knowingly. "Let me guess: 'While You Were Sleeping!'"

"No.' Some Like it Hot.' Mack why do you have on a wool overcoat? It's almost sixty degrees outside and at least seventy-two in here."

"The weatherman said it was in the thirties last night."

"It was. Last night. Outside. It's also freezing in Colorado, but you happen to live in Alabama."

He wiped beads of sweat from his forehead and upper lip, then pulled off the coat and laid it over the back of his chair. "It does feel a little warm. But I need your help, Deb. I brought a couple of suits in, and I want your opinion." He pulled the plastic wrapper off and held them up. "Which one?"

She lifted a shoulder. "Where do you plan to wear it? A masquerade party or a homeless shelter?"

"I can do without the sarcasm."

"So, maybe I guessed wrong. What's the occasion?"

"I have a date tomorrow night and it's been years since I've dated. That's why I pulled out the overcoat. I have no idea what to wear."

Debbie's eyes widened. "That's obvious. I've prayed for years for a swarm of moths to attack your closet. I must not be living right, because both suits are still around. Where are those pesky moths when you need them?"

His brows meshed together. "What's wrong with them?"

"Mack, I've wanted to say this for a long time, so it's way

overdue. But you need to pay attention to what men are wearing." She grabbed a leg to the gray pin-striped suit. "You could slit one of these wide legs and use it for a lightweight blanket on a queen-sized bed."

"Are you saying my suits are out of style?"

"Only by about fifteen or twenty years. The only nice thing I can say about either suit is that it's admirable that you can still fit into these clothes you wore in high school. I wish I could say the same."

"Then would you suggest I dress casual? Wear the slacks and shirts I wear to work?"

She bit her bottom lip and shook her head. "Since you asked—"

"I don't have anything else to wear."

"You will have. I'll go shopping on my lunch hour."

"Thanks, Deb." He pulled out his wallet and took out four twenty-dollar bills. "This should do it."

She shook her head. "Put it back in your wallet. I've got the company credit card."

He covered his face with his hand. "Uh-oh. I knew I shouldn't have given you that card."

CHAPTER 12

Maggie awoke from her hap early and was sweeping off her porch when she looked over at Liz's house and saw a strange car drive up. "It's Liz . . . with a man." Lifting her hand to shield her eyes from the sun, she stretched her neck, craning to see if it was someone she recognized.

What was Liz up to? If it wasn't a big secret, then why didn't she mention at lunch that she'd be going out? This couldn't be happening. Not now. Maggie had found the perfect guy, and it would be an awful time for Liz to get mixed up with the wrong fellow.

She ran back into the house and grabbed her glasses from off the kitchen table, then went back to the porch. With her glasses, she was able to read the sign on the side of the fancy automobile. *A Realtor?* Why would Liz be seeing a realtor? Well, there was only one way to find out. She'd go ask them what they were up to. Before she reached the car, Liz got out, waved and the man drove away.

"You're up early, Maggie. I thought you'd nap at least another thirty minutes."

"I guess I surprised you and you certainly surprised me."

She knew Maggie was dying to find out who he was, but she'd wait and make her ask. Knowing Maggie, it wouldn't take long. "Come on in. I have a fresh apple cake inside. It's an old recipe with a new twist. I'd like your opinion."

Maggie shoved her hands on her hips. "I'll be happy to give you my opinion if you'll tell me what you were doing riding around with a realtor."

A brief smile flickered across Liz's face. "Now, what makes you think he's a realtor? Maybe he's my new fellow."

"That's easy to answer. I can read, and there's a large sign on the side of that fancy car with the words Albertson Realty, so I can only assume you were out looking for property. What's going on, Liz? Why did you feel you needed to hide the truth from me?"

"I can see you're upset, Maggie, but the only reason I didn't want to tell you until it I knew for sure, was because I didn't want you to worry."

"Worry? Now, I *am* worried. hon. I know you've had a lot of unusual expenses in the past few months and if you're having trouble making house payments, I'll buy your house, and you can pay me back in smaller payments that you can afford."

"I'm doing fine. Honest. It's not the house."

"Then what?"

"It's a business decision."

Maggie's eyes widened, and she thrust her hand over her mouth. "Business? Oh, my lands, you're thinking about opening a bakery, aren't you? That's it! That's why you've been riding around with a realtor and it's why you've been trying so many different recipes. Well, hallelujah! It's about time. This town needs a good bakery and you're just the person to open one. It's time you began thinking big. Let's go sit down and have that cake. I want you to tell me all about it."

"Oh, Maggie, I've been so excited, I didn't know how much longer I could keep quiet."

Liz cut Maggie a big slice of Apple Cake and poured two cups of coffee.

Maggie swiped her finger over the cream topping. "Aren't you going to try it?"

"I'm not hungry. I'll trust your judgment. Tell me what you think."

Maggie forked a small chunk, then closed her eyes and moaned. "Oh m'goodness, hon, this is a Blue-Ribbon winner, for sure." She cut off another piece, tasted and smacked her tongue against the roof of her mouth a couple of times. "Is that black walnuts in it?"

"It is. I'm glad you like it." She pressed her lips together. "Maggie, do you know Allen Anderson?"

"The realtor? Only by reputation. I hear he's one of the wealthiest men in Alabama."

"Is that all you know about him?"

"I don't know the fellow personally, but there are a couple of ladies in my Book Club who are crazy about him. They say his wife died years ago, not long after they married, and he's never remarried. Not for lack of chances, I'm sure. He's not much to look at, but he must be very smart to have accumulated such wealth."

Liz frowned. "That's not nice."

"You must've misunderstood. I said he's smart and wealthy. What's not nice about that?"

"I'm talking about when you said he's not much to look at."

"Did I lie?"

The lines on her forehead vanished and a corner of her lip curled upward. "I guess not. But is that all you know about him?"

"I've never had an occasion to use his services. I've heard a couple of the ladies say he's active in his church and I'm sure you've seen all the articles in the newspaper, touting his participation in civic activities. I think he's quite the philanthropist." She stopped and stared. "Wait! Why all the interest?"

Liz was sorry she'd brought it up. Why didn't she wait until she'd come to a firm decision on her own instead of allowing Maggie to get all excited? Knowing Maggie, she'd be planning a wedding before nightfall.

"You haven't answered me. What's this all about?"

She'd gone this far. There was no backing down. "Allen has just asked me to marry him."

Maggie's face turned red. "He what? No. I don't believe it. You're pulling my leg, aren't you?"

"No. I'm serious and so was he. Don't get carried away, Maggie. I already know how you feel about me getting married, but I haven't made up my mind yet. I'm still thinking it over."

Maggie dropped her fork. "Elizabeth Blackstone, I'd be seriously worried about you if I thought you were honestly considering something so absurd. That's the craziest thing I've ever heard of."

Liz found her change of attitude to be puzzling. For years, Maggie had harped on all the reasons Liz should get married again. This sudden reversal was difficult to understand. "Maggie, why are you acting this way? You've just finished telling me what a fine man he is. It seems to me I'd be insane not to agree to marry him."

"I didn't say he was a fine man. I said he was rich, he goes to church, attends civic events and likes to have his picture in the paper. I know several shady politicians that I could say the same for. I can't remember what else I said, but I never once said I thought he was a fine man." She lifted her forefinger. "Oh, yeah, I remember the other thing. I said he's not much to look at. And that's the only thing about him that I can truly vouch for sure." She closed her eyes and shook her head. "Honey, please tell me you aren't seriously considering such a trumped-up proposal."

"I see no reason why I shouldn't."

Maggie shoved back from the table and crossed her arms over her chest. "It's preposterous. He's not your type."

"Not my type? Is that supposed to be a joke? I appreciate your concern, Maggie, but frankly, I don't think you know my type."

"Just because I got it wrong a couple of times is no reason for you to give up on finding the right one."

"This is bizarre. I was so sure you'd be planning the wedding before I finished telling you he proposed. I don't get you, Maggie. If you know something about Allen that you haven't told me, please don't hold back. But from everything I know, I couldn't possibly do better. I was flattered that he asked me. I'm sure he could have any single woman he wanted."

"But isn't he older than you?"

Her eyes hardened. "And that should bother me? How much older did you say Robert was than you? I don't understand you, Maggie. Ever since Carter died, you've warned me that I need to find a man and not live out my later years alone. Now, I've considered taking your advice, and you act as if I've lost my mind."

"Well, please just promise me that you won't make an impulsive decision. You've waited this long. What's the hurry? Until now, you haven't even been interested in looking around. As the old saying goes, haste makes waste. And there are plenty of fish in the sea."

"And lots of nuts in Peanut Brittle. Right?"

"I don't think I've heard that one, but there's truth there that can be applied. Sounds to me a little nutty that the man is in an awful rush to get married. Just don't let him push you into something."

"Maggie, I'm not in a hurry to make a decision, but I will let you know I find the proposal tempting. I can think of plenty of reasons why I should marry him and so far, I haven't thought of a single reason why I shouldn't."

Maggie lowered her cup to the table. "Tell me, Liz, do you love him?"

"Love? Are you kidding? I've loved before and look where that got me. I'm not looking for love, Maggie. I'm looking for security and companionship. It seems to me Allen can offer both."

Maggie dressed for bed and took her medicine. She walked back into the bedroom just in time to hear the little dinging sound, alerting her she had mail. She sat down at the computer and gave much thought to her response. It was important that she move the conversation to an even deeper level, even though she had a feeling Doyle Mackenzie had already fallen in love with Elizabeth.

No way could she let Liz ruin her life by marrying a man she didn't love, when true love awaited less than a week away.

CHAPTER 13

Mack's eyes widened when Debbie returned to the office at two o'clock with an armful of packages. "It looks as if you bought out the store."

"Oh, this is just the beginning. There are more in the car."

"My lands, Deb, where am I supposed to wear all these duds?"

"Everywhere you go. You need to pull everything from your closet when you get home and drop it all off at the nearest Goodwill bin. Then hang these new clothes in their place."

"Are you serious? Throw away my clothes?"

"I didn't say throw them away. I said give them away. There's a difference. I'm sure somewhere there's a man who is looking for cuffed pants, a few dress shirts with frayed collars and boring polyester ties. Think how you could brighten his day."

"But I can keep my suits. Right?"

She giggled. "No! That mustard-colored suit should be the first thing you put into the bag. It's got to go."

"It's brown."

"It's mustard."

"Okay, maybe brown with a hint of yellow."

"No, Mack. It's yellow with a tinge of brown. Every time I pull the spicy brown mustard from the fridge, it reminds me of you in that suit. I can't wait to show you what all I bought." She pulled the garment bags off each piece and laid them one by one on the conference table.

"I bought five pairs of casual slacks: Khaki, navy, gray, brown and black."

"Five? My lands, I won't live long enough to wear all these clothes."

She raised a shoulder. "Don't worry about it. If you kick the bucket before you get a chance to wear them all, I'll donate them to Goodwill. For every man looking for a mustard-colored suit, there are twenty others searching for something beautiful. They'll feel they hit the jackpot."

He flinched at the cutting words, though he didn't doubt their truthfulness. "Thanks, friend, your empathy is showing."

"Pay attention. I couldn't wait to get back to show you. I have vee-neck sweaters in red, black, yellow, light blue, bright green and white and—"

"Hold on. How many is that?"

"Sorry, I didn't realize you can't count past five." With her forefinger, she touched each shirt, counting slowly. "One . . . two . . . . three . . . four . . . five . . . six!" Without waiting for a snide remark, she picked up two packages of white tees. "These are to wear to work under your vee-neck sweaters."

"I have plenty of tee shirts."

"Wear them to sleep in."

"You're saying I can't wear them out?"

"I'm saying you've already worn them out."

"You're funny. Is that all?"

"Nope. Still in the car are two white dress shirts, two pair of dress pants, two sports coats and four new ties to wear to church or wherever more formal attire is required."

Mack rubbed his hand over the back of his neck. "Do I have enough money left to buy you dinner tonight?"

She gave a thumb's up. "I made sure of it."

"Well, this will be a practice run for that stupid date tomorrow night. I'd rather be thrown into a den of lions."

"If you don't want to go, why did you ask her out?"

"I didn't. She asked me."

Debbie laughed out loud. "You poor baby. But I'm sure you'll survive it. Who is she? Do I know her?"

"Remember that woman who called the other day and said her name was Jo Jenkins and that I was expecting her call?"

"Yeah, I thought it a little mysterious sounding. I've been dying to know who she was but didn't want to pry."

"You? Didn't want to pry? Forgive me for laughing. Since when did you care about prying into my personal affairs?"

She brushed his comment away with her hand. "Just tell me

how you met her."

"I haven't met her. At least if I have, I don't remember her. Luke set it up and it seemed important to him that I agree to take her out. She's his wife's cousin. So, what else could I do? I felt I owed him one."

"Mack you act as if he asked you to do a dastardly deed."

"How do I know he didn't?"

"You're being facetious. I'm sure you'll have a wonderful time."

"Which should I wear?" He picked up the red vee-neck sweater. "I like this."

"No, save that one."

"For what?"

"To wear Saturday."

"Why Saturday?"

"It's the fourteenth."

"Is that supposed to mean something?"

"February fourteenth? Hello? Doesn't that ring a bell?"

"Give me a hint."

"It's a holiday, Mack."

He snapped his fingers. "I get it. Father's Day, right? Thanks for reminding me, Deb. What would I do without you? Would you mind picking up something for me to give to Pop?"

"You're hopeless. It's Valentine's Day. I was saying it would be a good day to wear your red sweater."

"Whatever." Mack picked up the phone to call his father.

Jim's pulse raced, seeing Doyle's name pop up on his phone. "What's wrong, son? Are you sick?"

"Sick? Why would you think I'm sick?"

"Because you're calling me during work hours. You're alright, aren't you?"

"I'm fine, Daddy. I just called to tell you I'll be home late. I didn't want you to worry. I have a date tonight."

"A date? But why?"

Mack scratched his head. "What do you mean why? You've pestered me for four years to ask a girl out, and when I do, you act like you're disappointed."

"What makes you think this girl is right for you?"

"Daddy, I didn't say I was gonna marry her. I'm sure she'd love it if she were free to marry a hunk like me, but unfortunately for her, she's not free."

"She's in jail?"

"No. I mean she's not free to marry because she's already married."

"Son, you know I've tried to stay out of your affairs, but you're making it hard. Your mama would turn over in her grave if she knew you were out carousing around with a married woman. Come home and let's talk about this. I know you're lonely, but I have a feeling there's a wonderful, sweet, single girl out there, just waiting for you. I could almost guarantee it." Jim heard giggling in the background. "Who's that laughing?"

"My date. I'm crazy about her. She makes my heart go pitter-patter."

"She's with you now?"

"She's with me every day, Pop. She's my secretary."

"Aw pshaw. You were pulling my leg. I thought you were serious. Well, I approve. Deb is a sweet lady. I hope she tried that allergy medicine I told her about. I believe she said her husband was out of town for two weeks, so that's nice of you to take her to dinner."

"How do you know so much about my secretary?"

"Oh, we talk often."

"What reason would you have for calling her?"

"I don't call her. I call you, but she usually tells me you've given her instructions to say you're busy and can't talk, so we chat. She's got two grandchildren and she's excited that they'll be coming to see her on their Spring break."

"I didn't know that."

"Well, of course you didn't. All you know about is making money to invest to make more money. I wish you'd take more time to invest in lives, beginning with your own."

"I'll try to do better, Dad. I need to get busy."

"I know. You always need to get busy."

"I called to tell you not to fix dinner for me tonight."

"Bye, son." It was too late. Doyle had already hung up.

****

Mack stood when Debbie walked into the Salty Seas

Restaurant. "Wow! You clean up real good, girl."

"I suppose that's meant as a compliment, but you were right in saying we need to make this a practice run. Rule #1. That is not something you say to your date."

"Why not?"

"It seems to imply she was frumpy before, and finally got it right."

"No, no. That's not what I meant. I just meant I'm accustomed to seeing you in slacks, but that dress . . . well, it makes you look like a woman."

Deb popped her hand over her eyes. "Maybe we need to practice on how to give compliments before next Wednesday night." She glanced around the room. "Wow! What a swanky restaurant. I've never been here before."

The waiter came and after taking their order, Mack whispered. "How did I do? I'm not accustomed to dining with a lady. Did I do okay?"

"Perfect. If it's her first time in a restaurant and she doesn't seem to know what to order, but you've tried several dishes, it's good to suggest something."

"Yikes! I'm sorry. I could've done that."

"No, it's okay. When I saw Snapper throats, I knew that was exactly what I wanted. I was just saying to make a suggestion if she seems to be having trouble deciding. I'll have to tell David to bring me back here next month for our fortieth anniversary."

"Wow. Forty years with the same person. That's quite a

record."

"Mack, when you find your soul mate, time flies. It doesn't seem possible that David and I have been together that long. I really wish you could find someone to love, who loves you the way you deserve to be loved."

"I think that's about the nicest thing you've ever said to me."

"We joke around a lot at the office, but I want you to know my heart's desire is that you'll find someone to make you as happy as David has made me."

"Thanks. I'm not worrying about finding someone. I'm just hoping to get through Wednesday night."

"You'll do fine. Once you get there, the conversation will flow, and you'll see that you worried needlessly."

CHAPTER 14

Tuesday morning, Jim Mackenzie and George Dobbs met at the Senior Citizens Center for a game of dominoes.

"How's the love affair coming along between your son and that young woman you reeled in?" George asked.

"George, how can I thank you? She's the most wonderful lady I've ever known, Thelma excluded, of course. She's down-to-earth. Doesn't talk like all these young whippersnappers today. I can actually understand what she's saying. I read some of that stuff on social media written by the younger generation, and I can't make heads nor tails of what they're trying to say. I don't know if they even know. It's almost like they're speaking a different language. But Elizabeth is down to earth. She likes the simple things in life, like me. I hope my son is not so uppity that he won't realize a real prize when he meets her."

"I don't think you have to worry about Doyle not liking her, Jim. He probably won't even care if she's simple in the head after he gets a gander at what she looks like. Let me look at the picture again."

Jim proudly pulled a copy of Elizabeth's photo from his wallet and held it up for George to see.

He held it out at arm's length and whistled. "Now, that's one purty woman. You done real good, Jim. Just make sure you don't get so carried away you forget who she's falling in love with."

"You're funny, George. But it's amazing the things that pop in my mind that I hadn't thought of since my courting days. Of course, back then, I was quite the romantic cuss. I could make Thelma swoon with all my sweet talk. It's been so long ago, though, it took me awhile to get back in the groove. But, hey, I've got so good, I've been thinking it might be nice to find my own lady to try some of this out on."

"Why don't you, Jim?"

"Aw, shucks, I was just joshing. Elizabeth has me spoiled. I'd never find another woman like her or Thelma. Maybe I should just Sit Right Down and Write Myself a Letter." Jim whistled a little tune. "Remember that song, George?"

"Sure do."

"I'm gonna sit right down and write myself a letter . . . doo doop de do . . . gonna make believe it came from you—hoo," the men crooned, swaying back and forth.

"So, when are the two lovebirds getting together?" George asked.

"Sunday morning at a place called Heartie's."

"For real? I'll admit their hamburgers are hard to beat, but

103

couldn't you think of somewhere a little more romantic than a fast food joint?"

"I'm not talking about the fast food place, it's the name of a diner in Heartsboro. It may not be swanky, but I don't think the meeting place is gonna matter that much, when Doyle sees her for the first time. You may see fireworks all the way up here. They're crazy about one another."

"Jim! Aren't you forgetting Doyle hasn't met her? How can you say they're crazy about one another? She's been corresponding with *you*, not him, lamebrain."

"Well, you're the one who told me to do it this way. Are you now saying it was wrong?"

"No, I'm saying it seems to me you're the one getting stars in his eyes. I just don't want you getting hurt when Doyle gets the girl."

"Hogwash. I'll admit I've enjoyed the emails, but you make it sound evil. The only reason I've carried on all that love stuff was to win her over for Doyle, the way you taught me. I certainly don't want her for myself, ignoramus. I was joking about wanting to find me somebody. It's like I told you before—I'm still in love with Thelma, and I consider myself a married man, even if she has gone on to be with the Lord. I know she's waitin' for me up there."

"Well, Jim, my preacher said there ain't gonna be no marriages up in Heaven."

"Did I say I wanted to marry anybody? I'm already married, so it won't matter to me if there are no marriages up there. But just hush about all that. I don't want to hear any of your home-made theology about heaven. I've got my own ideas."

"Well, the Bible says—"

"George, stick to talking about something you know. I listen when you talk about fishing, because that's something you understand."

CHAPTER 15

Wednesday, February 12th

Crossing over the Florida Panhandle into Alabama, Mack glanced over at his father, and wondered how anyone could sleep while snoring so loud.

His throat tightened, seeing the road sign, "Welcome to Heartsboro, The Little Town with a Big Heart." He muttered, "Humph. The Place to Lose Your Heart would be a better description."

Jim roused up and blinked a couple of times. "I think I may have dozed off. Did you say something?"

"Nothing important. But look where we are, Pop."

Jim's chin trembled. "Ah, this looks mighty fine to me. Mighty fine. I've missed my old stomping grounds. Lots of memories were made here, weren't they son?"

"Yeah, Pop. Lots."

"Look, there's the ball field where you played ball all those summers. From the time you first went out for T-Ball, your mama started making Peanut Brittle to sell. She made sure we had enough money to pay registration, buy all your gear and to pay for camp. She worked night and day to make sure you had everything you needed, God bless her."

"I never knew that. I knew she made a lot of candy, and sold it at Church Bazaars, but I never thought about why she did it."

"Then when you got into Middle School and started playing basketball and going to dances and all the things young folks do, she started making Pound Cakes. Law, that woman could bake a pound cake that would melt in your mouth and people bought 'em as fast as she could take one out of the oven."

"Daddy, why didn't she ever tell me she was doing it for me?"

"Son, if she'd tried to tell you all she did for you, she would've had to give an account of every minute of every day. Everything she did was for you. She wanted to make sure you didn't want for nothing." Jim got a faraway look in his eyes. "There was only one thing she wanted for you that was left undone, but I made her a promise that I'd take care of it."

"You've mentioned a promise before. What kind of promise?"

"When the time comes, I'll tell you."

Mack didn't press him. He knew his father well enough to know if he didn't feel the time was right, there'd be no getting it out of him. He snapped his fingers when he realized he had the answer. "I know what it was."

"You do?"

"Yes. She wanted you to make sure I shaved every morning. Mama was a stickler about me shaving."

Jim reached up and rubbed the back of his hand against Mack's stubble. "Well, if that's what she asked me to do, I'm falling down on my job. My, how that woman did love you."

"I loved her, too, Pop. I'm afraid I didn't tell her enough."

"Aww, she knew it. Don't you worry about that. She never doubted it for a minute."

A few minutes later, they were driving into town when Jim clutched his hand over his heart. "Oh, m'goodness. Oh my!"

Mack slammed on breaks. "What's wrong, Dad?"

Jim pointed ahead, his eyes glistening. "There it is. The sign. Ain't that a sight for sore eyes?" He read aloud, "Heartsboro, Birthplace of Cupid."

Mack rolled his eyes.

"Me and yo' mama were newlyweds when the town took up money to pay for it. I sold bags of peanuts on the streets to help fund it, and there ain't another one in the world like it. Son, did I tell you about the day the Love Dust—"

"Only a thousand times."

Jim read the giant white banner with red letters stretched across Main Street: "When Hearts Come Home –Feb 12th – Feb 16th –Welcome to Heartsboro, The Little Town with a Big Heart." His cheeks glistened with tears. "My, my, this sure looks good to me."

Mack drove slowly through town, glancing from one side of

the street to the other. It was sad to see stores that were thriving businesses twenty years ago, now boarded up and the stores that remained in business needed a serious refurbishing. Didn't anyone buy paint anymore? It was good to see the Barbershop where he and his dad got all their haircuts was still thriving and the town newspaper, Heartsboro Legend, that came out once a week was still there. There was the Avon Theatre, the bank, the dime store, the hardware and Collins Department Store, where you could buy anything from fine China to fish bait.

It was the 1934 class that voted to change Homecoming from football season to basketball season and it always coincided with Valentines Day. Basketball was the main sport in Heartsboro. Seeing hundreds of giant heart-shaped balloons attached to every lamp post on Main Street and the paper hearts and angels plastered in all the store windows reminded him of his senior year, the night he and Liz rented a helium machine and blew up balloons to decorate the town. Strange, he still remembered the exact number. But there wasn't much about that night that he didn't remember.

He recalled the gang going over to Bonnie's house to cut out paper hearts and cupids and the brazen way Bonnie made a play for him. Liz had never given him reason to believe she was jealous, until that night. He finally convinced her he wasn't the least bit interested in Bonnie Bloodworth. It was the first and last real fight he and Liz ever had. If he'd known then, what he found out later, he might not have turned Bonnie down. But there are lots of things he would've changed, had he known the truth about Liz Farley back then.

He saw his dad pull a handkerchief from his pocket and take off his glasses. He dabbed at his moistened eyes and placed his glasses back on his face. He appeared to be taking in all the sights, but he didn't say a word.

A knot formed in Mack's throat. It was his idea to move his father to Point Clear. Maybe he was wrong to insist. And there was no getting around it—he did insist. Why did he come back? This was a mistake for them both. What did he expect to gain? Did he honestly think he'd be able to pick up where he left off? Sure, he had a lot of friends in high school, but time changes people. He knew them years ago. He didn't know them now and they didn't know him. Adding to his angst was the thought of going on a date that evening with someone he didn't know. Why did he agree? If it weren't for his dad, he'd turn around and head back to Point Clear, but it seemed the old fellow had an obsession about returning to his roots. Mack's throat tightened.

He wouldn't have his dad with him always. Feelings of shame overwhelmed him as he thought of how often he was short with his father. True, the old fellow got on his last nerve at times, but there was no denying his father loved him dearly and only wanted the best for him, even if he didn't always get it right. What if bringing him back to his hometown turned out to be his last request? Mack wouldn't have been able to live with himself if he refused him the last thing he ever asked for. No matter how much he'd like to turn the car around and head back, for his father's sake, he couldn't do it.

"Pop, are you okay?"

A smile stretched across the old man's leathery face, and at the same time, he dabbed at another tear rolling down his wrinkled cheek. "Okay? Son, I can't remember when I've been this okay. I have a real good feeling about coming back. Don't you love how festive everything looks, all decorated for Valentine's Day? Ain't it pretty?"

"It's decorated for Homecoming, dad. The school colors just happen to be red and white."

"Oh, yeah. I remember you telling me that. Remind me again. What is the mascot?"

Mack blew in his fist. He was quite positive his dad knew the answer to his own question, since he'd attended every baseball and basketball game that Mack ever played in. "It's Cupid. We're the Heartsboro Angels."

Jim nodded, knowingly. "That's what I was thinking. And I suppose those cute little red cut-outs with HHS printed on them in all the store windows are deflated basketballs and not Valentines?"

He rolled his eyes, at his father's attempt to make his point. "They're called Hearts, Pop . . . after all, this is Heartsboro. Get it?"

"I do get it, son. I'm just not sure you get it. I think it's wonderful the way the town celebrates such a special day, dedicated to love. It isn't a coincidence that Homecoming is planned during the month of February, or that the town is known as The Little Town with a Big Heart."

Mack chuckled. "And don't forget the important part, that it's the birthplace of Cupid." He recalled a time when he went along with the fantasy and pretended to believe, just as he'd pretended to believe in Santa, long after he knew better. No more.

Pop grinned. "Cupid's birthplace? Some say yes, some no. You can make up your own mind, but I have my own thoughts. I just wish you hadn't given up on love after that little girl went away to college and broke your heart."

Mack's fingers tightened on the steering wheel. He felt his father's hand reach around the seat and gently rub his back.

"Doyle, I know you soured on love, but I have a feeling that life is about to get sweet again. I think you're gonna meet your match real soon, son."

He forced a smile. "When pigs fly."

CHAPTER 16

Liz and Maggie packed the car and headed to Heartsboro. Maggie could hardly contain her excitement. She and Liz had been neighbors for fourteen years and in all that time, she'd never seen her truly happy. After her husband's death, Liz began to draw into a shell.

Maggie hoped seeing all her former high school friends would pull her out of that shell and prepare her to love again the way she once loved the guy who broke her heart. Although he could possibly show up for Homecoming, Maggie wasn't worried. It had been sixteen years since the college breakup. He'd be married by now, which would be exactly what Liz needed to see to get him out of her mind so she could move on with her life. The moving on would happen on Sunday morning when she and Doyle would discover one another. "I can hardly wait."

Liz turned. "What did you say, Maggie?"

"Nothing, dear."

"It didn't sound like nothing. I don't know what's going on in your mind, but when you get that look, it scares me."

"Why should it scare you?"

"It's the same Cheshire-cat look you had just before the biker turned up at my door. At least I can relax for a few days, since you don't know anyone in Heartsboro."

"You're exactly right, sugar. However, if you have as much fun as I hope you have while we're here, then the smile on my face may become permanent."

"Maggie, I pick at you a lot, but I don't know what I would've done without you, these last few years. In case I haven't told you enough, I appreciate all you do for me."

"Oh my!" Maggie pointed up ahead. "Looks like the police are stopping traffic. Do you have your Driver's License with you?"

"Of course, I do."

Liz pulled up behind the vehicle in front of her. The officer walked around the car, appearing to look at the tag, then handed something to the driver and motioned him on.

Maggie said, "It looks as if they're checking tags."

"Yes, I believe you're right."

The officer walked around Liz's car, then came back around and leaned in. "I see you're from Pike County. Welcome to Heartsboro, The Little Town with a Big Heart. Are you here for the Homecoming festivities?"

Before Liz could answer, he blurted, "Well, if it's not Liz Farley! Wow! Welcome home, stranger."

"Hi Blake, I thought I recognized you. I didn't know you were in Law Enforcement."

"A shocker, isn't it? The Jesse James of Heartsboro High turns cop. But who understands the criminal mind more than another criminal?"

"You were never a criminal. Just mischievous."

"So mischievous that your grandmother forbade me to come over to your house, isn't that so, Mrs. Farley?"

Liz cackled. "She isn't my grandmother. Blake Andrews, meet my neighbor, Maggie Askew. Maggie, Blake graduated two years before I did, and he lived down the street from me, growing up."

Blake said, "I should have known that pretty lady wasn't your grandmother. It's obvious I couldn't see her good or I would've known. Begging your pardon, ma'am, but I never got a good look at Mrs. Farley because she was always chasing me off. Looking back, I can't blame her. I was crazy about Liz. Some folks just said, I was crazy. Well, I'm causing traffic to back up." He handed Liz a welcome packet with two large Valentines. "Married?"

Maggie leaned forward. "Yes, young man."

"Good seeing you, Liz. . . and you, too, ma'am." He motioned them on.

"Maggie, when Blake asked if I was married, why did you say yes?"

"Because you were married. Once."

"You know that's not what he was asking."

"What difference does it make? You've never mentioned him before. Besides, you wouldn't want to give him the impression

115

you're available. I trust your grandmother's judgment and if she didn't feel he was good enough for her granddaughter, I'm sure she had her reasons."

"All Memaw knew about him was neighborhood gossip. She didn't really know him. It's true, he didn't always think about his actions, which often got him in trouble, but it was never anything serious. He was hilariously funny and could keep me in stitches. He was right about Memaw, though. She'd run him off with a broom when he'd come looking for me. I was only in the ninth grade, and he was in the eleventh and she thought I was too young to date."

"I'm sure that wasn't the only reason she didn't want him hanging around."

"For Memaw, that was the only reason she needed. She died at the end of the summer, and my sophomore year I began dating Mack and never dated anyone else after that." She paused, then added, "Until Carter came along, of course."

"Sugar, you've never had a chance to know what real love feels like. One day, and I believe it will be very soon, the right man will come into your life."

"You sound like you're reading from a fortune cookie."

"Mark my word. It's going to happen. I feel it in my bones."

"I'm guessing it feels a lot like rheumatism?"

"Poke fun all you like, but one day in the not-too-distant future, you're gonna say, 'Maggie, how did you know?'"

As they rode through town, Maggie oohed and ahhed over the

Valentine decorations. Red and white balloons were tied to every lamppost and cut-out cupids, angels and hearts were plastered everywhere. "I love this little town. These people go all out for Valentine's Day, don't they?"

Liz lowered her voice to a whisper. "You can't even imagine." She was beginning to feel sick on her stomach. She knew better than to come back here.

Riding down Main Street, Maggie pointed to a large banner hanging from one side of the street to the other. "Oh, m'goodness. Would you look. How cute is that? WHEN HEARTS COME HOME - Feb 12th – Feb 16th –WELCOME TO HEARTSBORO, THE LITTLE TOWN WITH A BIG HEART.'" She waited for Liz to respond, but when she didn't, Maggie said, "Don't you get it?"

Liz smirked. "I don't think there's a subliminal message there, Maggie. It's just a sign advertising Homecoming. They probably hang the same sign every February, since Homecoming is always planned around Valentine's Day."

"But don't you see? It's saying all those who left their hearts in Heartsboro are returning home to observe the one special holiday that's dedicated to hearts." She shivered and wrapped her arms around her mid-section. "I Suwannee, that makes chills run over my body."

"I'll turn up the heater. Maybe that'll help."

"Fiddle faddle. You know what I mean. It's so romantic sounding." She sang a few bars of "I Left My Heart in San Francisco," but changed the words from San Francisco to

Heartsboro. She reached over and poked Liz. "Don't be a stick-in-the-mud. We're here to have fun. Put on your happy face."

Liz shook her head disapprovingly. "Maybe I'd understand if I'd left anything here, but I didn't."

CHAPTER 17

Wednesday, February 12th

Liz rounded the corner and pulled up in front of a beautiful Victorian home with a sign out front, 'Latimer's Bed & Breakfast.' She parked the car and said, "Well, looks like we're here."

Maggie leaned her head down to get a better look. "Oh, my lands, sugar, it's absolutely gorgeous, and it's right smack in the center of town. How convenient. The picture on the Internet didn't do it justice. And look at that porch. Isn't it fabulous?"

Liz shrugged. "If you like that sort of thing. I can't imagine what I could do on a wrap-around porch that I couldn't do on my front stoop." As they walked up the steps, Maggie said, "Did you ever stay here?"

"I had no need to. I lived here. The Bed & Breakfast was here when I was in high school." The mere mention of high school sent shivers down her spine. What was she doing here? How did she let Maggie talk her into coming back to the last place on earth she wanted to be?

Maggie turned around, seemingly taking in everything in viewing distance. "I'm crazy about this porch. I'm sure I'll enjoy sitting out here in the swing, watching the people go by while you're out having fun with your classmates."

Liz groaned. "How about if I enjoy sitting in the swing and you go out and have fun with my classmates."

"Fiddle faddle. Stop being such a stick-in-the-mud, Lizzie."

"I don't even know what that means, Maggie. Do you?"

"Of course. It means the stick isn't going anywhere if it's stuck, and you're like that stick. You've been stuck in the same boring situation, way too long, missy."

Liz chose to let it go. What was the point in reminding Maggie her explanation didn't make sense? It would only lead to another nonsensical example.

As they walked up the tall concrete steps, Maggie pointed to a large clay container of tulips near the front door. "Would you look at those beautiful tulips. Someone here must have a green thumb. Liz, I want you to make a genuine effort to dispel with all negative thoughts and expect something wonderful to happen this weekend. If you're looking for nothing good to happen, you won't likely see it when it comes your way. Be optimistic. Expect something great to happen."

"Maggie, you don't know how I wish I could be like you, but I'm a realist. It must be wonderful to always see the bright side of life."

120

"Bless your heart, hon, you could too, if you'd try a little harder. You get what you expect, Liz. If you expect things to go wrong, they probably will. But if you take a positive view at life, you'll begin to see things in a totally different light. It's time to dispel with all negativity. Will you try it this weekend? For me?"

Liz reached up and rang the doorbell. It was a huge task to ask of her, but why ruin the trip for Maggie. "I'll try. I promise. But don't expect miracles."

A sweet lady opened the door and invited, them in. She introduced herself as Catherine and took them on a tour of the home. Liz remembered Mrs. Latimer had hosted one of their graduation parties in the beautiful parlor. She remembered wishing she could see the upstairs. Tonight, she'd have that opportunity.

The massive winding staircase with lush scarlet carpeting led to six bedrooms, baths, and a cozy sitting room.

Catherine said, "Liz, I believe another one of your classmates is staying in the next room—they both seem very nice, the 'McGinney's.

Liz hesitated, then shook her head. "The name doesn't ring a bell, but then it's been twenty years, since graduation."

Catherine walked them to their room. "Well, I need to get back to the desk. I hope you two are comfortable."

Maggie said, "Honey, didn't you say you brought your yearbook? Why don't we look up the McGinney's and put a face to the name?"

"But Maggie, I have no idea who the women in my class

married, so I wouldn't recognize any of their last names."

"I suppose you're right. I didn't think about that."

Liz and Maggie took their bags into their room and Liz sat hers down on the antique four-poster bed closest to the door. Glancing around, the room wasn't much different than what she imagined. Maybe a little larger than she'd expected, and the filled bookshelves were certainly a plus, in case she finished the two books she brought. She loved the high ceilings with beautiful crown molding and the tiny lilacs in the floral wallpaper. The theme of lilacs was carried throughout the room. There were lilacs on the lampshade, pictures of lilac fields on the wall, and sitting on the vanity was a small clay pot with silk lilacs that Liz had to touch to prove they weren't real. She sat down and bounced on the big antique bed. "I'm accustomed to a hard mattress. I'm afraid I'll sink down on this and smother to death, although it does feel good in an odd sort of way. I think I could get used to it."

Maggie's bed was near the window. She sat her bag on the luggage rack, opened it and pulled out a five-by-seven photograph of her late husband. She held it to her lips, kissed it and then placed it on the table next to her bed. "Well, Robert, we finally made it, and I do believe we're gonna have a lovely time, don't you, darling? I hope it isn't too warm for you, being so near the heater. I know how hot-natured you are."

Liz stood and opened her luggage. Without making eye contact, she said, "Maggie, I don't want to hurt your feelings, but must you do that?"

122

"What, dear?"

"That!" She pointed to the photo. "It's not normal and it bothers me to see you doing it."

Maggie's wounded expression made Liz want to stick a sock in her mouth, but she'd gone this far, she might as well say it. "Have you noticed how sometimes elderly people talk to themselves? It's weird, don't you think? Have you ever wondered how they got started?"

"Never gave it much thought. Why, dear? Do you have a theory?"

"I do, as a matter-of-fact. I think it probably begins by talking to inanimate objects until it becomes habit, and they eventually lose all sense of reality."

"Like talking to a photograph, maybe?"

"Exactly. It gives me the willies to hear you talking to that picture, as if you think he can hear you."

"Oh, hon, I'm sorry. I didn't realize it bothered you." She turned around and plunked her hands on her hips. "Did you hear that, Robert? Well, darling, I hope you won't think I'm upset with you if I don't talk to you until we get home, but we don't want to give Lizzie the willies." She leaned closer to the picture and cupped her hand over her ear. "What's that, sweetheart?" She popped her hand over her mouth. "Robert Askew! Be ashamed. You shouldn't say things like that about my dearest friend."

Liz glared. "What did he say?"

Maggie's eyes widened and her mouth gaped open. "Oh

123

m'goodness, did you just ask what Robert said? He's dead, dear. He can't talk." She walked over and placed the back of her hand on Liz's forehead. "Are you feeling okay, hon?" Maggie laughed until her eyes watered.

Liz picked up a pillow and threw it at her. "You think you're smart. But if you keep pulling those silly stunts, don't forget I have power of attorney and you and Robert can continue your conversations in the Nursing Home." Maggie's crazy sense of humor was one of the things Liz loved most about her, even though it sometimes drove her crazy.

Maggie finished unpacking and said, "Why don't we ride through town and locate a good breakfast place?"

Liz lifted the corner of her lip. "You're joking, of course."

"Why would I be joking? I'm serious. Let's see what we can find."

"What do you mean, what we can find? This is a B&B. Get it? A Bed *and* Breakfast. Stop being funny."

Maggie fidgeted. Why didn't she think of this when Doyle set up the appointment to meet for breakfast? Without her computer, there was no way to contact him to let him know she needed to change the meeting place. What if she couldn't convince Liz to eat breakfast at the diner Sunday morning? "Did I say breakfast? I meant a good little cafe where we might want to have lunch. Besides, I'd like to ride around and check out the town. I've never been here, and you seldom talk about it."

"Not much to talk about, really. But I can show you where I grew up, where I went to church, and my old school, if you're really interested."

"I'd love it." As they rode around town, Maggie kept looking for Heartie's Diner. She clamped her hand over her mouth when Liz shouted, "Oh look, there's the diner. It looks exactly the way it did back when we were in high school. They were known for their chili dogs."

Maggie breathed a sigh of relief.

"Maggie, why don't we stop in and see if the hot dogs are as good as I remember them."

"That's an excellent idea,"

After finishing her meal, Maggie now had a plan. She bragged about how delicious the hot dogs were. She even sent word to the cook that she'd never experienced such wonderful chili. "Why I could eat these delicious dogs three times a day."

"My, I never knew you were such a hot dog fan, Maggie."

"I've never tasted one quite like these. They're simply superb."

"We'll ride around town, and I'll show you some of the hot spots. I'll take you by my grandmother's house first, where I spent most of my childhood."

CHAPTER 18

Liz drove down Gilmore Street and almost passed her Memaw and Pawpaw's house. She backed up and pulled into the drive. Her chin quivered as she sat quietly behind the wheel, her wide-eyed gaze shifting slowly from the overgrown yard to the rotten boards on the unpainted house, to the torn screens, to the missing shingles.

Maggie said, "Is something wrong, hon?"

She licked her dry lips. "It looks much smaller than I remembered."

"Would you like to get out and look around?"

Liz shook her head. "I don't think so. I'd rather remember it with Memaw in it."

Liz drove and Maggie chatted nonstop, asking a million questions while taking in the scenery. When Liz turned down the road the church was on, an old familiar heartache returned. Her thoughts took her back to the scene, twenty-nine years ago, yet it was as vivid as if it were yesterday. Tears flooded her eyes, recalling the conversation: *No, granddaddy. No, please don't make me do it, granddaddy.* She could still see the two gray caskets with silver trim at the back of the sanctuary and could feel her granddaddy's strong arms lifting her up, insisting she kiss her mama and daddy goodbye. For years, Liz woke up screaming in the night, pleading with him to put her down. She still remembered the smell of the flowers and had never been fond of floral smells since that day.

She pointed to the cemetery next to the church. "I was only eight when my parents died. I hate that my most vivid memories are of seeing them lying in a casket."

Maggie reached over and placed her hand on Liz's shoulder. "I'm sorry, hon. It's still very painful, isn't it? Would it help to talk about it?"

"Not enough memories to talk about. Memaw and Pawpaw got rid of everything that belonged to mama and daddy, even their pictures, and scolded me if I asked questions. I suppose it was their way of coping. I wish I could've known my parents long enough to form lasting memories."

Maggie said, "Liz, I think I understand now, why you were so opposed to returning to Heartsboro. It's filled with sad memories for you. I'm so sorry, sweetie."

Liz knew Maggie thought she understood—but there was no way she could begin to understand just how many sad memories there really were. Heartsboro should be called Hurtsboro.

****

Jim said, "Son, do you remember that little eating joint called Heartie's Diner on Highway 27?"

Mack chewed the inside of his cheek. How could he forget? It was where he and Liz went every Thursday night after the Pep Rally. It was where he carved their names on a table. It was where he gave her a promise ring. And that was his big mistake. The promise was one-sided. He promised. He thought she did. How could something that happened so long ago cause his blood to boil every time he thought about it? Why couldn't he forget and move on?

"Mack? You look as if you're a thousand miles away."

"Nope, I'm right here, Pop. I heard you. And yes, I do remember the Diner."

"I remember they were famous for their hot dogs. I wonder if they still use the same chili recipe."

"I doubt it. It's been twenty years."

Jim's face scrunched in a frown. "Twenty years? But I've only been gone from here four years. What are you talking about?"

Mack rubbed his hand across the back of his neck. "You're right. Four years."

"After you graduated college, Mama and I used to go there every Saturday night and get us a hot dog. I thought she needed a night out. She cooked three times a day while you were growing up and we didn't have the money back then to eat out."

"Pop, you and Mama sacrificed a lot to send me to the University and I never considered how expensive it was for me to participate in sports, but you never complained."

"Aw, shucks, son, we were tickled to death when you made

128

the basketball team. and the scholarship was a big help. I don't know how we could've swung it, if it hadn't been for that, but I'm sure we would've made arrangements, somehow."

"I don't doubt it for a minute. I'm glad you shared with me about you and Mama making those special Saturday night memories."

Mack had never been fond of hot dogs, but he'd come down hard on his dad the last couple of days and the guilt was eating him up. He pulled up in front of the Diner. "Come on, Pop. Let's go in and have lunch. We'll find out if those hot dogs are as good as they were when you and Mama came here on Saturday nights

****

Liz and Maggie went back to the Bed & Breakfast. Liz glanced over the itinerary: Wednesday evening, Downtown Street Fair and Antique Car Show; Thursday morning; Assembly at Heartsboro High School and Downtown Parade after lunch; Friday night, Dance; Saturday night, Basketball Game. Unimpressed, she tossed it aside.

Maggie reached over and picked it up. "I'm so excited, aren't you, hon?"

Liz remembered her promise to keep a positive attitude. She gritted her teeth and said, "Yes ma'am, Maggie. I'm just tickled pink."

Maggie said, "Well, that's the attitude I like for you to have. According to the brochure, the fun begins tonight at sundown. It says there'll be a sidewalk café set up on Main Street, an antique car show and socializing in the streets to the sounds of the Original Bama Jama Band 'til midnight. Doesn't that sound like fun?"

Liz shook her head and pulled a book from her luggage. "That's for the younger set. I'm too old for that sort of thing,"

"Nonsense, honey, I'm at least fifteen years older than you and it sounds exciting to me."

"Yes, at least fifteen," Liz winked. Maggie seemed to sometimes forget Liz knew exactly how old she was.

****

After riding his father through familiar neighborhoods and revisiting a few childhood memories, Mack and his dad arrived back at the Bed and Breakfast. Mack hadn't mentioned to his dad that he had a four-thirty date. It wasn't that he was particularly trying to conceal it, but he had no desire to spend his time thinking about it.

"Pop, I'm going out for a little while. I hope you don't mind. I don't plan to be gone long."

"You go right ahead, son. Don't you worry about me. I'll be fine. It feels wonderful just to be back home, doesn't it?"

"I've been gone a lot longer than you, Pop. I don't look at it as home, anymore."

"Son, you must know how it breaks my heart to hear you say that."

Mack didn't try to hide the anger in his voice. "Are you serious? Why would you care where I call home? Besides, you live with me now. Point Clear is our home."

"No, Doyle. It's a beautiful place, but we've made no memories there. My heart will always be here."

Mack had patiently put up with his dad's grumblings in the beginning. He understood there'd be a period of adjustment, but after four years, it was time for the old fellow to realize that life moves on. Maybe Pop didn't have memories in Point Clear, but Mack had plenty. When he moved there, he had a small office on the backside of nowhere, with one employee. Now, he had a sprawling office building in Fairhope with fifty-two people working under him and another in Mobile. He had memories of purchasing his first piece of property on the water—a little one-bedroom cottage, built in 1952. Now he owned half-a-dozen beautiful prime waterfront condos, worth millions. He had made plenty of memories, but why argue? Nothing would be settled, anyway. "Pop, if you get bored while I'm gone, you can probably find a few good movies on TV."

"I'm not much of a TV fan. Too much filth on nowadays, but you run on and see if you can find some friends to visit with."

"Are you sure you don't mind?"

"Doyle, don't hurry back on my account. I've been looking forward to this weekend. I'm home. I can find plenty to do here. I have friends I can call, I can take a walk, or I can sit on that big, wrap-around porch and listen to the band playing downtown."

"Well, you might like to walk down the street and sit and watch the people. There's a little sidewalk café that's been set up specifically for Homecoming. It might be fun to sit at one of the tables and people watch. Who knows, you might find you a pretty lady to enjoy the evening with."

"Hogwash. You know your mama was the only woman for me."

"I was just teasing with you, Pop."

"But since you mention it, I just might take a stroll downtown. Maybe I'll see some of my old buddies hanging out around the Barber Shop."

"If you do decide to go out, you might want to pick up a sandwich and a bowl of soup at the café, or you can wait for me to get back and I'll take you wherever you want to go. I shouldn't be gone too long."

Mack went into the bathroom and came out wearing a new pair of gray slacks and a yellow vee-neck sweater.

His father turned and looked. His mouth gaped open. "Where are you going so gussied up?"

"I told you I was going out."

"Out where? You look like you've got a date, but I know better than that." He walked over and sniffed his neck. "You even got on smell-goody. What are you up to?"

His lip curled at the corner. "Okay, I might as well confess. I do have a date."

"Pfft, you ain't fooling me. Doyle, please tell me you didn't set up a business meeting for this weekend. Son, all you do is work."

"No, Pop. I told you I have a date. It's a blind date and I'm

132

going as a favor to a friend. I don't have time to chat. I'll barely make it there on time, now."

"But you aren't really interested in this blind girl, are you?"

Mack chuckled. "She's not blind, Pop."

"But you just said—"

"I know what I said, but a blind date just means you've never seen the person before."

"Then how do you know you have a date?"

"Because she called and asked me out."

"She called you?" Jim clicked his tongue. "Times have sure changed since my day. When I was young, the boy asked the girl out, not the other way around."

"Does it really matter who does the asking?"

"It would to me."

"I'm sure it would, but it's four-fifteen and I'm supposed to meet her at the restaurant in fifteen minutes. I'd just as soon go and get this over with."

Mack started toward the door, then stopped and turned around. "Pop, if you do decide to walk to town, be sure to wear your jacket and hat. It's turning colder."

"You act like I'm ready for the Funny Farm. By Jove, I'm not so old that I need you to tell me when to get out of the rain."

"I didn't mean to offend you. It was just a reminder. We've had a mild winter, but I think that's about to change."

Jim smiled. "That's not the only thing that's about to change."

CHAPTER 19

Mack drove to the Beckham Pecan Grove and saw a sign on the highway—"Andre's Epicurean Grill." He popped his palm to his forehead, unable to believe his eyes. There wasn't a Pecan tree in sight. The Beckhams two-story farmhouse built in the early 1900's was gone. Nothing left but an open field, and two rows of Date Palms lining either side of a long, winding drive leading to a large, ugly pink Art Deco style building. What could they possibly serve there that one couldn't get at The Old Mill Restaurant? It had been the go-to place for steaks and seafood for over seventy years.

His stomach knotted as he walked past concrete statues of frogs situated on either side of the door. Ridiculous. This might be fine for city folks, but not for a place billed as "The Little Town with a Big Heart." Was Heartsboro losing its small-town charm? He tried to shake it off. Why should it matter to him? This was no longer his hometown. But it did matter. In fact, it mattered so much he decided to do something about it at his first opportunity.

He handed the valet his keys, then walked into the restaurant and looked around. The hostess said, "Are you meeting someone, sir?"

"Yes, but she's probably not here yet."

"Perhaps she is. There's a lovely young woman in the back corner who said a gentleman would be joining her. Would you like to see if it's your party?"

"Thank you, I would."

It was so dark he wondered if he'd be able to see the menu. A little candlelight could offer ambience, but this was ludicrous. He spotted a woman alone and decided to introduce himself and hope he didn't wind up embarrassing them both. Why he agreed to do this baffled him. Surely, there were other ways he could've thanked Luke for his business. Before he was close enough to see her face, he heard his name called.

"Mack, I got here a little early. I hope you didn't mind me finding us a table. This is cozy, don't you think?"

He squinted his eyes. The voice was familiar, yet when his eyes adjusted to the darkness, he was convinced he'd never seen this woman in his life.

With a dramatic sweep of her hand, she brushed a headful of long, blonde hair away from her shoulder and licked her red lips. Luke was right. She was a beauty. His Adam's apple bobbed. *It couldn't be.* He walked closer and squinted his eyes. "Bonnie? Bonnie Bloodworth?"

"Yes, silly. Who did you think it was?" She jerked on the tail of his jacket. "For heaven's sake, sit down. Everyone is staring."

Everyone? Was she serious? There were only four other people in the dining hall, and all were seated at the same table. Mack rubbed the back of his neck, a nervous habit. "Sorry, but there's been a mistake. I'm supposed to meet someone here named 'Jo'."

"I am Jo." She reached for his hand. "I didn't mean to sound so curt, but I was beginning to feel like a pick-up. You know what I mean? Beautiful woman walks in restaurant alone, everyone stares, she waits, and then a gentleman comes over and yet he can't seem to decide whether to go or stay."

"But Luke called you Jo."

"If you recall, I was called Bonnie Jo in elementary school. Then, In high school, everyone shortened it to Bonnie, but I prefer Jo, so when I opened my law practice, I began introducing myself as Jo Jenkins." She patted the chair next to her. "Well don't stand there looking petrified. Have a seat."

He sat down and rubbed the back of his neck. "I knew you sounded familiar on the phone, yet I never thought about it being you. Listening to you now, your voice still sounds like the Bonnie I remember."

She reached over and laid her hand on top of his. "I've thought of you often through the years, also, Mack."

Also? He quickly tried to recall what he could've said that would've given her the idea she'd ever crossed his mind. Easing his hand from beneath hers, he picked up his napkin and placed it in his lap.

She said, "When Trudy told me Luke said you were planning to return for Homecoming, I was sure it was fate, bringing us together after all these years. I've always believed we would've been together if Liz Farley hadn't latched on to you like a leech in high school. Remember the night we were all at my house, cutting out paper hearts, and she walked in, just when you were about to kiss me?" Her shrill voice caused those around them to turn and look. Mack slinked down in his chair.

"You do remember, don't you?"

"Vaguely." He remembered it all right. He just didn't remember it the same way she did. He wasn't going to kiss her. Surely, she knew that. Had time warped her memory? She only slid close and puckered up when she saw Liz coming.

She smiled. "Don't kid me. I think you remember it as well as I do. I was glad when I heard you dumped her."

He picked up a menu and hoped he successfully hid his shock when he saw the prices. "Have you had an opportunity to decide what you'd like?"

She leaned in and laid her hand on his forearm. "What I'd like is sitting across the table from me."

Pulling back, Mack rubbed his neck while glaring at the menu. "The stuffed crab sounds good. I think I'll try it." Though his focus remained on the menu, he could feel her glaring eyes.

Bonnie appeared miffed, though he couldn't imagine why. She motioned for the waiter. "I'll take the Snapper Pontchartrain with a twice-baked potato, asparagus, and the House Salad with extra dressing."

The waiter turned to Mack. "And you, sir?"

"Bring me the stuffed crab, garlic potatoes, marinated beans and . . . I guess I'll take the slaw."

There was an awkward silence as they waited for their meal. Not that he minded. It wasn't nearly as awkward as having Bonnie pretend that they were somehow romantically linked in the past, while making a vain attempt to rekindle a romance that never existed. She was a good-looking woman, but she made him nervous. He tried to initiate a conversation. "Do you have any pets?"

"No." She cut her eyes away from him.

"Me either. I had a German Shepherd named Rusty, but he died of old age two years ago. I haven't wanted to get that attached to another animal."

She shrugged, then took a sip of water.

He'd begun to question Debbie's dating tactics. Apparently, there was something she forgot to tell him, because this wasn't going so well. He wore the right clothes; it was impossible for him to make a menu suggestion since he'd never eaten there, and he didn't tell her she cleaned up good. There was no conversation taking place. Nothing was going the way Deb predicted.

He took another stab. "How's your fish?"

She nodded. "Mushy."

"Is that a good thing?"

She glared at him as if he had horns on top of his head. "What

138

do you think?"

"I don't know. I've never had it before. What did you call it? Snapper Pontchartrain?"

She gave a curt nod, then lifted her hand high in the air and motioned for the waiter.

"Something wrong, miss?"

"Yes. Please take this plate back to the kitchen. The fish is mushy, and the asparagus is overcooked."

"My apologies, ma'am. Could I get you something else?"

"That's a stupid question. I came here to enjoy a good meal."

"Yes ma'am. What would you like?"

"I'd like the same thing I ordered, but at these ridiculous prices, I expect it to be cooked to perfection. Is that too much to ask?"

Her rude behavior caught Mack by surprise. After she made such a spectacle, he was glad there was no one in the restaurant who knew him.

The young man walked away with her plate, and Bonnie slammed her napkin on the table. "I declare I don't know what they teach at Culinary Schools today. One would expect to get a decent meal in a five-star restaurant."

Mack leaned in, keeping his voice low. "Bonnie, I can't help wondering if it was the way your food was prepared that upset you, or if you took your frustration out on the waiter, because you were upset with me."

She reached in her bag and took out a tube of lipstick and a small mirror, then preceded to paint her lips. Glancing up, she said, "Oh, well, I suppose I did overreact, but we won't let that little episode spoil our time together, will we? I've thought of you so often through the years, Mack."

Mack planted his elbows on the table, with his hands clasped under his chin. "Bonnie, if I hurt your feelings, believe me, it was unintentional. But frankly, you made me uncomfortable bringing up a past I'd like to forget. Tell me what you've been up to since high school. I assume you've been married, since your last name was Bloodworth when we were in school. I believe Luke said you practice law. Here in Heartsboro?"

The tension eased when she was offered the opportunity to share her impressive life's story. She married a guy who was a partner in the law firm of Jenkins, Taylor and Hughes. Since she made a point of trying to impress Mack with her ex-husband's importance, he nodded as if he knew all about him. She rambled on, giving details of her divorce before and after.

She said, "The divorce was very amiable, and I got everything I wanted."

"That's nice." Mack reached up and rubbed the back of his neck. "I didn't mean it was nice. I'm sure divorce is never nice. I simply meant—"

She took a swallow of water and glared. "It's okay, Mack. I can see you're nervous. Do I do that to you?"

"It's not you, Bonnie. I mean, Jo."

"It's okay to call me Bonnie. It sounds romantic, the way you say it."

"Maybe I am nervous. It's just that I haven't dated since—well, since college."

"Why not? You're still a very handsome man, and you've apparently made a name for yourself. I'm sure you've had plenty of chances."

"I haven't had time. I've been building a business."

She reached up and stroked his cheek with the back of her hand. "Well, I hope you'll allow me to change that pattern. All work and no play could make Mack a very dull boy. We wouldn't want that, now would we?" She leaned in and whispered. "I'm a good playmate. Just saying."

Mack pulled his arm back when the Chef came to their table and introduced himself. "My sincerest apologies, ma'am. I'm truly sorry that you didn't enjoy your meal. Since I only prepare the Pontchartrain one way, I can only suggest that you choose another entrée. I'm sorry the asparagus wasn't to your liking, and it will be no trouble to prepare it according to your specifications."

"I don't want anything else. I've eaten the fish here more than once and it was always delicious, so either you prepare it properly, or bring nothing at all."

"As you wish, madam. Your meal will be extracted from you bill. I'm so sorry we were unable to please you."

The skin around her eyes tightened. "You must be new here."

"No ma'am, I'm not only the chef, I'm the owner and the only one who has ever prepared the Snapper Pontchartrain. Perhaps

141

your tastes have changed."

"Well, I've never been talked to in such a discourteous manner. You are not only a poor excuse for a chef, you're a very rude man."

Mack glanced at the chef and mouthed the words. "I'm sorry." He reached in his pocket and pulled out his wallet to retrieve his credit card. The chef walked away, and the waiter came over and took his card.

Bonnie said, "Bring us a to-go box, please and make sure my meal is removed from the ticket."

Mack shook his head and held up his palm. "No, a box won't be necessary, and I'd like to pay for what we ordered. My meal was delicious and far more than I could eat. Give my regards to the chef."

Bonnie's bottom lip poked out. "A box, please. I wasn't asking for you, Mack. I haven't eaten, and I plan to eat your leftovers when we get to my apartment."

The waiter came back and handed Mack his credit card and Bonnie her box.

Mack couldn't get out of there fast enough. What a horrible night. If this was a taste of modern dating, he was glad he hadn't been exposed before now. "Bonnie, I'll walk you to your car. I'm afraid I need to get back to the B & B and check on Pop."

"Aww, Mack, it's still early. Let's go to my apartment. I'm sure your father will be fine. He's probably sound asleep."

"I'm sorry, Bonnie, but I feel responsible for him, and I don't like to think about him at his age in that room all by himself. I hope you understand."

Bonnie poked out her bottom lip. "This night has certainly not gone the way I expected, but I don't suppose I have a choice. I guess that means you'll be sitting with your old man Friday night and won't be attending the Cupid's Ball, since it doesn't begin until eight o'clock. Oh, Mack, I'm so disappointed. I'm on the decorating committee and the gym will be beautiful. Cupid shows up every year and it's so much fun. Please say you'll change your mind."

"Thanks, Bonnie, but we do what we have to do."

"Are you sure you don't want me to help find a sitter for the old man?"

He bit his lip to keep from smiling. "Oh, trust me, Pop would never go for that." He slid her chair out, helped her with her coat, then walked her to her car.

CHAPTER 20

Maggie grabbed Liz by the hand and tried to pull her off the bed at the B&B. "Come on, hon, you can read later. Don't be a party-pooper. Let's walk downtown where the action is."

Liz refused to budge. "Really, Maggie, I'm tired, and I don't care about watching antique cars chugging along down the street or socializing with a bunch of strangers. If that sounds appealing to you, then why don't you go sit on the porch, where you can see most of what's going on. Or walk down the street and find a seat at that little sidewalk café and watch the people. But honestly, I'd much rather stay in the room and read."

Maggie thought better than to push her luck. "Fine, honey. I may do that a little later. You rest up for the Assembly in the morning. I believe the itinerary said it starts at eight-thirty."

From the porch, Maggie could see the antique cars lining up on Main Street. She walked down the block to find an empty table at the sidewalk café. It seemed the perfect spot to people-watch, and she supposed the tables would fill quickly.

Several large tables had reserved signs, but she spotted a small wrought-iron table up front, where she could see everything.

When the waiter came around with a menu, Maggie regretted ordering the chili dog earlier. Never had she suffered such a serious heartburn, and the menu touted a wonderful selection of specialty salads, which would've been much better on her digestive system. She handed the menu to the waiter. "What an interesting list of options, but unfortunately, I've already eaten. Just a cup of hazelnut coffee, please."

Just as she anticipated, the tables filled quickly. What an uplifting atmosphere, as she watched old friends greeting one another with warm hugs and lots of laughter. Maggie loved it. People-watching was one of her favorite pastimes.

She noticed a well-dressed older man stroll past. He appeared to be searching for a place to sit. Would he think her forward if she offered him a seat at her table? It seemed selfish to take up a table for four, and not share it, when tables were scarce. She watched as he wandered on down the street. He walked with an uneven gait as if he might have a bum leg.

A few minutes later, the gentleman ambled past her table once again. He walked a few paces, turned around and limped back. He stopped in front of Maggie, and said, "Ma'am, please don't think I'm some old geezer trying to pick you up, but it seems every table on this street is filled. I noticed you're alone. Would I be out of

line if I asked if you're waiting to share your table with someone—
and if by chance you aren't, would you mind if I sat in one of the
chairs? My dogs are killing me."

"Be my guest," Maggie picked up her handbag from off the
table and sat it under her chair.

"I sure thank you, ma'am. And just so you won't be sitting
with a strange man, my name's Jim."

"Hi Jim. I'm Maggie."

"Well, Miss Maggie, that's a mighty pretty name."

She loved the way he talked. She figured him to be a Texan,
not that she'd ever been to Texas, but she'd watched enough
Westerns on TV to know what one was supposed to sound like.
"Thank you. Maggie is a nickname. My given name is Margaret
Alice Askew."

"Well, howdy-do, Miss Margaret Alice Askew. It's a
pleasure."

Jim told Maggie he was from Heartsboro. The conversation
flowed as if they'd known one another for ages. He had many
interesting stories about his days growing up in the small town. He
talked about his stint in the Navy, and some of the crazy stunts his
buddies pulled on him. He was quite a storyteller, and such a sweet
man. Maggie felt comfortable, almost as if she'd known him for
years. He told her all about himself. He'd been happily married to
a wonderful woman for fifty-one years, who passed away a year
ago. They had one child, a son, who moved away from Heartsboro
after college.

"You're such a good listener, Maggie, but I've been doing all the talking. Tell me about yourself."

"I'm afraid my life hasn't been nearly as interesting as yours. I married young, and my husband was a Real Estate Broker. We had a wonderful marriage, but Robert died over fifteen years ago. I still miss him terribly."

"Children?"

"Unfortunately, no, but I now have an adopted daughter. Well, I haven't legally adopted her, but I think of her as my own."

Maggie and Jim spent over two hours enjoying one another's company, when Maggie said she'd best get back before her daughter called the FBI. "She's a real worry-wart." It made her feel good to speak of Liz as her daughter. She took her napkin from her lap and laid it on the table. "Jim, it's been nice chatting with you. Thank you for the lovely evening."

"My, my but ain't you sweet? The pleasure was all mine. I haven't sat down that long and talked with a woman since Thelma passed on, God bless her. It was mighty refreshing just to have someone to sit and share a cup of coffee with. I have a friend named George, and we meet for coffee every morning at the Drug Store, but I'll have to admit he's not nearly as interesting or as charming as you."

"Aww, you're making me blush." She giggled like a schoolgirl. "I hate to end such a pleasant evening, but I'd better get back to the Bed & Breakfast. My daughter will be wondering what happened to me."

"You're staying at the B &B? What a coincidence. I'm staying there, also. I'd be tickled if you'll allow me to walk you there."

As they approached the home, Jim pulled out his key, opened the front door and they walked up the stairs together. Even with his stiff leg, Jim managed the stairs with the agility of a much younger man.

"This is my room," Maggie gestured as they were about to part ways. *Oh, dear! I hope that didn't sound forward.*

"Well, what d'ya know, I'm just next door. Good-night, Maggie."

CHAPTER 21

Liz had a mind to check out of the Bed & Breakfast first thing in the morning if she had to put up with the inconsiderate galoots in the next room for one more night. The manager had been apologetic when Liz reported the obnoxious noise but instead of them quieting down, one annoying racket was replaced with another.

She sat up in bed and laid her book down when the door opened and Maggie tiptoed in. "Welcome back, Miss Night Owl."

"I thought you'd be asleep, Lizzie. You would've enjoyed the band. They were really good."

"At least one of us had a good night. I'm just glad you're back. I expected you hours ago. I'd begun to worry about you."

"You always worry." Maggie kicked off her shoes and sat down to rub her aching feet. "Oh, Liz, I had such a wonderful time. I don't know when I've enjoyed myself as much. Thank you for inviting me to come with you."

Liz sighed, knowing she'd have a tough time if she had to

convince Maggie to leave, now. "You must have found lots of good-looking men downtown to have stayed out until this hour." She snickered at her little joke.

"Actually, I did meet a handsome gentleman tonight. He was so sweet."

"Really?" Liz picked up her book. "If that's supposed to make me regret staying home, it didn't work. Personally, I'd rather read about other women's romantic escapades, rather than experiencing them for myself, but it's really nice to know that you found such a handsome man to keep you occupied."

"You think I'm joking, but I'm serious. I had a lovely evening. I hated for it to end. I wouldn't mind seeing more of him."

Liz closed the book, and her voice took on a somber tone. "You aren't serious. Are you?"

"Why would I joke about it?"

"You met a man? From Heartsboro?"

Maggie hesitated. "Hmm . . . he said he was from here, but now that I think about it, I wonder why he'd be staying at the Bed & Breakfast if he lives in town."

"Maggie, that should be a red flag. You are too trusting for your own safety. Please, stay away from that man. He could be roaming the streets, looking for an unsuspecting older woman. I've warned you about wearing your diamond rings in public. It's like having a sign on your back, saying, I'm wealthy. Rob me."

"Hogwash!" She snorted when she laughed. "If I don't wear them in public, what fun is it to wear them in private? I love bling and nothing says bling, bling, bling like a few diamond rings."

Liz squealed. "Oh, m'goodness, did you really say, 'hogwash?' What backwoodsy hick did you pick that up from? Your new boyfriend, I suppose."

"He's not a hick. Redneck, maybe, but I happen to like rednecks. They're *real* men." Maggie smiled. "Jim—the fellow I met tonight—is not my boyfriend, and he's not looking to rob me. He's really sweet, Liz. He told me all about his deceased wife, and how much he loved her. I was touched."

"In the head, maybe. Which room is your friend staying in? You know—the one who's from Heartsboro, but rents rooms by the night at a B&B?"

"He's right next door."

"You're kidding. Next door? Are you sure?"

"Of course, I'm sure. I watched him go in."

Liz's eyes darkened. She sat straight up in bed with her arms crossed around her midsection. "Maggie, I'm dead serious. Stay away from that guy. He may be a widower, but he's got a woman in that room with him."

"Fiddle faddle. How do you know? Did you see her go in?"

"No, but don't you remember when we checked in, Catherine told us a couple was staying in that room? His lady friend probably didn't know where he was, while he was out flirting with you. Or maybe she doesn't care. She's been playing loud music over there all night. It was classical and I might've enjoyed it, if it hadn't been so obnoxiously loud. I couldn't concentrate to read. I knocked on the wall a couple of times, but it didn't help, so I called Catherine and asked her to go next door and say something. She apparently did, because the music stopped. But then it sounded as if the woman started doing jumping jacks. I'm gathering she's quite hefty, since the glass of water on my bedside table was rocking back and forth. I figured she did it to aggravate me, because I complained about the music. It was so annoying, I couldn't concentrate on what I was reading."

Maggie's face contorted. "Well, I'll admit, I don't know what to think—I do remember Catherine telling us that a couple was staying in there." She clicked her tongue in a tsk. "His smooth-operator style certainly had me fooled. Shucks, do you think maybe he was trying to pick me up?" Maggie snickered.

"It's not funny and I don't know why you seem to think it is. I don't know what his intentions were, but I don't want you hanging around him this weekend. That scares me."

"But Liz, everything scares you. I had an empty seat at my table, and he needed a place to sit down, so I offered to share my space."

Liz's eyes widened. "You didn't."

"I did. And I'm glad I did, because we had a wonderful time. I know he enjoyed it as much as I did. If you had met him, you'd agree he's a gentleman—"

"Yes, and I hear the Boston Strangler was a good ol' Joe. Be careful, Maggie. You're too trusting. I'm just glad you didn't hear any more from that stupid dating service. Now, *that* really frightened me. I still shudder when I think about it. Please don't ever do anything like that again."

"Yes, dear," Maggie replied mockingly.

CHAPTER 22

Thursday, February 13th

Thursday morning, a beautiful centerpiece of yellow tulips, Blue Willow China and cut-glass goblets graced the long formal dining table at the Latimer's B&B. Catherine brought out hot, buttered cat-head biscuits made from scratch with homemade pear preserves.

A nice middle-aged couple, Larry and Sue who were on their way to visit their new grandbaby sat across the table and naturally, their entire conversation revolved around the new baby. Liz tried hard to appear interested, but she had other things on her mind—like going back home. What was she thinking when she agreed to come?

Maggie, said, "Liz, aren't you going to eat a biscuit?"

"Not hungry. Juice and coffee are all I want." She took another sip of coffee and slid her chair back. "I enjoyed the conversation. Please excuse me."

When Maggie came up later, she said, "Liz, according to the itinerary, the program begins at 8:30. You might need to leave now if you want to get a good parking place."

Throngs of people had already arrived when Liz drove up, Not yet convinced she was ready for this, she remained in her car, waiting to see if she recognized former classmates. Her gaze focused on five cheerleaders over near the gym. They all circled around one tall, handsome guy wearing a red and white jacket with the letter "H" on the front and a basketball patch on the arm.

She watched as the young man's attention centered on one particular girl—the way he wrapped his arm around her waist and led her away from the group. The way their faces lit up when they stared into one another's eyes, and he leaned down and kissed her hair.

Memories rushed in like a giant tidal wave. *I was once that girl.* Once upon a time, a lifetime ago, she stood in that very spot, giggling and flirting with the school's star basketball player. Life was exciting at seventeen. She was so trusting. Too trusting. And now, at thirty-seven, she might as well be seventy-seven. Maggie was older in years, but younger in spirit. How Liz envied her. How does one recapture that zest for life when it's been stolen?

Liz turned when someone tapped on her window. She opened her door and tried to see the girl's name tag without being obvious. "Ada Barker?" Ada was on the cheering squad with her the last two years of high school.

"Liz Farley, girl, you look terrific. You can sure tell your husband is taking good care of you."

Why go into the details? She'd never see her again and Ada had never been interested in anyone but Ada.

"Thank you, Ada. It's been a long time, hasn't it? Do you still live in Heartsboro?"

"No, we moved to Birmingham over ten years ago. I haven't seen you here before. I try to come back every year."

"This is my first time back."

"Why don't we go inside. It's almost time for the Program to start."

The high school auditorium looked just as it did twenty years ago. Same seats, same curtain over the stage. The only thing that appeared to change were the faces in the crowd. Although she recognized quite a few, there were others that she had no clue who they were.

Ada leaned over. "I wonder if Bud Granger is here. I didn't want to wear my glasses. Look around and see if you see him."

Liz was almost afraid to turn around. Afraid of who she might see. She took a few short glances, then said, "I don't think he's here. I watched a lot of people going in, but I didn't see anyone that looked like him. Didn't you and Bud date in school?"

"Yes, we dated almost two years, but after I went off to college, I met my husband and I was young and eager to get married, so when Richard asked me, I said 'yes.' Not that I regret

156

it. Like all marriages, we have our ups and downs, but he's a good provider and we've had a good life."

"I'm glad you're happy."

Ada had a wistful expression. "Did I say I was happy?" She nudged Liz. "Don't look so shocked. I may not be happy, but I'm contented. That's more than a lot of married couples can say. What about you? Happy or contented?"

Liz was glad that The President of the Senior Class stepped up to the podium when he did. She wasn't sure what took place on the program, because her mind was replaying the conversation with Ada.

Happy or contented? Liz mulled the question over in her head and concluded she didn't really fit into either category. In three more years, she'd turn forty. She shuddered. *Allen wants to marry me. What woman couldn't be content living with someone with such a sweet, gentle spirit?*

Following the Assembly, Liz mingled with her classmates in the school library.

She noticed a woman walking slowly down an aisle of books, yet she never pulled one out to look at it. It became obvious to Liz that she only pretended to be searching for a book. Liz understood because that's exactly how she reacted when placed in an uncomfortable situation. If Mack were to walk in, she'd be doing the same thing.

She walked over in an effort to engage her in a conversation.

Liz stood beside her and pulled out a book. "I've never read anything by this author. Have you?"

She shook her head.

"Is this your first time to come—" When she turned around, Liz recognized her. "Oh, Haley, I didn't recognize you."

"Hi, Liz. It's the scars. I was in an automobile accident a few years ago."

"Scars? I don't see any scars. You look great."

Haley lifted her bangs, then pulled on her turtleneck sweater. "I've had five surgeries, but I still feel like a freak."

"Oh, Haley, no. I promise you they're only noticeable to you. Why don't we go sit on the concrete bench under the big oak?"

"I'd like that."

The bench was occupied by young lovers, so Liz suggested they sit in her car since it was parked out front. "Haley, you were the smartest girl in our class. I believe you were voted 'Most Likely to Succeed. I've wondered many times what happened to you."

Though she gave a short laugh, it had a sad ring to it. "You guys messed up on that one."

"I don't understand."

"I don't consider my life being a success. Oh, I love my job, but I'm thirty-seven and every time I go to church, or we have another family reunion, every parishioner, or every aunt, all the way down to cousins-twice removed, ask the same question: Why aren't you married? I don't even like to be around people anymore.

I don't have an answer for them."

"Hey, you think you're hounded. You should meet my neighbor. That's all I ever hear from her. I'm a widow and she's constantly trying to set me up."

"I'm sorry, I didn't know about your husband. But don't you get tired of it?"

"Sure, but I know her heart. She only wants me to be happy."

"I understand, Liz, but why can't people believe we can be happy, even if we aren't married."

"Haley, just remember we answer to no one but the Good Lord and ourselves. If you're happy being single, then don't let the questions weight you down."

"That's just it. I'm not happy and I resent that it shows. I was perfectly satisfied with my single status, and then met a man when I was twenty-seven. He gave me a ring and we set a wedding date. Then two weeks before the wedding, I had the accident, and the wedding had to be postponed. My face was badly scarred, and he couldn't stand looking at me. Of course, there was a lot of swelling and bruising that slowly went away, but he took a job in another town, and I haven't seen him since."

"Oh, Haley, you are even more beautiful than you were in school. You need to take a good look in the mirror. You said you love your job. What do you do?'"

"I'm a court reporter. I can't imagine wanting to do anything else."

When people began to file out of the building, Liz said,

159

"Looks like everyone is leaving. I'm staying at the Latimer's Bed & Breakfast. My neighbor came with me, and we'll be going out to lunch as soon as I get back. Would you care to join us?"

"Thanks, but I'm staying with my eighty-five-year-old grandmother, and I need to spend as much time as I can with her. Liz, I wish we lived closer. I could really use a good friend, and I can't imagine a better one than you. Do you have your phone with you?"

"I do."

"Here's my number. If you're ever in Middle Tennessee, give me a call."

CHAPTER 23

Liz returned to the B&B and filled Maggie in on all the details. "Once I realized Mack really wasn't going to show up, I relaxed and had a great time. I talked to several former classmates, and you were right. We seemed to pick up where we left off."

"Didn't I tell you?"

Liz gave her a little hug. "Yes, you did, so go ahead and gloat. I'll admit, I'm glad you insisted I come."

After lunch, Maggie helped her choose an outfit to wear to the parade. Though she balked, Maggie convinced her to wear make-up and insisted on styling her hair. Blotting the lipstick, Liz stared at her reflection in the mirror. "Who is that lady staring back at me? Where has she been for the past ten years?"

Maggie wrapped her in a hug. "She's been there all the time, honey. You've kept her hidden."

"I think Allen would approve of the new me. You were right, Maggie, when you said I wasn't taking care of myself. But if I'm to ever become Mrs. Allen Albertson, I'll need to pay more attention to my appearance, since he's always in the spotlight. I'm considering accepting his proposal. Did I tell you that?"

"You're what? When did that come about?"

"This morning. I know Allen can make me . . . uh, I know he'll be good to me and I'll be . . . contented. He'll see that I'm taken care of."

"Contented? Elsie the cow is contented but I've never heard a commercial claiming she's a happy cow. You know why?"

Liz rolled her eyes, "No, but I think you're about to tell me."

"Because she's not in love with that ol' Bull." Maggie wagged her finger in Liz's face. "And I don't think you are either. I listened to what you said just now, and you didn't say you love him. I'm worried about you, Liz."

"Worried? Why?"

"You may be having a nervous breakdown."

"Oh my lands, Maggie. That's crazy and you know it."

"I'll tell you what's crazy. Saying you'll marry him because he'll take care of you." She threw up her hands. "Who are you? That doesn't even sound like you, Liz. You're a strong woman. Always have been. That's one of the things I admire about you. Look what all you've managed to do on your own. Don't sell yourself short at this point in your life by thinking you need a man to take care of you."

She crossed her arms over her chest. "That coming from a woman who signed me up on an internet site with a bunch of freaks. Then when I find a real gentleman who is willing to provide me with security as I grow older, I don't see that as being weak. I see it as being sensible."

"Liz, it's not that I'm opposed to Mr. Albertson. From all appearances, he's a very nice fellow. But I have a feeling if you'll be patient, a man will come along very soon that will love you the way you deserve to be loved . . . the way I loved Robert and the way he loved me. I want that for you, hon. Is that so wrong?"

"Maggie, I have learned from experience that there are more important things in a relationship than emotions that can swing in any direction at any given time. I'm looking for something that lasts."

"Like money to buy a bakery?"

Liz's mouth gaped open. "That's not fair. If it was about taking money from someone else, I could've taken yours, but I didn't, did I? And I won't take Allen's. If I can't open a bakery on my own, I won't do it."

Maggie walked over and threw her arms around her. "Oh, honey, let's don't argue. I want you to have a good time this weekend. We'll talk about you and Mr. Albertson when we get home, but for now we're putting that conversation on the back burner."

Liz's eyes clouded. "I know you want what's best for me, Maggie. I'm just having a hard time figuring out why you keep changing your mind about what you perceive to be best."

"Well, don't mind me. I'm just an old lady. I'm entitled to act a little eccentric at times. Now, scoot! The parade lineup will start in a few minutes, and I don't want you to miss it, so you go on now, and have fun."

Liz practically ran the two blocks from the Bed & Breakfast to the church parking lot, where the parade was scheduled to begin. The firetruck led the parade. It was then she spotted her class's float and realized the procession had begun to creep forward.

Awed at the beautiful red and white floats decorated with hearts, angels and cupids, she stood spellbound until someone yelled. "Quick, Liz, jump on."

Two hands reached out, grabbed her, and pulled her up.

"Thanks, Jerry. I'm glad you're strong enough to help an old lady onto a moving vehicle."

Huddled together like sardines, Liz attempted to hide her shock, when she realized she was wedged between Jerry Lyons and Mack Mackenzie.

Jerry said, "Old? What are you talking about? We aren't old. Besides, you look as beautiful as you did the day we graduated. Doesn't she Mack?"

Her heart pounded like a jackhammer. He was even more handsome than he was in college. Same wavy hair, square jawline, broad shoulders and trim waist. The only difference she noticed was the twinkle in his eyes had disappeared. His eyes darkened as he glared straight ahead. Feeling that old familiar pitter-patter in her heart return, frightened her. She waited for his response to Jerry's question.

Without glancing her way, he muttered, "Yeah, I guess."

Why it felt as if she'd swallowed a serrated knife, Liz couldn't imagine. She hadn't let herself pretend that he cared for her—if he ever did. Still, it felt as if the jagged cut went in one side of her body and came out the other. Pulling her arms tightly across her chest and crossing her legs, Liz attempted to take up a minimum of space. Chills ran over her body at the thought of having any part of Mack Mackenzie touching her.

As the float moved past the Heartsboro Bank, an attractive blonde made her way to the front of the crowd. Waving enthusiastically, she yelled, "Mack, baby, I had a great time last night. Give me a call. I've got something for you, sweetheart."

Mack thrust his arm in the air in a hearty wave. "Yeah, it was great. We'll have to do it again, sometime."

It was then that Liz recognized the girl to be Bonnie Jo Bloodworth. *Bonnie and Mack? What a fine pair. I'll just bet she's got something for him.* Her teeth ground together, as she recalled the night twenty years ago when she caught Bonnie practically sitting in his lap with her eyes closed and her lips puckered. Mack convinced her at the time he wasn't interested in Bonnie and didn't see it coming. Liz clenched her teeth together. *The only thing he didn't see coming, was me!*

CHAPTER 24

This Homecoming thingy was turning out to be no different than what Liz had expected. Why did she let Maggie talk her into coming? If only she'd held her ground and stayed home.

As the float bumped and inched slowly down Main Street, her instinct was to jump off, run back to the B&B and head for home as fast as she could go. But what kind of signal would she be sending? No way would she give Mack Mackenzie the satisfaction of thinking she still cared. Because she didn't. She sat rigid in uncomfortable silence, as Jerry and Mack carried on a conversation about basketball.

Finally, Jerry directed his attention to her. "Liz, I believe this is the first time you've been back for Homecoming since we graduated. Is that right?"

"Yes, I've been meaning to come back, but you know how it is. Life gets in the way." Liz wasn't sure why she made such an absurd statement. What life?

He said, "Well, I hope in the next few days, you'll see what you've been missing and will make a point to come again next year. We always have a blast. Mack, I don't remember ever seeing you here, before, either. Is this your first time, also?"

"As a matter of fact, it is, but I've been having a ball, renewing old friendships, so I'll make a point to come back next year."

Liz felt a pain in her jaw from clenching her teeth. She knew exactly what old friendships he was referring to. If she were on speaking terms with Mack Mackenzie—which she wasn't—she would inform him that Bonnie Bloodworth wasn't the only one who had something for him. She'd like to give him a piece of her mind and let him know what a jerk she thought he was.

Jerry's head turned slightly to his left, then to his right. "So, is it a coincidence you both decided to come this year for the first time, or did you plan it this way?"

She knew exactly what she wanted to say but chose to wait for Mack's response. If he chose to answer amiably, she'd attempt civility for Jerry's sake, though it would be difficult.

A low, sarcastic chortle bolted from Mack's lips. "Plan it? Of course not. I haven't seen her in years. I have no idea what her plans are. As a matter of fact, I never have known."

His snarky reply left her with plenty to say, but it was neither the time nor the place, and if she were lucky, there'd be no other time nor place. Clamping her lips tight, Liz struggled against the anger building inside her.

She had the distinct feeling Jerry was attempting to push her and Mack into having a conversation. Perhaps he meant well, but she refused to be manipulated.

Jerry said, "Well, I'm glad you're both back. Tell me, Liz, what have you been doing with your life for the past twenty years."

She sucked in a deep breath and prayed she wouldn't start crying. No way would she give Mack Mackenzie the satisfaction of knowing how much he'd hurt her. With her head held high, she upped the volume in her voice, making sure Mack didn't miss a single word. "Oh m'goodness, where do I start? Life's been a trip, for sure, Jerry. One exciting adventure after another."

"How so?"

She'd hoped he wouldn't ask. "Let's see . . . after college I married a remarkable man. Simply remarkable." Why mention she was a widow and have Mack feeling sorry for her? "Carter was Principal where I interned, and I was blown away when he began to actively pursue me from my first day there. It was a whirlwind romance."

"Cool. Did you get caught?"

"Caught? For what?"

"I don't know, I assumed there would've been a regulation against a Principal dating one of the employees. Lucky for you there wasn't."

The possibility that there might've been such a rule had never crossed her mind. What if? How different would her life have been if such a regulation had existed. Quickly shifting her thoughts back to Jerry's last comment, she said, "You're right. Lucky for sure." She felt the lump in her throat growing. If it didn't slow down, she feared she'd choke on it

Jerry said, "Too bad your husband couldn't come."

"Yes, too bad." Liz felt a gnawing discomfort in the pit of her stomach, having been caught up in her own web of deceit.

Mack appeared bored. He stiffened his back and cracked his neck.

Wanting to shift the subject away from Carter, Liz said, "What about you, Jerry? What have you been up to?"

"I married my best friend thirteen years ago and we're still on our honeymoon. She's the best thing that ever happened to me."

 Liz breathed easier, now that they were no longer discussing her and Carter. "How did you meet?"

"Cindy and I began dating our second year of college. We hung out together for five years before we realized what started out as a fantastic friendship turned into something more. She's not only my wife, she's my confidant, my guidance counselor, my lover and my best friend. But if I'm understanding you, then you and your husband began your relationship based on physical attraction. I'm guessing you became lovers first, and later developed a deeper relationship as friends. Not saying there's anything wrong with that."

His expression, however, said otherwise—as if it were an odd way to begin a marriage. She was glad he didn't voice it aloud, because she would've had to agree. Liz would've settled for either in her marriage, a lover or a friend, but Carter had no desire to be either.

Her thoughts were interrupted when Jerry said, "I hope he can make the next reunion. He must be a super guy to make you fall in love with him so quickly."

Her stomach churned. She'd been deceptive, and it wasn't like her to lie. It was all Mack's fault, and she resented him for it. One lie had led to another and as much as it pained her to think about it, she knew the only way to stop it would be to tell the truth. "Jerry, the reason Carter isn't here is because he—"

There was a sudden jolt, and the flat-bed trailer bumped. She looked around and realized Mack had bounded off the moving truck.

Jerry yelled, "Hey, Mack. Did we crowd you off, buddy? Hop back on. I'll give you a hand."

"No thanks. I meant to jump off. I'm heading back to the room. Catch you later."

"Yeah. See you at the game Saturday. All you single kids have fun tomorrow night at the Cupid's Ball and make sure when you leave, you're with your perfect match. Cindy and I will be with the old married folks at the Yoked-Together Dance."

Mack made no comment but threw up his hand and walked through the crowd in the direction of the bank.

There was little doubt in Liz's mind where he was headed. He apparently couldn't wait to get with his precious Bonnie, who "had something for him." Liz tried to dispel the surge of jealousy rising up. Why did it still bother her after all these years?

"Wonder what's wrong with him?" Jerry remarked. "He looked green. Maybe he gets motion sickness. This truck does seem to jerk a lot as we stop and start. I wonder where he's staying. Cindy and I are at the motel, and he isn't there. Where are you staying, Liz?"

"I'm at the B&B."

"Oh, I forgot about that place. How is it?"

"It's great. I love it."

"That must be where Mack's staying."

"No. He's not staying there." She answered quickly. Maybe too quickly. She didn't like the smirk on Jerry's face. It was obvious he wanted to keep this conversation going. Why didn't he just come out and say what he was thinking?

"I believe his mother died, but I suppose his father still lives in the same house. You and Mack were a real item when we were in school. I always expected the two of you to wind up together."

Liz didn't respond.

"Hey, I didn't mean to open a can of worms. I hope I didn't offend you."

"Offend me? Of course not. That was long, long ago. Lots of water under the bridge, as they say." She felt the prick of tears behind her eyes.

"I believe you were saying something about your husband when Mack interrupted you by jumping ship."

"My late husband, Jerry. Carter died three years ago."

If he attempted to hide his shock, he failed miserably. "Oh,

Liz. I didn't know. I'm sorry."

"Thanks."

"An accident?"

"Cancer."

"I had no idea. I've asked several classmates about you through the years, but it seemed as if you'd dropped off the face of the planet. No one knew anything about you. Someone on the committee said they finally located you through the Teachers College in Cottonvale and were able to get an address to send an invitation."

****

Mack left the parade and tried to call his dad on his cell to tell him to be ready. They'd be leaving town. He'd had enough of Homecoming to last him a lifetime. Aggravated when the phone kept going to voice mail, he went back to the B & B and stomped up the stairs.

"Daddy," he yelled. "Your phone is dead again. You have to plug it in once-in-a-while." He beat on the bathroom door. "Pop? You in there?"

Realizing his father had left, he grabbed his keys and decided to ride around town until he had a chance to cool off. He wound up going into the same little theatre where he and Liz shared their first kiss. Why did he come back? Everywhere he went in this town brought back painful memories. He bought a ticket, popcorn and a root beer. His throat tightened seeing a box of Sugar Buddies in the glass counter. They never went to the movies that Liz didn't ask for a box of Sugar Buddies.

He could've sat anywhere he chose, since he was the only one in the theatre. He walked up the steps and sat down on the back row to watch the only movie in town, "The Killer Potatoes."

CHAPTER 25

The excruciating agony of seeing Mack again and having old wounds reopened, which she thought—or at least hoped—were healed, was more painful than Liz could bear. Though by nature she was a very private person, Maggie was the one person Liz could always go to when she needed a sounding board. However, she'd learned from experience that Mack Mackenzie was a subject best not discussed with Maggie.

She couldn't go back to the B&B. Not yet, anyway. It would be impossible to hold back the tears in her present frame of mind and Maggie wouldn't let up until she had her admitting the problem was Mack. Liz shivered. She was in no mood for a lecture. Why did it still hurt so much after sixteen years? The answer wasn't one Liz was willing to admit.

Convinced that all she needed was to be alone long enough to have a good cry, she drove out to the park, but quickly pulled away when she spotted Ada walking toward the car. Going to Heartie's Diner was definitely out, since it would be a favorite gathering place for alumnae.

A movie? Of course. What better place to unwind than in a dark theatre, but so many businesses had closed since she left home, Liz was confident the only theatre in town would be gone. It was a relic, eons ago, when she and Mack shared their first kiss on the back row. With nowhere else in mind, she turned and drove down Pine Street. Her pulse raced when she spotted the familiar Avon Marquee flashing, "Killer Potatoes."

"Seriously?" She shook her head, groaned and drove past, but after weighing her options of (1) Killer Potatoes or (2) An inquisition from Maggie, she turned around and parked in front of the theatre.

Did it matter what movie was showing? She wasn't interested in being entertained. She simply needed a dark, quiet place, where she could sit and cry until the pain subsided, without having to answer to anyone. It didn't even matter that the movie was probably half-way over.

She walked inside, bought a ticket, a soda and a bag of popcorn. The kid behind the counter said, "Madam, you bought the Special. Candy comes with it. What kind would you like?"

The lump in her throat prevented her from speaking. She simply pointed.

"Great choice. Sugar Buddies are my choice, also. Hope you enjoy the movie. You're getting a private showing . . . well, I think there may be one other person in there, but it's been on for ten minutes. It's a good movie. You might want to stay and see the beginning. It's creepy."

"Thank you."

The theatre was so dark, it was impossible to see, but she followed the tiny floor lights leading up the stairs to the back row. Here she could let it all out. Stumbling in the dark, she spilled her popcorn, but it didn't really matter. She wasn't there to eat. She just needed a good cry. Liz didn't wait to sit down before she began boohooing.

It felt good to cry. She'd held it in way too long. She jerked straight up in her seat when she realized she had sat down next to the only other person in the dark theatre.

He whispered, "Ma'am, please don't cry. Take my popcorn. I don't even know why I bought it."

Horrified that the kind gentleman assumed she was crying over popcorn, she sucked in a heavy breath, snubbed a couple of times and said, "Thank you, but I'm not crying because I spilled my popcorn."

"Liz?"

Her jaw dropped. "Mack!"

"Oh, Liz, I'm glad you followed me here. I needed to apologize. I felt awful after I jumped off the float. It was stupid."

"The only thing stupid is your thinking that I followed you here."

"My bad. I suppose you've been looking forward to seeing the Killer Potatoes?"

Liz didn't know why she laughed. It wasn't funny, but once she started, she couldn't stop.

Mack joined in.

Catching her breath, she said, "It wasn't funny, you know."

He nodded. "I know." He reached in his pocket and pulled out a box of Sugar Buddies. "Here, these are for you."

She held up her box and the laughter began again. "Thank you, I have some." Their eyes met. Liz said, "But you never liked Sugar Buddies."

"Still don't."

"Then why—?"

"It just seemed the right thing to do."

"Mack, Carter's dead."

He jerked around in his seat. "What did you say?"

"I said my husband is dead."

Mack sucked in a lungful of air and blew out slowly. "Wow. That caught me by surprise. I'm . . . I'm so sorry, Liz. When you first sat down, I didn't know it was you, but I could tell you were very upset. Now, I understand why you were crying. I thought it was because you spilled your popcorn."

Her stomach tightened. "You *know* why I was crying?"

He nodded. "I'm sure the news came as a terrible shock."

"What news?"

"Liz, are you all right?" His voice reeked with a sympathetic tone. "You may be in shock."

"Why would I be in shock?" It was then she caught on and covered her mouth. "Oh, did you think he just died?"

"He didn't?"

"No. Carter died three years ago."

"But on the float you said—"

"I know what you're thinking. On the float, I led you to believe he was alive. If it makes any difference, I realized how childish I was acting and had begun to apologize when you jumped off the float. If you'd waited, you would've known."

"I don't get it. Why did you want us to think you were still married?"

"Maybe I wanted to pretend I was happy. I don't expect you to understand."

"But I do understand. Liz. I haven't found anyone who could make me happy since you and I broke up."

Warning bells sounded, reminding her of the past lies. "Really? You sounded rather happy today when you were gushing over Bonnie Bloodworth."

"Liz, I tried to tell you years ago—"

She pushed her palm forward. "Stop it, Mack. Please don't go there. You don't owe me an explanation and I don't want to hear one. Why can't we let the past stay in the past and settle for friendship."

"I can do that if you can."

"I can."

"So, we're starting fresh, from here?"

Liz nodded. "Sounds good to me." She opened her Sugar Buddies, and suddenly felt his warm breath on her neck. She jerked around. "What are you doing?"

"Remembering what it's like to start fresh."

Her breath caught in her throat. Struggling to recall the reasons she shouldn't trust him, her mind went blank. She knew she should stop him. Wanted to. But the scent of the masculine cologne filling her nostrils had a paralyzing effect. What else could account for her lack of will power? "You're crazy, Mack Mackenzie," she whispered.

"Crazy about you, Liz Farley. Always have been, always will be."

CHAPTER 26

The dark theatre, causing Liz to stumble to her seat when she arrived, didn't seem nearly as dark now that her eyes had adjusted. Seeing the passion on Mack's face caused Liz to search for words, but they were locked inside her beating heart. His hand touched her face, then gently turning her head, she felt his stubble rub against her cheek. Their lips met and Liz pondered if the moment was real or if she'd possibly fallen asleep during the movie. It wouldn't be the first time she had dreamed of his lips caressing hers and his arms wrapping around her. If this was indeed a dream, she'd take the concession stand kid's advice and stick around for it to begin again.

The movie ended, but the beating in her heart hadn't slowed from the moment he touched her cheek.

"Liz, there's somewhere in town I'd like to take you. Do you mind leaving your car here, and I'll bring you back to get it in an hour or so."

"This sounds mysterious. Is it far?"

"How far can it be? We're in Heartsboro."

"You have a point."

Never had he looked so handsome as he did tonight, while walking her to the car. The light from the full moon reflected in his twinkling eyes, while accenting his square jaw and perfectly shaped lips.

Liz couldn't take her eyes off him as he drove through town. She didn't ask him where he was going. Did it matter? She would've gone to the moon with him if he'd asked. He pulled up in front of Heartie's Diner and switched off the engine. "Remember this place?"

Her lip quivered. After trying to hate Mack Mackenzie for sixteen years, it was difficult believing she was sitting beside him, holding his hand. "How could I forget?"

He reached across the seat and pulled her close, kissing her once again.

She couldn't breathe. This was happening so fast.

He said, "Let's go in. I hope our booth is empty."

They walked in the door, and the first person they saw was Jerry.

"Hey, guys, I thought I saw sparks on the float, earlier. It's good to see you two together again."

Mack shook his hand, thanked him, then led Liz to the far booth in the corner, and helped her take off her coat.

The first thing they both did after being seated was to look for their initials. Though the table was marred with many other carvings, Mack pointed theirs out quickly. Tears mulled in Liz's eyes. Her head told her to tread slowly, but her heart beat out a different message.

"Do you remember that tacky little Promise ring I gave you the night we graduated?"

"It isn't tacky. It's always been my favorite piece of jewelry and I've never taken it off." She wiggled her pinky on her right hand.

"Liz, I've thought a lot of times about your goal to open a bakery. How's it working out for you? Are you still baking those awesome pecan pies?"

"I still love to bake."

"But you do own a bakery, don't you?"

"I have a kiosk."

"A kiosk?"

"You're frowning. What's wrong with a kiosk?"

"Nothing. It's just that years ago all you could talk about was the day you'd have your own bakery. I would've thought it would've been a priority."

"It was and it still is. As they say, life got in the way. The kiosk has provided a great outlet for me, but I'm now ready to turn the dream into a reality. In fact, I have a realtor who has been working overtime with me for five or six weeks to find the perfect place that I can afford." She paused. "Well, maybe that's an oxymoron—a perfect place I can afford. Naturally, I want the perfect place, but I had no idea property was so expensive. I've lived in the same house from the day I married, so I've had no reason to keep up with market prices. I was lucky to find such a dedicated realtor."

"I hope you thoroughly checked her out. Just because a realtor passes the exam doesn't mean they're a fit for everyone. You really need to be able to connect and make sure she's someone who gets you and knows exactly what you're looking for."

"Actually, she's a he. But he's been fantastic. If it weren't for him, I would've given up by now, but he's relentless. I can't tell you how many properties we've gone to see, but he keeps saying, we're not going to give up until we find the perfect property."

"He sounds like someone who knows his business. That's good advice. Don't give up. You've held onto this dream too long to let it die."

The waitress came around. "Do you need menus?"

Mack said, "No, I think we know what we want."

She held her pad and pen, ready to write.

"We'll take an ice cream float and two straws, please."

Her face scrunched into a frown. "You want a *what?*"

"An ice cream float with two straws."

"Never heard of it. All we have is chocolate and vanilla ice cream."

Liz glanced at Mack and winked. "Never mind. I ate two boxes of Sugar Buddies at the movie. I couldn't drink one if they had it."

"If you don't serve ice cream floats, I think we're good, thank you."

When the waitress walked away, Mack said, "Liz, I'm glad to know you have a realtor who is encouraging you. I hope he isn't only doing it for his own gain, but that he's genuinely interested in helping you make your dream a reality."

"Oh, I sometimes think he's as excited over the prospects of me opening a bakery as I am. You two would get along famously. He's very thoughtful and loves what he does."

"Awesome. Do you still bake those wonderful Sour Cream Pound Cakes that melt in your mouth?"

"I do. I'm surprised you remember."

"Sweetheart, there's nothing about you that I don't remember. Liz, believe me when I tell you there's never been anyone since you."

"Are you sure about that? What about Bonnie Bloodworth?"

"Oh, puh-leeze! Especially not Bonnie, but I thought we had an agreement to leave the past in the past."

"So, we do, but I'm not referring to the past. I'm talking about—"

He nodded. "I know. You're referring to that little tit-for-tat at the parade today."

"That's exactly what I'm referring to." The warm and fuzzy feeling she'd enjoyed until now, turned cold and sticky, as she recalled Bonnie yelling what a wonderful time she had last night and Mack's unmistakable, enthusiastic response. Had she subconsciously put it out of her mind until now? Did Mack really expect her to believe there was nothing between them? How naive did he think she was? "Mack, I heard it all, so why would you try to deny it?"

She slid over in the booth and glanced at her watch. "Please take me back to my car. It's later than I thought."

"Liz, you have it all wrong."

"Do I? Fool me once, Mack, but don't try to fool me twice. I heard her tell you what a wonderful time she had with you last night and you agreed it was great. I believe those were your exact words. And don't forget she has something for you. I hope you get everything that's coming to you."

She grabbed her coat. "I think it's time we should go."

"No. Not until you listen. Just as you pretended that your husband was at home, wishing he could be by your side—"

"I never said that."

"No, but you implied it, and you did it to make me believe you were happily married. Well, I get it, because when Bonnie yelled at me, I didn't want you thinking I was still pining over you, so I pretended there was something between us and that I was enjoying it."

"Are you saying you didn't date her last night, because if you are, I find it hard to believe."

"No, I had a quick four-thirty dinner with Bonnie last evening, as a favor to a friend. It was a blind date, and he said the girl's name was Jo Jenkins. How was I to know her name was Bonnie Jo and that Jenkins was her married name?"

Liz bit her lip to keep from smiling. He was so cute trying to explain and she found herself believing him.

"I was shocked when she called my name. That's when I saw her sitting at the table and realized she was my date."

"So, she's married?"

"Divorced, but it wouldn't matter to me. I'm not and never have been interested in Bonnie."

"Well, one more question, if I may. Did she give it to you?"

The expression on his face revealed his confusion. "What are you asking?"

"Surely, you heard her say she had something for you. Did she give it to you?"

"No. I haven't seen her since the parade, and I don't plan to see her. I'm telling you, Liz, the girl means nothing to me. She never has. It's always been you. Please believe me."

"I do believe you, Mack." She reached for his hand and felt their fingers curl together. "I think we were both wanting to make the other jealous on the float, because of decisions we made years ago."

He nodded. *We?* It wasn't his decision. The memories, both good and bad flooded back. Was she saying she made a bad decision when she chose the other guy over him? Or was she simply acknowledging now that her husband was gone, he was her second pick? He'd once considered himself to be the luckiest guy in the world, being able to claim Liz Farley as his girl. Looking at her now took him back to their high school years. He recalled the cute little red short skirts and white fitted tops the cheerleaders wore back then and had no doubt she could still fit into the uniform as beautifully as she did at seventeen. If she'd changed at all, it was only because she was more beautiful than ever. Her long, dark hair hung loosely about her shoulders and the way she'd toss it back with her hand made him want to run his hands through it, the way he did years ago. He still remembered the fresh smell of her shampoo, which he considered more enticing than the most expensive perfumes. Did she still use the same shampoo? Her beautiful green eyes were as bright as they were when they'd sit in silence for hours in a booth at Hearties, staring, when words weren't necessary. His throat constricted. Then, four years later the last thing in the world he would've ever dreamed would happen, did happen.

She leaned over and pecked him on the cheek. "I really need to get back. My neighbor came with me and although I think she's done well to find things to do when I'm not with her, I've already been gone much longer than I anticipated. She's old enough to be my grandmother and she's quite the worry-wart."

"I understand. My dad's the same way. He still treats me like I'm twelve. He was forty when I was born, and with Mama gone, he seems to think he's got to help me plan my life. I love him, but I do wish he'd realize I'm capable of making my own decisions. Maybe I'll get to bed early tonight. There's a squalling baby in the room next to mine and kept me awake half the night."

Mack drove back to the Avon parking lot for Liz to get her car. "Are you planning to go to the Cupid's Ball?"

"Are you asking me for a date?"

"I wish I could, but if you read the rules, everyone goes stag."

"I remember. I've just never understood why."

"Tradition. Every year, Cupid pulls out his arrows and if your arrow matches a guy's, then he's declared to be your match."

"What if Cupid matches you with someone you don't want to be matched with?"

"He won't. He's Cupid." Then laughing, he said, "Sounds crazy, I know, but there's no denying an awful lot of Heartsboro couples claim they were brought together by Cupid at the dance."

Liz laughed. "It's fantasy, of course, but it does sound like a fun little tradition." How long had it been since anything sounded fun? Liz had her zest back. It hadn't been stolen, after all. Just put on hold until now.

CHAPTER 27

Thursday, February 13th

Jim had enjoyed spending Thursday afternoon with three lifelong friends. It was good being back in the old hometown. He had called Gus, Al and Hank earlier and they sounded genuinely happy to hear from him. Al suggested they all meet at the Downtown Drug Store for a game of dominoes, for old time sake.

It was sad seeing the way Gus's health had declined in the four years Jim had been away. He was glad he had the opportunity to spend time with him, since he presumed it would be the last time they would ever be together. If only he could convince Mack that he'd be better off living in familiar surroundings than in Point Clear. Not that it wasn't a lovely place, because it was a Paradise—but there's nothing like being home.

He put his money on the table to pay for the coffee and stood. "It's been therapy, seeing you ol' codgers again, but my son will be sending the law after me if he gets back to the B&B and discovers I'm not there." He winked. "He thinks I'm old. Imagine that." He hugged each one and saw the tears in Gus's eyes as they said their goodbyes.

As he rounded the corner, he noticed Mack's car was gone. He was ambling up the walk in front of the Bed & Breakfast when a young woman pulled up at the curb and yelled, "Excuse me, sir. I'm looking for a guy who moved from Heartsboro several years ago who has come back for his high school reunion."

Jim eyed her over and didn't particularly approve of what he saw. "I'm not sure how I could be of help."

"Well, I think he may be staying here. I've checked the hotel, and he isn't there."

"Maybe he's staying with kinfolk."

"I don't think he has relatives living here, because he has an invalid father and I'm sure if he had folks in town he could drop the old fellow off with them for the weekend. He doesn't seem to have any time to himself, poor guy. I thought they might be staying at the B&B. It's important that I get a message to him."

"I'll keep my ears open. What would his name be?"

"Mack Mackenzie."

"Mack Mackenzie? Shucks. Yeah, I know him. You say his old man is an invalid? That's a crying shame. I have a message for him, myself. What would you like for me to tell him?"

"That's fantastic. Thank you, sir. Being that you're from out of town, I don't suppose you would know, but Valentine's Day is the most important day of the year around here. Legend has it that—"

"Don't waste your breath, young woman. I know all about the legend, but what does that have to do with Mack?"

"Everything. I never put much confidence in the Heartsboro Legend until fate brought Mack back into my life last night." She giggled. "Now, I'm a believer."

"Zat so?"

"I hadn't seen him in years until last night, when he took me on a dinner date at the most expensive restaurant in town."

Jim stiffened. "A dinner date? Well, now ain't that grand? How did it go?"

"It was very romantic, though I wish we'd had more time together. I invited him to go to my apartment, afterward, so we could catch up on lost time, and all, but—"

Jim slapped his thigh. "Well, by Jove, I'd say you're mighty accommodating, miss. I'm sure you two had a right nice time, catching up on lost time . . . and all."

"I only wish it could've turned out that way. Sadly, he was pressed for time and had to leave early. Being the only child, the burden of taking care of his father has fallen on him.

Jim fumed. "Well, how selfish of the old goat to be so inconsiderate that he'd come between his son and true love. The old codger ought to be put in a home, wouldn't you say?"

"You're very understanding. I thought the same thing, but I didn't want to voice my opinion on our first date. It might come across as if I were trying to interfere in Mack's affairs."

"Does he have a lot of affairs or are you his only one?"

Her brow shot up. "I'm not sure I understand what you mean."

"Forget it."

"Sir, are you sure you'll see him tonight?"

"I can guarantee it."

"In that case, would you mind giving him this box of chocolates?

Jim took it and peeked inside. "What message would you like for me to give him?"

"Oh, it's in writing. I taped it to the box."

"Fine. I'll make sure it gets in the right hands." Jim regretted not reading Lemuel's letters to his son in Proverbs, warning about such women. Thelma certainly would not have approved of the bleached blonde with more skin on the outside of that sweater than there was on the inside.

Jim glanced at his watch, and for fear that Mack would be back soon, he said "I'm late, so excuse me please. Gotta go take care of business, but don't you worry your little head over a thing. I'll be sure to tell Mack everything he needs to hear."

"Thanks, mister. I'm decorating for the dance and I'm already late. Just tell him Jo sent it and if he decides he wants me to recommend a sitter for his father so he can come to the Ball, then give me a call and let me know. I took it upon myself to line one up, in case he changes his mind."

"A sitter? Well, now ain't you thoughtful."

"Thank you, but it's the least I could do. I've tried to call him, but I think he must've changed phones. The number I have apparently isn't working, since I haven't been able to get an answer." She stopped, chewed on her thumb knuckle, as if she might've left out something important. "Do I need to go over any of the instructions with you again?"

"Young lady, I may be old, but I ain't deaf."

"Oh, I didn't mean to offend. I really appreciate you taking care of this for me. I wish I could wait, but I'm chairman of the committee and I'm already running late."

"Well, you just go take care of business, and don't worry about a thing." With that, he rushed upstairs and hid the candy.

CHAPTER 28

Maggie was quiet, as she and Liz trekked down the front steps of the B&B and walked toward the car. With so much finagling going on in her head, she wouldn't be able to breathe freely until after breakfast Sunday morning. Until this moment, Maggie was convinced she'd done the right thing. Doyle had sounded so perfect. But slowly, her confidence faltered. Dozens of things could go wrong.

Dreadful scenarios invaded her thoughts. Why did Mr. Albertson have to show up in Liz's life at such a crucial time? She didn't want Liz confused when she and Doyle would finally come face to face. Maggie could understand how thoughts of marrying the richest, most eligible bachelor in Alabama could certainly provide a distraction.

She felt a rumbling in her stomach and couldn't discern if it was from hunger or if it was caused from worry. What if she was making a huge mistake? Doyle said he owned his own business, but had she bothered to ask what kind of business? She tried to think. No, she was sure he didn't say. He could be a ditch-digger and own his own shovel, for all she knew.

Liz backed out of the driveway and drove through town. Maggie expected her to stop at the Corner Café, but she kept driving until she reached Heartie's Diner. "Maggie, this will probably be your last opportunity to ever eat here, and I don't ever remember seeing you enjoy anything as much as you seemed to enjoy your meal last night."

"Well, aren't you sweet?" Maggie feigned a smile. "It was a humdinger of a chili dog, for sure." If only she'd thought to bring her anti-acid pills. An acute bout of indigestion hadn't waned from last night's acid-laden dinner.

The waitress came over with menus, but Liz let her know immediately there'd be no need for menus. "Please bring my friend a chili dog, all the way and two cups of coffee."

The taste of bile rose to her throat. "Aren't you planning to eat?"

"No, coffee is all I want. I ate two boxes of candy after the parade today and I couldn't possibly hold another thing. Maggie, I want you to know I feel awful for leaving you alone all afternoon. I'm sure you were bored. We can leave for home first thing in the morning."

"Heavens no, child. I don't get away often and this is a real treat for me. I wasn't bored at all. It's been years since I've enjoyed myself as much. There's a wonderful little library in town, and I watched much of the parade from the window. I spent a couple of hours there, reading and I enjoyed chatting with the librarian. She is such a lovely person, and I learned so much about the history of Heartsboro from her. Did you know this little town is the birthplace of Cupid and—"

Liz groaned. "Yes, and I suppose she also told you this is where he shot his first arrow?"

"That's right. You never told me that."

"Why should I? It's fiction."

"Annette—that's her name—she called it a legend."

Liz's frown deepened. "That's what I said."

"No, honey, you said—"

"It's the same thing, Maggie. Surely, you know that. A legend is nothing more than a dumb story that's not true that keeps on circling among gullible people."

After woofing down the last bite, Maggie could hardly breathe.

Liz said, "I've been meaning to ask . . . that creep you met last night in town . . . have you seen him today?"

"He was no creep, but no I haven't seen him all day. I'm thinking he may have checked out. Why do you ask? Did you think I might be sneaking around having a secret rendezvous?" Maggie cackled.

"Of course not, silly, but I wondered if he was the man I saw leaving this morning."

"This morning? You didn't say anything."

"I'm not sure it was him. But there was a nice-looking older man, wearing a camel sports coat, neatly pressed Dockers and a sharp looking fedora. He was walking out the front door, just as I headed toward the stairs."

"That was him, Liz. That was him. Oh, I was hoping he'd be staying through the weekend. So, what did you think?"

"What do you mean, what did I think?"

"Never mind. I know what you were thinking, but I think you're wrong. Isn't he handsome?"

"Maggie. I learned long ago that it's the handsome ones you should beware of. They get on this ego trip and don't care who they hurt, as long as they get their way."

"Oh, honey. I wish you wouldn't be so skeptical of every man you meet."

"I'm not. Only the good-looking ones."

Liz shivered when they arrived back in the room. "Do you mind if I raise the thermostat? I think it's colder in this room than it is outside. These high ceilings don't help."

"Sure." Maggie's mind appeared to be elsewhere as she plundered through her bags, then dumped the contents of her purse on the bed.

"Lost something?"

"I can't seem to find my meds. I know I brought them." She slapped her palm to her forehead. "Fiddlesticks! Now I remember, I left them in your car."

"I'll run down and get them for you."

"No, honey. Thanks, but I know exactly where I left them. I'll run down and pick them up."

Maggie hurried down the steps, then rammed her hand under the car seat and retrieved a small bag. Heading back up the steps, her stomach quivered when she spotted Jim sitting in the porch swing. She garbled something about not noticing him on her way to the car.

His lips stretched from one side of his face to the other. The swing creaked, moving slowly back and forth. Why was he smiling like that—it made her nervous—it was as if he could read her mind.

"Hello, Maggie. I was sitting in this same spot when you zipped by me and ran down those steps like a spry teen-ager. I was hoping you might like to join me."

He looked even more handsome tonight than he did last night. "Uh, well, yes, I would . . . I mean, no, uh . . . I've got to get back and tend to some things," she muttered. That sounded ridiculous. *I'm letting Liz's paranoia rub off on me.*

His shoulders sagged. "That's too bad. I thought I'd take a stroll downtown. Got me a hankering for a cup of hazelnut coffee and hoped you might see fit to join me."

"Hmm . . . hazelnut coffee." Maggie bit the inside of her lip. She shouldn't. Liz would be furious with her. "Hold on, Jim. I'll be right back as soon as I run this bag upstairs." Maggie's heart pounded as she hiked up the stairs and rushed into their room.

"Liz," she panted. "I think I'll go for a . . ." She caught her breath. "For a walk. Uh . . . downtown." She huffed. "For coffee."

"You're out of breath. You must've run all the way to the car."

Maggie pounded her fists on her chest. "Good for the old ticker, you know. Now, I'm ready to take a stroll downtown."

Liz glanced at her watch. "Now?"

"Yep! That little sidewalk café serves wonderful hazelnut coffee. You know how I love my coffee, dear. Especially hazelnut."

"Of course. Enjoy, and try not to pick up any strange men while you're out," she added with a wink.

"If I do, I'll make sure I bring him home with me."

Liz cackled. "You're a hoot, Maggie Askew."

Maggie hurried into the bathroom and came out wearing yellow pearl-studded sweater and navy slacks. "How does my hair look?" she asked, as she dabbed a bit of blush on her cheeks.

Liz walked over and smoothed the back of Maggie's sweater. "Wow, if I didn't know better, I'd say you really were hoping to snag a fellow. You look terrific."

"Thanks." She glanced in the mirror and fluffed her hair.

"Maggie, you're amazing. I wish I were more like you."

"Land sakes, honey, what makes you say such a thing."

"You know how to enjoy life. Even something as minor as walking downtown to buy a cup of hazelnut coffee can excite you. Your life is never dull."

"Well, I could arrange your life so yours would never be dull either, but you won't let me."

"I certainly haven't been able to stop you from trying, now have I. I didn't mean to infer I wanted you to help spice up my life. But it's the simple things in life I want to enjoy—the way you do. Have fun."

"Thanks, I intend to, honey." Maggie took one last look in the mirror, then scurried out the door.

Jim sat waiting on the porch. He stood and gave a cat-whistle when she walked out. Maggie noticed he picked up a large shopping bag, but she didn't feel it her place to ask, even though the curiosity was driving her crazy.

"My stars, Miz Maggie, let me take a gander at you. I Suwannee if you ain't pretty as a June bug."

"Oh, how you do go on, Jim. I thought it might be a little cool in the night air, so I decided to slip into this old sweater."

"Yes'm, you look mighty spiffy in that get-up."

Maggie's heart raced. No man had said she looked 'spiffy' since Robert died. That was his favorite word for her. A lump formed in her throat. She wondered if Robert would've approved of her taking a stroll down the street with a virtual stranger. Wouldn't he want her to have a good time? Of course, he would. So why was she nervous?

"The moon's beautiful tonight."

A queasy feeling swept over her. Was it because she felt she was slipping around behind Liz's back, knowing she wouldn't approve? She squeaked, "Yes, it's very bright."

"No wonder there've been a passel of love songs written about the moon or the stars. There's something strangely romantic about a moonlit night, don't you think?"

Maggie swallowed hard. The answer was yes—but she dared not reply. After all, they'd just met. She stepped up the pace.

"Hey, Maggie, this bum leg's holding me back. I can't keep up with you, sugar."

She stopped to let him catch up. "Sorry. I'll slow down. We'll turn back if you like."

"Nothing doing. These old joints are about worn out, but it's been 'coon ages since I've enjoyed anything as much."

When they finally reached the coffee shop, Jim pulled out her chair, then sat the shopping bag on the sidewalk next to his chair.

Maggie let out a soft sigh, relieved to end a romantic subject she deemed inappropriate for strangers of the opposite sex. A waiter came around and took their coffee order.

Jim reached down and pulled out a large Valentine-shaped box from the shopping bag. He hadn't noticed the small envelope taped to the front of the box until now. He pulled it off and snuck it in his pocket. "I hope you like chocolates."

Her mouth gaped open. "Oh, Jim. How sweet! We'll share them with our coffee."

He blew in his cup, then took a sip. "I enjoyed thinking about all the love songs written about the moon and I've been coming up with a few more while sitting here."

Maggie squirmed.

"How many can you recall, sugar?"

Sugar? Had she been too quick to disavow Liz's warnings? Was he flirting? Of course, he was. Maybe she should leave. Faintly, she replied, "Off hand, I can't seem to think of a single one."

"What about Blue Moon? Remember that one?" Jim hummed a few bars.

Sure, she remembered. Robert sang it to her all the time. He had such a wonderful voice. "I do. It's one of my favorite songs."

Jim stopped humming and stared at the night sky. The awkward silence made Maggie even more uncomfortable than all the talk about the moon.

His eyes clouded. "My Thelma loved that song."

Maggie exhaled a long-held breath. "You must've loved her very much." She was hoping.

"You ain't wrong, sugar. My Thelma was quite a woman. I miss her something awful. But I expect you understand, being as how you've lost your first love, too."

"Robert wasn't only my first love, he was also my only love and my last love."

CHAPTER 29

The muscles in Maggie's neck relaxed. Somehow, it seemed to make everything all right as long as she and Jim discussed Thelma and Robert. She opened the box of chocolates and pushed it toward him. "They look delicious. Please take one."

Jim bit into a dark chocolate with pink cream filling. "You and my Thelma would've been great friends. Yes ma'am, Thelma woulda thought the world of you."

"That's very sweet of you to say, Jim. And I wish Robert could've met you. He would've approved." She wanted to cram her fist down her throat. Why did she say, 'approve,' as if there was something to approve of? However, it didn't seem to offend, and she was glad.

"My Thelma was a plain woman, but she was beautiful to me, from the inside out. She mostly wore cotton print dresses and always had her apron on unless she was heading to church. I tell you what's the truth, that woman had more aprons than a hound has ticks. Made 'em herself."

When his eyes filled with moisture, he looked up at the moon.

Maggie knew how he felt. She was feeling it, too. They both had suffered a great loss. He pulled a toothpick from a small cylinder on the table, stuck it in his mouth and chewed on one end.

Making an effort to change the somber mood, Maggie said, "Let's have another chocolate."

"I was hoping you'd ask." He reached in the box and held up a piece wrapped in foil. "I wonder what this one is."

"I think it's probably a chocolate-covered cherry."

He shuddered and put it back in the box.

Maggie's eyes widened. "You don't like chocolate-covered cherries? They're my absolute favorite."

"I'm not surprised. They were Thelma's favorite, also." He mumbled. It was so low she wasn't sure if he meant for her to hear it or if it was for his ears only.

Maggie placed the top back on the box of chocolates. "Jim, I think you're right. I think I would've loved your Thelma."

"I'm sure of it. You're alike in some ways but very different in other ways."

She didn't know if she should ask him to elaborate, but before she finished debating the question, with his eyes still focused on the moon, his face lit up in a smile. "No one would ever call you plain. You look like you could model for a magazine, so that's why it's amazing to me that you're so down to earth. I think that's real admirable. Most women of means walk around with their nose stuck in the air. But not you. I noticed that right away, how sweet and gentle you are."

204

"Jim, can I tell you something about myself?"

"Oh, forgive me, Maggie. I've been doing all the talking, haven't I?"

"I love listening to you, but I need to clear something up. I'm not sure what you meant when you referred to me as 'a woman of means. I was one of twelve children, daughter of a sharecropper. Mama and Daddy didn't have electricity until after I left home. I was sixteen when I got me a job at the Five & Ten, and one day this cute guy came in and asked for change to put in the peanut machine. For a quarter, you could get a bag full of hot, salted peanuts."

Jim nodded. "Many a time, I've bought me a bag of peanuts out of one of them machines."

"I gave him change for a dollar and the next day, he was back and needed change again. For a solid week, he came in just to buy a bag of peanuts, but he always needed change. I could tell he was shy, so the seventh time he walked in I handed him a quarter and said, 'My name is Maggie, what's yours?' I don't know to this day if he would've ever said something first, but I got tired of waiting. He asked me out the next week, and three weeks later, we were at the Court House getting married."

"Well, that's a real nice story. I reckon me and your Robert were about the two luckiest fellows in the world to wind up with two of the best."

A blush rose to her cheeks. "I don't know about that, but Robert was a hard worker, and he had a head on his shoulders. He started off small. He bought us a little house, fixed it up and sold it. He discovered he had a talent for it, and through the years, he acquired a lot of property, which he turned around and sold for a hefty profit. But I'm still the same Maggie that I was when we lived in that first little bungalow."

She turned to face him. "Do you know what I'm getting at, Jim?"

He gazed into her eyes. "I'm thinking you want me to see you as plain."

She nodded. "Exactly. I wear aprons, too."

They both laughed, though Maggie hadn't intended for it to sound like a joke."

She thrust her hand over her lips and gasped when the clock on the courthouse struck nine times. "I suppose I should go, Jim. My daughter is such a worry-wart."

"Be thankful. Shows how much she cares."

As they walked back to the Bed & Breakfast, Jim said, "You look worried, Maggie. Did I say something wrong?"

"No, Jim. Nothing you said. But there is something I need to ask, and I hope you won't be offended."

"Why, I can't imagine you asking anything offensive."

"I don't know how to say this, tactfully, so I'll get it over with. I heard there's a woman staying in your room, but I didn't want to believe it." She cringed. He'd have every right to tell her it was none of her business. She attempted to smooth over her blunder

206

with, "I meant to say, if it's true, you should've invited her to have coffee with us.

Maggie bristled when Jim cackled and slapped his thigh. With her hands on her hips, she blurted, "Did I say something funny, because I certainly didn't intend to."

"So, you think I have a woman locked up in my room, while I'm out carousing around, do you?"

"Maybe you think it's funny, but I've heard from two reliable sources that there's a couple staying in the room next door to me and my daughter."

Jim did nothing to hide his amusement. "As I understand it, it takes two to make a couple, and yes ma'am, there are two of us sharing a room. I'm here with my son. I was glad when he said he booked a room for us at the Latimer House. It's a beautiful old home, don't you agree?"

"It certainly is, and I knew all along that there had to be a sensible explanation." She couldn't wait to tell Liz that a couple occupied the next room, all right—but a couple of men. Related. Father and son.

Maggie breathed a sigh of relief, after convincing herself that she never for a moment believed he had a woman stashed away in his room.

****

Maggie walked upstairs and quietly opened the door, expecting to find Liz in bed asleep. "You're still up? I thought you'd be in bed by now."

Liz sat at the vanity, rubbing lotion on her hands. "Couldn't sleep. Did you enjoy the coffee?"

"I did, but I enjoyed the company even more."

"Company? So, you met someone?" She picked up the hairbrush and ran it through her hair. "I'm not surprised You make friends easily."

"Oh, I didn't meet him tonight. I knew him already."

"Really? You ran into someone you knew? Small world, isn't it? At least you didn't pick up any more strangers. You gave me a scare last night, but I sometimes think you delight in doing that."

"Honey, if I scared you last night, you should be terrified tonight." She pressed her lips together to keep from laughing.

Liz didn't look amused. "What do you mean?"

"I mean I spent a lovely evening with the pervert."

"Maggie Askew. If you're trying to shock me, it won't work. He left this morning. I watched him leave."

"You're wrong Liz. He didn't leave. And that's not the only thing you were wrong about. He has someone in the room with him, all right, but it happens to be his son. Now don't you feel ashamed?"

"Maggie, that's impossible. Catherine said—"

"I know what Catherine said. She said there was a couple in there . . . she didn't say a married couple. He's spending time with his son, Liz."

Her eyes squinted. "Are you sure?"

"I'm quite sure. I told you there was nothing to fear. I hope you get a chance to meet him while we're here. I've never met anyone quite like him before. I don't know how to describe him, other than to say he makes me feel comfortable, like we're a fit. Do you know what I mean?"

"I think so. He reminds you of an old shoe."

CHAPTER 30

Friday, February 14th

Friday morning, Mack awoke before sunrise and his dad was already up and dressed. "Pop, it looks like you've been shopping since we've arrived. That's a new derby, isn't it?"

"Yeah, I bought it at Collins Department Store, yesterday." He pulled it off and spun it around on his finger. "Looks right spiffy, don't you think?"

"I can think of no better adjective. It's certainly spiffy, all right. Let's go downstairs and eat breakfast."

"I don't think they start serving until seven o'clock. It's only six-twenty."

"Then we'll drive over to the Corner Café. I have an appointment with a guy at seven-fifteen this morning, and I don't want to keep him waiting."

"Doyle, aren't you ever gonna slow down? It ain't good for a man to work all the time."

"Dad, you think you know who I should date and when I should work and how often. I'm a responsible adult. Don't you believe I'm capable of making simple decisions?"

"I'll admit, son, I do tend to want to help guide you sometimes, but if I do, it's just because I'm an old man and I won't be here forever. I want to see you happy before I draw my last breath."

"And you will, Pop. As a matter of fact, I'm happier now than I've been in a very long time."

"I'm glad to hear it. There's just something about coming back to your roots that does that to us, don't you think?"

"Could be." Mack cranked the car and backed out of the drive.

"Doyle, I haven' seen much of you since we've been here. I'm thinking maybe we ought to spend a little more time together."

"I'm sorry if I've neglected you, Pop. I thought you were having a good time on your own."

"And I am. I'm having a great time, but tonight is the Annual Cupid's Ball and I'm sure you don't plan to go since you ain't into that sort of thing. Maybe it would be fun if we took in a movie. Remember when you were a kid, and we'd search under sofa cushions for enough change to go to the Saturday matinee at the Avon Theatre? Those were the days." His voice lowered. "Your mama never cared much for the picture show. It was how she was raised, I reckon, but she would've bent over backwards to make sure me and you got there."

211

Mack glanced over at his dad. "I remember, Pop."

Jim blotted the corner of his eye with his finger. "Yessir, bobtail, those were some good times for sure. How 'bout it, son? You wanna go watch the late movie with your old man? I've got plans earlier, but we could go to the last showing."

"No thanks. I've seen The Killer Potatoes and I know how it ends, but why don't you call up one of your buddies to go with you?"

"It's not for me. I can always find things to do in Heartsboro. Just thought you might not want to be alone on Valentine's night."

"I appreciate it, but I don't plan to be alone, Pop. I'm meeting a friend at the Cupid's Ball. Maybe we can take in a movie when we get back home."

Jim bristled. "Home? This is home, Doyle. You mean Point Clear?"

Mack's lip curled. "You really have enjoyed coming back, haven't you, Pop?"

"More than you can imagine. But I wanted you to have a good time, too."

"It's been fantastic. I can't believe I almost didn't come."

Jim cringed. He didn't know what kind of spell that woman put on Doyle at dinner Wednesday night, but he hadn't seen his son act this moonstruck over a female in years. Not since his college days, in fact. He pulled out the note she had attached to the box of chocolates and shook his head and blushed as he read it for the third time. Now was not the time for Doyle to allow that

Jezebel to turn his head when beautiful, sweet Elizabeth would soon enter the scene. He stuck it back in his pocket. "Doyle, you aren't seriously interested in that woman you're planning on meeting tonight, are you?"

Mack's eyes lit up. "Pop, I'm very interested."

There was no way for Jim to hide his disappointment. He wasn't normally one to worry, but this was something to worry about. Jim knew her kind, and she wasn't what Thelma had in mind when she made him promise to help Doyle find a good woman.

"Dad, you've been acting very strange, lately. Why don't you come out and say what's on your mind?"

He wanted to tell Doyle what he knew, but if he did, he'd have to admit he purposely didn't give him the message or the candy—and not only that—but he read the obscene note she wrote, and he and Maggie ate the candy. No, there was no way he could admit the truth. "Son, suffice it to say, I know who she is, and I want you to know your dear Mama would not approve of you seeing that woman."

Mack threw up his hands. "Dad, that's crazy. Let me remind you, I'm thirty-seven years old and capable of choosing my own friends. But what prompted you to make such an absurd statement? Mama knew her when we were in high school, and she liked her a lot. She told me so."

"Well, maybe she did, back then, but I can assure you, she wouldn't approve of her now."

213

"Explain to me, please, why you're making such an assumption? She's a wonderful person. I'll admit we had some problems, but that was a long time ago and I think we can work through it."

"I didn't want to bring it up, Doyle, but I saw her yesterday and I can tell you, she's not the girl for you."

Mack tried to keep his cool, but it was becoming extremely difficult. "Why would you make such a snap judgment. It's not like you, Pop."

"Well, maybe I know something you don't. I wish you wouldn't see her again, Doyle."

"I'm sorry you feel that way, but I'll be seeing her at the Cupid's Ball tonight, so don't expect me home early." Mack tried to think where his dad could've possibly seen Liz, yesterday. It had to be before they went to the movie. Could it have been at the parade, after he jumped off the float? "Pop, were you downtown, yesterday?"

"I was. Why do you ask?"

"Just wondered." Liz looked beautiful yesterday. What was it that could've caused his dad to create such a bad opinion of her? Mack didn't like the questions pushing their way into his thoughts. His dad had his faults, but he'd always been a good judge of character and wasn't one to make snap judgments about people. There had to be something that turned him off when he saw Liz. He knew his father was very vocal about women using foul language or showing too much skin in public. Liz was dressed very appropriately, so it wasn't her attire, and she had never approved of off-color jokes.

Mack couldn't remember her even using mild slang. What was it with Pop? Chills ran up his spine. Didn't she fool him once? He wouldn't have believed back then that she'd be making a play for another guy while wearing his engagement ring. But she did. Did he really want to take a chance on being fooled twice? He hated the doubts, but they wouldn't go away.

After breakfast at the Corner Cafe, Mack dropped his father off at the Bed & Breakfast and rode over to the Mayor's office.

Mayor Lindsey met him at the door. "Come on in, Mack. I'm sorry I had to set the appointment up so early, but with this being Homecoming weekend, I have a full schedule. I hope it wasn't too inconvenient for you."

"Not at all. As I mentioned on the phone, Dad is with me, and if he ever slept past six o'clock, I'd be worried about him. This worked out perfectly."

"Good, good. I'll have to tell you, I've looked at your revitalization plans for downtown Heartsboro and shown them to the council. We are very impressed with your ideas."

"It's a rough draft, but it gives you an idea of what I have in mind."

"Mr. Collins is very excited. He remembers what the town looked like in the mid-fifties and agreed that bringing back the nostalgic look of yesteryear would be a boost, not only to our citizens, but would help to bring back businesses. As you can see, the town is beginning to look deserted. After the shopping center opened in the west part of Heartsboro, people started shopping there and the local Mom & Pop stores couldn't compete. We have several empty stores downtown and the old hotel is almost beyond repair. None of the present store owners have been willing to make repairs and I understand. What good would it do if those around you aren't interested in keeping their end of the block up?

Darby Sails has retired and moved back, and as you may remember, she spent several years in Hollywood studying acting. I don't think she ever landed any major roles, but she was in a few productions. We invited her to the meeting, and no one is as excited as she is about having the hotel restored. She said she'd like to teach drama and hold dinner theatres in the dining room every summer. We all thought that was an excellent idea."

"The Miller family still own the Avon Theatre, and they are also excited at the idea of Heartsboro getting a new 'old' facelift. They like the idea of the external looking fiftyish but agree the inside needs enlarging. They're considering six different viewing rooms. I sure thank you for having this vision, Mack. I've never seen so much excitement among the council and I'm sure the entire town is going to be supportive. As Darby remarked last night, 'Tennessee has their Gatlinburg, Georgia has their Helen, but Alabama is gonna rock The Little Town with a Big Heart.'"

"I appreciate your interest, Mayor, and I'll be getting in touch with you as soon as I can draw up the plans. I'll bring my team

216

down here in a couple of weeks to answer any questions."

"So, you're serious about moving back to Heartsboro?"

"Very serious. Not that I don't love being near the water and Point Clear is as good as it gets. But Dad left his heart here when he moved in with me, and I'm beginning to think it's time to come home."

****

Mack was pleased the way the meeting went, but he couldn't stop thinking about his dad's reaction when he found out he'd be seeing Liz again. What could Pop possibly have seen that would've made him have such a low opinion of her? Was she with another man? Whatever it was, did he really want to know? He rode back to the B&B.

Catherine waved him over when he walked in. "I missed you and your father at breakfast. We had blueberry muffins and there were several left over. I can box them up for you if you'd like to take them to your room."

"That sounds great, Thank you."

"How about a cup of coffee to go with them?"

"You're an angel. I have a lot of work to do, and blueberry muffins and hot coffee will make it a lot more pleasant."

When Catherine asked if he'd met the two nice ladies in the room next to his, he politely answered that he hadn't had the pleasure. He didn't bother to mention he had no desire to meet them after they so rudely reported him for playing his music. He considered himself lucky that he hadn't run into them.

217

She handed him a box with four muffins and a large coffee. "Hope you enjoy."

Not surprising, his dad was not in, which was good since Mack had a lot of drawings he needed to work on, and it was difficult when Pop was around, constantly talking. His father's flip-top phone was on his bed. "Lot of good it did to get him a phone. He never has it with him or if he does, it's dead."

Jim came in around lunch. "Well, I don't know which is worse—seeing you working when you should be enjoying yourself with friends or worrying if you might be out with that woman."

"Dad, I resent you calling her 'that woman.' I wish I knew what you had against her."

"If you have to ask, then you aren't as clever as I gave you credit for. I suppose you're still planning to take her to the Ball?"

"I won't be taking her, since it's traditional for everyone to go stag."

Jim nodded. "Oh, yeah. I remember something about that, although me and Thelma never went. She didn't take to dancing."

"The idea is to wait and see who Cupid matches you with, but I know who my match is. I'm just sorry that you have such a low opinion of her because I happen to believe that I couldn't do better."

"Then heaven help you is all I can say." Jim meant it with all his heart. Things weren't going according to plan, and it was beginning to look as if divine intervention would be the only way to save Doyle from making a huge mistake.

CHAPTER 31

Friday, February 14th
Cupid's Ball

Luke McGallagher arrived at the Annual Cupid's Ball at six o'clock, aggravated at his wife for promising her cousin that he'd run around the dance floor wearing a silly diaper, and wings. "Bonnie, I don't see why I had to come early if it doesn't start until eight."

"Stop being so ornery, Luke. The Committee needs to make sure you know what the role of Cupid entails."

"I don't know how I let you and Trudy talk me into this. Tell me again how I got so lucky."

"Luke, you can't tell anyone, but we've had a disastrous thing happen this year and we can't afford to let the news out. For generations, the Garden Club has sponsored the Cupid's Ball and every year, a man shows up dressed as Cupid. No one knows who he really is, not even anyone in the Garden Club, but it's always been assumed that one of the town's civic clubs is responsible for providing a Cupid."

Luke huffed. "The only club I belong to is the Quarterback club, and we have nothing to do with this silly tradition, so why am I here?"

"Stop ranting and I'll tell you. Yesterday, the committee received a letter and a package with Cupid's costume inside. Hold on. I'll let you read the letter." She reached in her bag, pulled out a folded piece of paper and handed it to him.

Luke read aloud:

Dear Friends,

I regret to inform you that I will be unable to perform my duties at the Cupid's Ball this year, since I am urgently needed at the Royal Palace in Anakooga to prevent the Crown Prince from making a terrible mistake that could affect the whole country. However, I sincerely hope you can find some kind gentleman who will act as my double. I realize there will be mistakes in love matches that I'll need to correct at a later date, but I can handle it. The dance must not be cancelled because of my absence.

This is truly regrettable since it's the only time in over a century that I've not been able to uphold my duty to find love for the wonderful people in my hometown of Heartsboro."

Love and Kisses,

Cupid

Luke shoved the letter back into her hands. "Very funny. Who sent it?"

"We honestly don't know. We've contacted every civic organization, and none claim to know anything about it, though I have a theory."

"You wanna know what happened, Bonnie Jo? I can tell you what happened. Whatever club has been responsible for finding a man willing to act like a stupid comic character has run out of suckers."

"I think you're wrong."

"So, what's your theory?"

"You're gonna laugh, but after reading the letter, I've had thoughts that Cupid might be the real deal. There are a lot of married couples in Heartsboro who have said it for years, and I never bought into it, but now I'm beginning to wonder."

Luke slapped his palm to his forehead. "Not you, too. You're smarter than that, Bonnie Jo. People believe what they want to believe, and they want to believe the words to that old song. . .." He sang a few bars: *They say for every boy and girl there's just one love in this whole world.* He shook his head. "It's a gag, Bonnie."

"Whatever. I only said I've been wondering. I didn't say I believe it. But you didn't tell anyone you'll be playing Cupid, did you? It's the mystery that makes it fun."

"No, but I don't see how you'll manage to disguise me. I think anyone who has ever seen me would recognize me."

"Oh, they won't when we get you outfitted. You're sure you didn't tell? Not even Mack?"

"I haven't seen Mack since I've been here. By the way, how did your date go, the other night?"

"Very romantic."

"Really?"

"You act surprised."

"I guess I am, a little. When I talked to him, he sounded as if he had soured on women. He got burned years ago, and I wasn't sure he'd agree when I told him you wanted to go out with him."

"You underestimate my charms, ol' boy. Follow me to the back and I'll show you your costume and the props."

Jo opened a large box and pulled out a pair of pink tights, red bloomers and a red Tee shirt with the words, "Cupid Always Aims to Please."

Luke backed away. "Oh, no you don't. You don't seriously think you're going to get me to wear silly pink tights and those . . . those blousy things, whatever they're called."

"They're called bloomers."

"They look more like my grannie's underwear. I'm sorry, Jo, I can't."

"You can't back out now, Luke. Look! Here's the mask you'll wear over your eyes, a cute short curly wig, and angel wings."

"A yellow wig?"

"You don't want anyone to recognize you, do you? When you put on the wig and mask, they'll never guess. Didn't you ever attend a Cupid's Ball before you and Trudy married?"

"Never, and I wish I wasn't coming to this one. What am I

supposed to do, anyway?"

"You should never say a word. Nodding your head or shaking it is okay, but don't speak. You'll flit around the room, then sit on your cloud." She pointed to a tall platform in the back of the room. A billowy-looking cotton cloud sat atop the platform.

"Unless these wings really work, I don't know how you expect me to get up there."

"There's a ladder in the back. You'll flit around to the back, climb up the ladder and sit in the chair. All they'll see is from your waist up. The cloud hides the chair."

"We have another problem."

"Nothing we can't solve I'm sure."

"I don't know how to flit. Never heard of it."

"You've seen Ballerinas, haven't you? You do as they do." Jo flitted about the room, then had to catch Luke before he went out the door. "You can do it, Luke. You'll have fun once you get the hang of it."

One of the committee members walked over. "You'll be perfect, Luke. Here's your quiver."

"My what?"

"Your quiver. You'll have a helper who'll stay hid behind the cloud and she'll keep your quiver full. It holds twenty-four arrows, so after you've handed out arrows to twelve couples, you'll need to flit back up to your cloud. Sit there for a while as if you're looking for matches."

"Do I get to do what I want to with the matches? I have a

couple of thoughts."

"I'm talking about matching up couples."

"Why can't we let them choose who they want to match up with?"

"Because you're Cupid. It's your job to put lovers together. Now, go in the Restroom, put on your costume and go sit on your cloud."

After fifteen minutes, he yelled, "These stockings are too little."

Jo yelled back. "No, they aren't. Now hurry and dress."

"I'm telling you they're too little."

"Luke, do you need me to come help you get them on?"

"No. I think I've got it."

CHAPTER 32

Liz was sitting cross-legged on the bed, reading when Maggie came in at four-thirty, Friday afternoon, holding a garment bag. "Looks like you've been shopping all day. Why am I not surprised?"

"Not all day, but I did pick up a snazzy-looking cocktail dress, before I came home. Can't wait to show it to you."

"A dress? Maggie, you brought enough clothes with you to wear for a month."

"But Hank and Merle have invited Jim and me to go with them to their Church's Valentine Banquet for Senior Adults and I wanted to wear something special."

"Who is Hank and Merle?"

"Longtime friends of Jim's. I had such fun today. I'm glad you no longer suspect Jim of being the Boston Strangler."

"Well, if I was wrong about him, I apologize, but I know how naïve you are."

"Naïve?"

"Yes, when it comes to making judgments about people, you

tend to trust everyone, but we'll be leaving soon, so if you can stay out of trouble until Sunday, I'll breathe much easier."

"You're hilarious, Liz." Maggie fell across her bed and looking like a teenager experiencing her first crush, she gushed, "Oh, Lizzie, I've never met anyone quite like him." For fifteen minutes she talked nonstop: "And then Jim and I walked over to the Senior Center and played cards with Hank and Merle. Lovely people. We did more laughing and talking than we did playing, but I don't know when I've enjoyed myself as much. I felt sixteen again. I love this place and these people. I'll hate to see the week come to an end. I feel awful knowing I'm having all the fun while you're spending most of your time in the room alone, reading your books."

"Maggie, I haven't been alone as much as you might think. You've been gone so much, how would you know whether I've been here or not?"

"Because I know you. You're a hermit. I want you to learn how to have fun, but if my hunch is right, and I believe it is, things will look up for you, very soon. Don't lose hope."

"You've said that more than once, lately. I'm beginning to believe there may be something to women's intuition."

"Well, you just keep on believing, hon, because it will happen. I feel it."

Maggie knew Liz was only pretending to be enjoying herself to keep her from feeling guilty about leaving her alone so much. She hated to go off and leave her again, but Jim would be waiting in the lobby at six and she still needed to shower, fix her hair, do her makeup and put on the new dress she bought to wear to the banquet.

Maggie walked out of the bathroom at five-forty-five, looking like a gorgeous model for Mature Magazine.

"Oh, Maggie, you look beautiful. That dress is stunning on you."

"It should be, as much as they charged for it, but I'm glad you like it. I hope Jim does."

"Maggie, I'm glad you're having fun, but I'm beginning to worry that you might be letting yourself get too involved with that man. You don't know much about him."

"I know enough to know that we enjoy one another's company, and that's enough for me. I wish it was enough for you."

Liz brushed it off with her hand. "It is. Don't mind me. I don't mean to put a damper on your fun. I'm really glad you're having a good time, but then, I've never known you to not have fun."

She glanced at her watch. "It's a few minutes early, but I'm going to run on downstairs and be there when he comes down. Goodnight, hon, and don't wait up. I don't know what time the banquet will be over."

"Don't hurry back. I'll be going out, also, so you may beat me home."

"Oh, Liz, really? That makes me happy." Maggie started out the door, then turned around and came back. "You don't have a date with that officer, do you?"

"What officer?"

"The bad boy who stopped us on the way in."

"You mean Blake." Liz giggled at Maggie for referring to him as the bad boy. "No. I haven't seen him since we've been here."

"Good."

Liz found it curious that Maggie had been so eager to marry her off and now, suddenly, she'd become overly protective if a man showed an interest. Maggie insisted she hadn't changed her mind, but simply wanted to make sure she found the right man. Liz wanted to tell her she *had* found the right man. That she found him years ago, but she wasn't ready to hear what Maggie would say, though she had no one to blame but herself. Now, even though she'd forgiven him, Maggie would have a hard time forgetting Mack was the one who had broken her heart.

The minute Maggie closed the door, Liz ran in the shower and washed her hair. After putting on makeup, she pulled out the winter-white satin sheath—the dress Maggie bought her, which she thought she'd never have an occasion to wear. She decided to wear her hair up, with a few tendrils falling softly around her face. Staring into the mirror, she gasped. Who was this gorgeous female looking back at her? Liz hadn't felt this giddy since Senior Prom.

For thirty minutes, she sat in her room, waiting for time to go. She didn't want to be too early, nor too late. Maybe around five past the hour would be a good time to walk in.

At precisely five after, she drove up and gasped to see such a long line. Who would've thought there would be that many singles

229

in the entire county? She parked and walked across the parking lot in the six-inch heels Maggie bought for her. They were beautiful, but very difficult to walk in, on gravel. Standing in line, her eyes searched for Mack. Her hopes for a future together soared as she recalled hearing her parents' story of being matched by Cupid at the dance. How cool would it be to make it a family tradition? A tinge of sadness swept over her when she acknowledged that any family traditions ended with her, since Carter had been opposed to having children. In the first couple of years after their marriage, he claimed they needed time to get to know one another since their courtship was so brief. After two years had passed, he told her they couldn't afford a child and should wait another couple of years. Liz finally realized he'd never agree, regardless of how many times she pleaded or how many tears she cried.

Eyeing three young women in their late teens or early twenties in front of her, caused her to shake her head in amazement. Did she act that silly at their age?

It was an eye-opener when she realized if she and Mack had married when they finished high school twenty years ago, it would've been possible for them to have a child old enough to be attending the Cupid's Ball, by now. And instead of being here at a dance for singles, they'd be on their way to the Yoked-Together Dance on the other side of town. She felt like a relic, when she realized at least two-thirds of the people standing in line were much younger than her thirty-seven years.

As she inched closer to the front of the line, the louder the music blared, if one could call it music. If it hadn't been for meeting Mack, she would've turned around and driven back to the B&B.

When Liz finally reached the door, the young lady selling tickets informed her she was free to mingle and dance with as many hopefuls as she cared to dance with. But at some point during the evening, if she were lucky, Cupid would seek her out and give her an arrow with a number on it. Some fortunate fellow would receive an arrow with the same number and she and her perfect match would then spend the remainder of the evening dancing the night away. The young woman said, "After you are matched, Cupid will hang a Valentine around your neck and the neck of your partner, as a sign to the other dancers that you've been chosen."

Liz tried to dismiss the apprehension. After all, this crazy game had been going on for generations and in all these years, no one had attempted to put a stop to it. There were countless success stories that began with couples' receiving Cupid's arrow. What was there to worry about? There was little chance of Cupid missing the cues. She loved Mack and she was confident that he loved her. It couldn't be more apparent if it were written on their foreheads in bold letters.

The first person Liz recognized was Claire, the little girl she babysat in high school. Only she was no longer a little girl. Liz recalled helping with Claire's tenth birthday party her senior year. She winced at the thought that the little pig-tail child who once sat in her lap while she read her stories, could now be thirty years old.

Claire ran over and hugged her. "Liz, I'm glad you came. I saw you riding the float in the parade. I couldn't believe it was you when Mom pointed you out. I was hoping I'd have a chance to see you while you were in town."

"Thanks, Claire. It's good seeing you, again."

"Isn't this exciting?"

"How's that?"

"Look around at all the good-looking guys. Cupid could close his eyes and shoot an arrow at most any male in this room, and we couldn't go wrong. I've never seen so many single hunks in one place."

Liz wrung her hands. Where was Mack? The dance had already begun. What if Cupid presented her with an arrow before he arrived?

"Claire, how do you suppose Cupid knows who to put together?"

"I've heard he sits on his cloud and watches the body language as people dance together. I don't think it would be difficult for anyone to see if two people were really connecting. You know, the way their gaze is fixed on one another; the way she puts her head on his shoulder; or how he pulls her close and she closes her eyes, looking dreamy. I wouldn't think it would take a degree in psychology to see the signs."

"I suppose you're right." Liz went over all Claire's instructions in her mind: Be aware that Cupid could be watching, so send out the right signals. If her dance partner was not the one she wanted to spend the remainder of the night with, she should play it cool. Dance at arm's length and let her eyes wander around the room. However, when Mack asked her to dance, she should remember to laugh to show they were having a great time, and remember to gaze into his eyes, then lay her head on his shoulder and close her eyes. She relaxed, realizing it wouldn't take acting for her to pull it off. It would be real, and Cupid would know it. She had nothing to worry about.

Blake Andrews walked over, looking fine in his uniform. "Liz, may I have this dance?"

She quickly glanced at the door searching for Mack. Where was he? She turned back around to see Blake standing there holding out his hand. "Uh . . . yes, thank you."

He took her by the hand, walked her out on the dance floor, then held her at arm's length, gazing at her. So far, so good. She glanced about the room, hoping Cupid was watching. Blake swung her around, then jerked her close. "Liz, I was hoping you'd be here."

"Really?" She pushed back to make space between them.

"It's the only reason I came."

"Oh, Blake, I'm no longer the freshman girl on Gilmore Street."

"And I'm no longer the wild kid who couldn't keep his eyes off you. I'm now a man who can't get my eyes off you. You're even more beautiful than I remember."

Liz looked up at the cloud, hoping Cupid wasn't seeing the same thing in Blake's eyes that she was seeing. The band stopped playing a romantic melody and a loud recording of Stupid Cupid, Stop Picking on Me, blared over the speakers. Every couple on the dance floor froze, waiting for Cupid to make his move. Liz breathed easier, when she realized he'd hung an arrow over the neck of an unsuspecting male, who turned to locate his perfect match. Liz watched as they strolled across the room and met in the center, both holding up their arrows with matching numbers. Cupid hung hearts around their necks and the crowd applauded when the two kissed.

Blake said, "Greg must've paid Cupid."

"Why would you say that?"

"He's on the force and he's been wanting to date that girl for ages, but he's so shy he wouldn't ask her out. Way to go, Cupid."

"You're saying your friend paid Cupid?"

"No, that was a joke, but I wasn't joking about him wanting to date her. I suppose this will go down as another lasting romance that began at the Ball."

Once again, the band struck up and dancers filled the floor, doing the Cupid's Shuffle. Liz shook her head when Blake suggested they give it a try. "Thanks, but I'll sit this one out." Cupid was in the center of the line, shuffling with the best of them.

Liz turned to look toward the door and saw Mack crossing the dance floor, wearing a beautiful red vee-neck sweater that accentuated his broad shoulders and trim waist. *"Wow!"* Feeling a warm blush paint her face, she hoped she didn't blurt the exclamation aloud, but there was no denying the years had been good to him. Very good. He was handsome at twenty-one, yet even more good-looking at thirty-seven. His fine physique confirmed he was no couch potato. Her knees felt shaky.

CHAPTER 33

Blake's eyes darkened. He looked first at Liz, then at Mack who was making his way over. His smile appeared forced. "I guess this is where I came in."

Liz said, "You're leaving?"

"You don't have to be Cupid to see Mack Mackenzie still owns your heart. Thanks for the dance, Liz." He kissed the back of her hand.

Mack gave the box to Liz, then thrust out his hand toward Blake. "How's it going, man?"

"Not so good. Story of my life. I'm sure you two will be wearing your hearts on your back in short order. If Cupid misses this one, he needs to retire."

Mack gave a thumb's up. "That's what I'm thinking. Thanks for taking care of my girl, Blake. I couldn't find a parking place. Looks like the whole County turned out."

Liz opened the box and pulled out a beautiful rose wrist

corsage. "Oh, Mack, it's beautiful. Thank you."

"I hope you still like roses."

"I do. It was sweet of you to remember. I pressed the rose corsage you gave me the night of the Senior Prom and kept it in a scrapbook for ages." She wouldn't bother to explain the reason she no longer had the scrapbook was because Carter burned it.

Mack tossed the box the corsage came in, in the nearest trash barrel. "Shall we dance?"

She shook her head. "Sorry, but I'm afraid I haven't kept up. I don't shuffle."

At the next slow dance, he pulled her close and planted a kiss on the side of her cheek. "You look stunning, Liz. Wow!"

For the first time since arriving, she relaxed. His head tilted, and when he looked at her with a longing in his eyes, she knew there was no way for Cupid to get this wrong.

She glanced up at the cloud, hoping it wouldn't take long for Cupid to see what she was feeling. *Where is he?* How could he see Mack pulling her close, kissing her, if he spent his time flitting around on the dance floor and not sitting atop his cloud?

It was their third dance. Liz's head was on Mack's shoulder, her eyes closed, when suddenly the band stopped playing "Unchained Melody" and the recording of "Stupid Cupid, Stop Picking on Me," blared over the speakers. Everyone on the dance floor stopped dancing. Her eyes opened wide to see Cupid handing Mack an arrow with #78 attached. Liz's pulse raced as she waited for hers.

Cupid whispered, "You can thank me later, Mack."

Standing behind Cupid was Bonnie Jo Bloodworth, holding arrow #78 high in the air, and squealing with delight.

Even in the darkened room, Mack's red face glowed like a Christmas light. His voice quaked as Cupid hung a heart around his neck. "Luke? No. No, what are you doing, man?"

Cupid hung a heart around Bonnie's neck and the crowd applauded. The band began to play, once again and the crowd chanted, "Kiss her, kiss her."

Mack squeezed Liz's hand, before she jerked away. He whispered in her ear. "I'm so sorry. I don't understand."

"I think I do." She turned and hurried toward the door. He'd managed to do it again. How could she have been so blind to what everyone else could apparently see? She turned at the sound of Blake's soothing voice.

He said, "What does Cupid know? I just had my heart broken shortly before you did. I'm through here. I think I'll drive over to Heartie's and order the biggest banana split they can make, to ease the pain. Could I interest you in sharing it with me?"

The lump in her throat was choking her. "Thank you. I would love to leave."

"Do you want to take your car to the Bed & Breakfast now, or come back and get it later?"

"I guess I'll come back later to get it, but how did you know where I'm staying?"

"There aren't many choices in this town, but I make my living knowing how to investigate people." He winked. "The truth is, I called and asked if you had reservations, the day you rode into town. I've ridden by several times a day, hoping I'd catch you walking out and I could pretend it was coincidence that I happened to pass by at the right time."

"You're sweet, Blake. You always have been." She forced a smile, though the pain in her chest made it hard to breathe. "Instead of bringing me back here later, how about if I meet you at Hearties?" He was walking her to her car, when Mack ran out the door and yelled her name.

"Liz, wait. We've got to talk."

She tried to close the door, but he grabbed it and held it open. "Please listen."

Blake pointed behind him. "Mack, I believe Cupid is looking for you."

Mack turned around when Luke laid his hand on his shoulder.

He jerked away. "Do you know what you've done? Why don't you stay out of my life, Luke? I went out with Bonnie as a favor to you, but I don't owe you anything else."

Luke pulled off his wig and ran his fingers through his hair. "Look, man, I don't know what's going on here, but Jo told me you two had a very romantic evening together and she led me to believe there was a real connection between the two of you. I thought I was doing you both a favor."

Liz had heard enough. "You did me one, Luke. Thank you. Now, close the door, Mack. I have a date, and I don't want to be

239

late."

Mack thrust the arrow into Luke's hands. "Cupid, you missed your mark. But the dance must go on. I believe you have a job to do. You're finished out here."

"I wish you'd let me explain, Mack."

"I believe you just did."

Blake said, "I'll be waiting for you, Liz."

The dejected look on his face told Liz that Blake knew exactly what she knew—even though she vehemently denied it, she was still in love with Mack Mackenzie. How could it be, after the humiliation he'd caused her? Never had she felt so violated, and in front of all those people. She was so angry she could bite a ten-penny nail in half, and didn't she have every right to be? But with whom? Mack? Bonnie? Cupid? Or herself? Maybe all four. Mack for kissing her at the theatre, leading her to believe he still cared. Bonnie for being the thorn in her flesh that never went away. Cupid for not aiming at her, but she was angry with herself for letting her guard down. If she hadn't been so vulnerable, not Bonnie, nor Cupid nor even Mack could've hurt her.

Luke plopped the wig on his head and ambled back inside.

With a sad smile, Blake trudged back to his truck and drove away.

Mack stalked around to the front of Liz's car, jerked open the door on the passenger side and sat down. "You owe me the right to explain."

"Owe you? I owe you nothing. I should've known better than

to believe you when you tried to tell me there was nothing between you and Bonnie." Liz slammed her fist on the steering wheel. "I can't believe I was so stupid. Even though I heard you both admit at the Parade that you had a wonderful time on your date, I foolishly allowed you to lie your way out of it. I'm done."

"Liz, it's not how you think."

"Don't tell me how I think. You aren't my ventriloquist and I'm not your dummy, so please get out of my car. I don't need you or your lies. In fact, I came here debating whether to accept a recent marriage proposal. You've helped me come to a decision."

"Liz, I love you. Please believe me. The only man you're going to marry is me."

"You're wrong, Mack. I want to be able to trust the man I marry, and I know I can trust him. You, not so much."

"Don't be like that, Liz. You and I both know you're only trying to make me jealous, and I would be if there was anyone else. But I know you're still in love with me, and I am with you. We can't let Bonnie mess this up for us."

When his eyes met hers, she looked away. Was he so conceited he couldn't imagine she could choose another man over him? "You don't believe me? His name is Allen Albertson and he's begging me to marry him. I should thank you for helping me make up my mind."

Mack covered his face with his hands. "Red Albertson? You've got to be kidding. Liz, please tell me you're not mixed up with that low-down rascal. He's a crook."

"I didn't know you knew him, but obviously you don't know him well or you'd have a better opinion of him. I've never heard a negative word spoken about him."

"I'm sure you haven't. That's his mode of operation, to create a pseudo personality."

"Speaking of pseudo personalities, you don't have room to talk. I believed every lie you told me. Not once, but twice. Never again. Now, please get out of my car."

Mack's voice lowered. "Just answer one question for me, Liz. How in the world did you get mixed up with Allen?"

"He's my realtor, and I'm not mixed up. Not anymore. Things have suddenly become very clear to me."

He popped his palm to the side of his head. "No, it can't be."

"I'm afraid it is. Allen has spent hours, trying to help me find the right place for my bakery and I've been very grateful for his help."

"Liz, even if you don't give me a chance, please, get away from Allen Albertson as fast as you can. I know him personally and he's bad news."

"As if I can believe anything you say. I'm ready to go home to let him know I no longer have any doubts. I know he'll be good to me."

"He's a cad, Liz."

"Stop it, Mack. I love him, and I didn't realize how much until a few minutes ago. After comparing the two of you, I don't know why I almost let you ruin the best thing that's ever come into my life."

"You really think he's gonna marry you? I know at least three women who have moved in with him through the years, believing it would lead to marriage, but it only lasted until he found his next victim. Now it looks like that would be you."

"That's an awful accusation, Mack. I never knew you to be so hateful."

"Watch what comes next, Liz. He'll be handing you the keys to his condo and promising the ring will come later. Don't hold your breath."

"Mack Mackenzie, why are you making up these things? He loves me but I don't think that's something that you can understand."

"You may be right. It seems there are quite a few things I fail to understand. You led me on this weekend, although you were romantically involved with that sleaze ball. What else is it you forgot to tell me, Liz?"

"Get out."

When he looked up and saw Bonnie walking toward the car, he got out and slammed the door.

CHAPTER 34

Maggie was glad Hank and Merle invited her and Jim to their church banquet. She was meeting so many wonderful people and couldn't help wondering what it would be like to live in this little town where everyone seemed so happy. But it wouldn't be the same without Jim and he'd soon be going back to Point Clear. Jim told her more than once she was beautiful—or "a sight for sore eyes," as he put it, but she knew what he meant. She hadn't had anyone to look at her the way he looked at her, since Robert died. The dress was worth every penny she paid for it.

The Dining Hall was decorated with hearts of all sizes hanging from the ceiling. The centerpieces consisted of red roses and greenery, with a half-dozen red and white balloons tied to each bouquet. Tiny candy hearts with messages were scattered about the table.

Hank picked up the first one. He took his glasses from his shirt pocket to read the tiny print. "This one's for you, my sweet Merle." His eyes rounded as he glared at the candy. He rubbed the back of his bald head, "This doesn't make sense."

Merle said, "Read it."

It says, "go pitter patter . . . that's all. Just, 'go pitter patter.'"

After the laughter at the table died down, Merle said, "Turn it over, Hank. I think you read the back first."

"There's a back?" Turning it over, he read, "To the one who makes my heart." Hank laid the candy in his wife's plate, then reached for her hand. "My darling Merle, you are the only one who could ever make my heart go pitter patter, and you still do.

Maggie felt a good cry trying to push its way out. "That was very sweet, Hank." It was the kind of thing Robert would've done. She glanced over at Jim and thought how much alike he and Robert were in some ways, yet how totally opposite in others.

Robert was a stickler for proper English. With Jim, not so much. Yet there was no doubt in her mind that Robert would have approved of her enjoying Jim's company. She wondered what it would've been like if she and Robert had lived in Heartsboro and had been privileged to know these wonderful friends.

Jim certainly had many fascinating stories to tell of the experiences he had when living in the Little Town with a Big Heart. He never mentioned why he moved away, and she didn't want to pry. Liz was right when she said Maggie didn't know much about him. He mentioned from the beginning that he came back with his son, yet he never elaborated. Did his son have business in Heartsboro or were they taking a holiday to visit in the old hometown? Not that any of it mattered. She was simply curious, that's all.

The meal was wonderful. Steak, baked potato and asparagus, yeast rolls and a choice of chocolate silk pie or cherry cheesecake. When she couldn't decide, Jim suggested she get the silk pie, he'd get the cheesecake, and they'd split them.

As they finished the meal, a wonderful quartet entertained them with a medley of love songs. Then, the preacher stepped up to the microphone and said they were going to play a little game to see how much the couples knew about one another.

"I need four couples to volunteer. We'll have two sides with two couples on each side."

Hank raised his hand. "Our table will volunteer."

Maggie looked at Hank and shook her head. "It wouldn't be fair to the other couple on our side, since Jim and I know very little about one another."

Hank ignored her. "It's just a game. Come on, let's have fun."

The preacher put four chairs on one side, and the other four facing them. "Hank, how long have you and Merle been married?"

"Fifty-four years, Preacher, and working on the next fifty-four."

He turned to the couples across from them. "Gus, what about you and Anne?"

"We've got them beat. Sixty years next March." The crowd applauded.

Then the preacher said, "Jim, how long have you and your lovely date known one another?"

Maggie was still blushing over the word 'date,' when Jim responded, "If we can count tonight, it makes three nights in a row."

"Oh, I'm sorry. I'm sure this little game would put you at a disadvantage, so if you'd prefer to have someone else take your place, I'll understand."

Hank said, "No way. Don't take away my partners."

The preacher shrugged. "Okay, then let's get started. Hank's team will be the Red team, and Gus's team will be the white team. I'll ask a question, and your partner will write her answer on a slip of paper. Then after I've finished asking the questions, I'll see how well you gentlemen know your sweetheart."

Maggie hoped she wasn't blushing.

"First question: What is your sweetheart's favorite song?" Maggie saw Merle hesitating, but she knew this one, and wrote "Blue Moon." She could only hope the next ones would be so easy.

"Second question: What is her favorite food?" Now, Maggie was the one hesitating. Then she let out a little giggle and wrote, "Chocolate-covered cherries."

"Next, if not with you, who would she choose to go on an excursion with?" She wrote, "Liz." Then marked it out and wrote, "My adopted daughter."

"Now, what is one of the most romantic things she's ever said to you?" That was a tough one, since she didn't consider anything that she'd said to Jim to be romantic. She closed her eyes and tried to remember their conversations, then wrote, "I said he reminded

247

me of my late husband." She was sure Jim wouldn't get this one, because he had no way of knowing just how romantic she considered that to be. No man had ever reminded her of her sweet, romantic Robert, but Jim came very close.

"Last question: What would she like to say to you at this very moment?" Maggie felt she and Jim had lost already, so it didn't really matter what she wrote, but she knew exactly what she would like to say—and she would before the night ended. She wrote, "I wish we had more time to spend together."

When it came time for Jim to answer what he believed Maggie had written on her paper, he said, "Her favorite song is Blue Moon."

The preacher halted as if he might've given a wrong answer. "Are you sure about that?"

"Absolutely positive."

Maggie hid her smile behind her hand.

"Next question.' What's her favorite food?'" Jim looked at her and winked. "Chocolate-covered cherries."

There were giggles and the preacher said, "Would you like to change that answer?"

"No sir. My answer stands."

The preacher read the next question: "Who, if not you, would she choose to take an excursion with?"

"I don't recall her name, but it would be her adopted daughter."

The preacher stuck his tongue in his cheek." Okay, let's see if you get this one: What is the most romantic thing she's ever said to you?"

"I considered it very romantic when she compared me with her Robert, since I know how much he meant to her."

Maggie's lip quivered.

The preacher read the last question. "Now, what would she like to say to you at this very moment?"

Jim reared back in his chair and looked into Maggie's eyes. "I'm not sure what this sweet woman would like to say to me, but I know what I want to say to her—and I'd like to believe it could possibly be in her thoughts."

The room grew silent.

The preacher, said, "Well, don't keep us in suspense."

Jim said, "I ain't got no way of knowing, but I'll be hoping she wishes the week wasn't coming to an end so we could have more time to spend together."

After the preacher read all the answers, he said, "Well folks, looks like the Red team won. And even though three of our four couples have enjoyed a combined one-hundred-seventy-two years of marital bliss, the couple who has only known one another for three nights came out the big winner. Jim nailed every one of Maggie's answers. I think that's incredible. Let's give them all a hand."

CHAPTER 35

Mack's head was spinning. He turned and walked Bonnie back into the gym and suggested they sit and talk things out. He'd tell her what he should have told her Wednesday night when she so rudely chewed out the poor waiter at the restaurant—there was nothing between them and never would be.

When they walked in together, Bonnie plastered a fake smile on her face and threw up her hand, waving at the curious eyes. She whispered, "They're all staring. Can't we at least dance?"

"Not until we talk." He pulled out a chair for her and they sat over in a corner.

"I'm sorry," he whispered. "But Bonnie—"

Her eyes welled with water. "Mack Mackenzie, I've never been so humiliated in all my life? How could you have embarrassed me in front of all my friends by walking out on me to follow Liz? This has been the worse night of my life. I can never forgive you."

"I didn't mean for it to happen this way, and it wouldn't have if you hadn't given Luke reason to believe there was a connection between us. You know there isn't and never has been."

Her lip quivered. "How could I have known that, when you were sending out signals all night on our date?"

"Signals? Please explain."

"You took me on a date and purposely led me to believe you would've gone with me to my apartment and stayed late if you hadn't needed to get back to your invalid father."

He chewed on his bottom lip. "Did I really give you that impression? Because if I did, I apologize. It wasn't my intent." Maybe she was right. He could've told her he had eyes for someone else instead of using Pop as an excuse to leave the restaurant. A dishonest excuse, at that.

"You know that's the impression you gave, Mack. I bore my heart in the note I attached to the box of chocolates, so there was no way you could not know how I felt about you. You could've at least thanked me for the forty-dollar box of candy."

"What candy?"

"Don't try to pretend you didn't get it because I know that sweet elderly gentleman at the B&B gave it to you. I could tell he could hardly wait."

Mack had a sneaky feeling he knew the sweet, elderly gentleman. "I can't seem to do anything but apologize, Bonnie, but whether you believe me or not, I know nothing about a box of candy."

"Doesn't matter now. Nothing matters. I live here and work

among these people. I won't be able to ever show my face in town again. For years, everyone will be talking about the first time Cupid's choice was turned down on the dance floor, forcing her to watch her perfect match go running after someone else." She lifted her gaze, then quickly lowered her head. "I should get my coat and leave. I can't stay here and know they're all whispering behind my back."

"Don't go. We'll dance and try to look as if were enjoying ourselves. That should squelch any gossip."

"Oh, Mack. You'd do that for me?"

He stood and extended his hand. "Shall we dance?"

Mack flinched when Bonnie pushed her body against his and rested her head against his neck.

She whispered, "Kiss me, Mack. They're all staring."

Glancing around the dance floor, he realized she was right. They were suddenly the center of attention. But kiss her? Wasn't dancing with her enough to satisfy their curiosity?

"Kiss me."

He had never felt as hemmed in, not only by Bonnie, but by the crowd of dancers who seemed to be pushing closer and closer. They hardly had room to move. Maybe Bonnie was right, and he'd acted like a real cad. He couldn't find justification for furthering a false image. *I can't do it. I won't.* He leaned down to whisper it in her ear, when she quickly turned her head and planted a kiss on his lips.

Mack rubbed his hand over his mouth. "What are you doing?"

He glanced to his right when he heard clapping. It began with only a few people, but within seconds the whole room was looking in their direction and applauding. Bonnie looked up at him, smiling.

"Bonnie, I've got to go. You can either walk out with me or stand here on the dance floor alone, but I'm getting out of here. I feel as if I'm suffocating."

She grabbed his hand and clasping it in hers, she lifted their arms in the air while displaying a huge smile.

When they reached the parking lot, he said, "Why did you do that?"

"I told you, they were all waiting for it. I gave them what they wanted. I'd like to go the basketball game tomorrow night. I thought you might like to take me."

He stopped, turned and glared. "Bonnie, we're done. Okay? Done. I'm in love with Liz and always have been. I realize I've blown it. I wanted to blame you or Luke, but I see now I handled things the wrong way. But even if Liz never speaks to me again, she'll always be the one who holds the key to my heart. I'm sorry if you can't accept that, but it's just the way it is."

"I can accept that, Mack. What I couldn't accept was having people believe you chose her over me. Now that we've set them straight, we can part as friends."

"Goodnight, Bonnie." All the way to the B&B he thought about her crazy statement. *What I couldn't accept was having people believe you chose her over me.* Why dwell on it. It was over with him and Bonnie. At least he could hope.

253

When Liz arrived at Heartie's there were only two other people besides Blake there.

He stood when she walked in. "I wasn't sure you'd come."

"I'm sorry it took so long. I tried to get away."

"Am I right to assume you and Mack didn't make up?"

"Oh, Mack has made up a lot, but I won't ever believe anything else he makes up."

"I'm sorry, Liz."

"Don't be. I'm not. Blake, could we sit near the window?"

"Sure. Are you looking for him to come?"

"No, I promise you, I'm not." She didn't want to admit it was difficult sitting in the booth that she and Mack referred to as their booth.

She looked around the empty room. "I've never seen Heartie's this empty."

"All the businesses in Heartsboro fold up around 6:00 PM every year on Valentine's Day. The people are either at the Cupid's Ball, the Yoked-Together Dance, the High School Dance or at one of the Senior Adult Banquets at the various churches. Sometimes I wish Cupid had been born in another town. It's painful for a few of us."

Liz hoped he wouldn't go there. She liked Blake but she could never be in love with him, yet she knew too well how painful it could be to love someone and not have it reciprocated. Perhaps she shouldn't have come. She didn't want to give him false hopes.

The Heartie's manager walked over and sat a huge banana split with two spoons in front of them. "You two didn't go to the Cupid's Ball?"

Blake pressed his lips together and nodded. "We did."

"Well, congratulations."

"For what?"

"Finding your match."

"I'm afraid you don't understand. We're the rejects."

"From the look in your eyes, I'd say Cupid goofed."

Liz was grateful that Blake had rescued her, but she felt guilty that she couldn't return the affection he had for her. She would if she could. How naïve she was to think Mack had changed. "Blake, do you remember Haley Newsome?"

He took a bite of the banana split. "Haley? Funny, you should ask."

"Why is it funny?"

"When I realized your Memaw would never let me come near your house, I got this huge crush on Haley."

"Really? Did you ever date her?"

"Oh, no. She never knew. It was one of those torches I carried for a long time, but she lived up on the hill. I knew better than to ask her out."

"What did living on the hill have to do with it."

"Everything. I never tried to kid myself into thinking I was in the same league with Haley. You may remember her dad was Chief of Police and there was no doubt in my mind that he had me pegged as trouble. I was sure he'd never allow his daughter to go out with someone of my caliber and frankly I didn't want him having to tell her why. Maybe she knew already that I wasn't good enough for her, but if she did, she never showed it." He looked down and said, "Haley Newsome. She was one of the sweetest girls in school. I always wondered if she would've gone out with me if her dad had approved."

"Why don't you find out? She's here."

He jerked his head around to look, but except for the two of them, the room was now empty. "What do you mean, here? Are you saying she's in Heartsboro?"

Liz nodded. "Yep. Staying with her grandmother."

"I haven't seen her since high school, but I'm sure she's married by now."

"Nope. She's single."

"I'd love to see her, but she wouldn't remember me."

Liz handed him her phone. "Why don't you call her and find out?"

He looked down at Haley's name in Liz's contacts and glanced at his watch. "It's getting late. I wonder if it would be okay if I gave her a call."

"I'm sure it would. I need to leave, anyway."

Blake took down the number and walked Liz to her car. "Thanks, Liz. You're the best."

CHAPTER 36

Liz went back to her room and noticed she'd missed two calls while driving back to the Bed & Breakfast. One from Haley and one from Allen. She called Haley first.

"Haley, what's going on?"

"I had to call and thank you, Liz. Blake and I just hung up."

"Don't leave me hanging. What did he say?"

"He's on his way over and we're going to Heartie's. He told me he didn't finish his banana split you two shared, and I assured him I could help him woof one down. Liz, you had no way of knowing because I didn't tell anyone, but I was crazy about Blake our Senior year. I remember Daddy saying to Mom at the supper table one night, 'That young boy, Blake has had a hard time, but he can be as tough as nails or as gentle as a lamb. No one will ever run over him, but he'd put his own life on the line for anyone in need.' I was glad Daddy understood him because I didn't think many adults did."

"Oh, Haley, I played a hunch, and it seems to have worked out beautifully. You two make a perfect couple. Blake is a sweetheart and such a fun guy."

"I agree. I missed our Prom, waiting for him to ask me. It never happened. Now, I find the only reason he didn't was because he thought Daddy didn't like him. He had no idea Dad was the one who was instrumental in seeing that he got into the Academy. Oh, he's at the door. Gotta run. Thank you, Liz. My heart feels like it's about to beat out of my chest."

"I'm glad I could help. Now, go have fun." At least one good thing had come out of this horrible night. She hung up and listened to the second message.

"Please call me, Liz. I've tried several times tonight and haven't been able to reach you. It's late. Where are you?"

Her hand shook as she punched in his number and waited for him to pick up. "Allen, is anything wrong?"

"You might want to ask me that in person."

"I want to know now. What's wrong?"

"Hey, I didn't mean to upset you, pretty woman. I've just pulled up in front of the Bed & Breakfast."

"What Bed & Breakfast? You don't mean here in Heartsboro, do you?"

"Unless someone has pulled a joke and put a sign that reads Latimers Bed & Breakfast in front of the building that I'm walking into, it's the same one."

"What are you doing here?"

"I've tried to call for hours to let you know I'd be coming. Why didn't you answer my calls?"

"I'm sorry. My phone was turned off."

"I finally got tired of waiting and decided to surprise you. What room are you in? I'm walking in, now."

She grabbed her robe, tied it at the waist, then opened her door, stepped out and looked down. When several people from the lobby looked up, Liz quickly stepped back inside and closed her door.

"Allen, I'm already dressed for bed. Give me time to change and I'll meet you in the lobby."

"Liz, the lobby is swarming with people. I need to see you in private. It's important. Are you alone?"

"Yes."

"Then I'm coming up."

"I don't know. Maggie should be back soon. If what you have to say is of a personal nature, I'd rather meet in a crowded room than in a room with her. Give me five minutes to dress."

"Why? I saw you standing in the atrium. You have on a robe. What's wrong with that?"

"Nothing, I don't suppose. Okay, the rooms aren't numbered, but I'm in the Scarlett O'Hara room. First door on the right as you top the stairs. You'll need to make it quick. I want you gone before Maggie gets back."

Liz opened the door and offered him a seat on the sofa. She sat

259

in the desk chair, fearing that Maggie would come in any minute and get the wrong idea if the two of them shared the sofa. "What brings you here, Allen?"

"You, my love. Isn't that enough?" He handed her a bag with "George's Candy Shoppe" written across it. She pulled out a large heart-shaped box of chocolates.

"I couldn't let such an important day as Valentine's Day pass without giving you a box of chocolates."

"Oh, Allen, you shouldn't have driven here to bring me candy, but it was awfully sweet of you."

"It's not the only reason I came. Liz, I'll be going to New York in two weeks, and I've already made our flight reservations and booked a room at one of New York's finest motels. We'll take in a Broadway show and see the sights." He handed her a plane ticket.

Mack's words played loud and clear in her head. *Watch what comes next, Liz. He'll be handing you the keys to his condo and promising the ring will come later. Don't hold your breath.*

Her forehead creased. "Allen, I can't go with you."

"Why not?"

She shoved her hand in his face. "Tell me, Allen, do you see a ring on my left hand?"

"Oh, sweetheart, don't be so archaic. The ring will come later. I promise."

"No, Allen. You aren't hearing me. I'm not going. You've been very good to me, and I hate I've wasted your time, but I'm not going to marry you."

"Okay. Fine. We won't get married, but that doesn't stop us from having a good time does it? I enjoy your company, Liz. I'd like to keep seeing you."

"It's late and I think you should go." She handed him the plane ticket.

He laid it down on the table. "I'm leaving it with you. I think when you've had time to think about what you'd be turning down, you'll change your mind. When you do, call me."

He started to walk out the door, turned back and hesitated. "By the way, I have a surprise for you. I purchased the perfect building for a bakery."

"Allen, we discussed this. I want to do this on my own."

"Hey, I think when you hear the details, you'll thank me. It's been a small café for the past thirty-five years, but the owners retired, and I had to move fast so I bought it from them to keep it from going on the market. As your realtor, I knew this was what you've been searching for. The location is perfect. It was formerly called The Lunch Counter."

"Oh, Allen. The Lunch Counter? You aren't serious. I know the place. I didn't realize it had closed."

"So how would you like to open a bakery there?"

"Oh, my goodness, it would be perfect. I'd love it. I hope it's affordable."

"Didn't you get the part where I said, I bought it? I'll make sure you can afford it."

"Allen, I don't want you doing me any favors. I want to pay you what it cost you, plus commission. That is if I can swing it, and I sure hope I can."

"Honey, I knew it was perfect, and we didn't have time to wait for your bank loan to go through, so I snatched it up before someone else could buy it out from under you. The elderly couple who owned it were asking an arm and a leg for it, but I knew it was exactly what you needed, so I gave them what they asked for. What are friends for if we can't help one another?"

"But it's strictly a business deal, right?"

"Strictly. I'll keep it off the market until you're financially prepared to purchase it. You do understand it could take months. I hope that won't be too disappointing."

"Of course not. Just knowing it's finally coming together is exciting. I can't thank you enough."

****

Mack left the dance and drove back to the Latimer's Bed & Breakfast. Walking through the Dining Room, he stopped at the fruit basket to pick out an apple when he happened to look up in time to see Allen and Liz walking out of an upstairs bedroom together. He felt he was going to be sick. He stepped away from the stairs to keep from being seen. Every muscle in his body tightened. Red Albertson—how could she? Maybe Luke had done him a favor, after all.

He heard Liz thank Allen for buying her the Lunch Counter building. *What?* Mack clinched his teeth and felt his temples pulsing. Allen Albertson was such a liar, but what else was new? Mack's stomach knotted when Liz gushed and called him a good man, hugged him, then told him she'd be home Sunday. Red told her he couldn't wait and warned her not to leave the plane ticket in the room when she checked out.

Every muscle in Mack's body tightened. So, it had gotten to that, had it? She was flying around the world with him. If he hadn't heard it with his own ears, he wouldn't have believed it. Her words to Red kept playing in Mack's head. *I'll be home? She lives with the scoundrel? Why should I be surprised?* After all, she walked out of the room in her bed clothes.

He owed Pop an apology. If only he'd not been so blind, surely, he would've seen the signs, also.

When Allen came bouncing down the stairs, with an uncanny grin, Mack stepped from behind the wall. "How could you stoop so low, Red?"

"I don't know what you're talking about."

"I think you do. I just heard you lying to Liz about owning the Lunch Counter. You don't own it and never will. It's no longer on the market."

Red snorted. "I suppose you think you're doing it to spite me, but I couldn't be more pleased. I have no use for it, so you'll be doing me a favor by taking it off the market. Liz thinks she wants a bakery, but I have other plans for us. What's it to you, anyway?"

"Nothing. I just wish you would've told me who the widow was you were so concerned about."

With a smirk on his face, Allen said, "Hey, you're sweet on my girl, aren't you? What a hoot. I should've known. It's all over your face. Well, you can forget her. Like your tacky little property over on High Street, she's been taken off the market."

His chilling laughter made Mack want to sock him. "No, you have it all wrong, Red. You can have her. I don't care what she does."

"Good, because you couldn't get her if you tried—and I have a peculiar feeling that you have. Liz and I share a little something that will hold us together like glue and I'd appreciate it if you'd stay out of our lives. She's going back to bed, and I've got to get back home, so get out of my way. I have an early appointment in Cottonvale, or I wouldn't be leaving."

Mack's mouth felt parched. Allen had come from her room, but he still found it hard to believe. But what did he mean by the crack, "a little something held them together like glue?"

CHAPTER 37

Jim walked Maggie to her door. "Goodnight, Maggie. Thank you for a wonderful evening. I ain't had that much fun in years. My Thelma was a good woman and I ain't taking nothing away from her when I say what I'm about to say. Truth is, she was good as gold and smart as a whip. She could out-iron, out-cook, out-clean any woman in the County and there wasn't nothing she wouldn't do for nobody. No woman ever loved her family any more than Thelma loved me and the kid. All that to say, she didn't hold to having fun—not the way we did tonight. I don't know when I've laughed so much. Fact of the matter is, I'm not sure I ever have. I like being around you, Maggie. You make me feel young again."

Maggie reached for his hand. "Thank you, Jim. I like being around you, too."

"Can I see you tomorrow? I thought if you like, we could go back over to the Senior Center. I enjoyed playing dominoes with you. Maybe we could do it again, and then walk over to the Corner Café when we get hungry."

"I'd like that. I sure would. Why don't I meet you in the lobby at ten o'clock?"

Maggie tiptoed in and found Liz in bed when she opened the door. "Are you asleep?"

"No."

"Good, we can talk. I had so much fun tonight. We played this game at the Banquet and—" She stopped short and walked over and sat on the side of Liz's bed. "Oh, honey, what's wrong? You've been crying." When Liz failed to answer, Maggie took her hand. "Oh, sweetie, I'm such an idiot. I was hoping you were going out and would find friends to spend time with. I've been very insensitive lately, thinking only of myself. I should never have left you."

"I'm just feeling a little blue, Maggie, but it has nothing to do with you. I'm glad you went out. Really, I am."

"Sweetie, I wish I could explain why I am so sure but trust me when I say I know that a love like you've never experienced before is coming your way very soon and I pray you'll be receptive."

"I think you may be right. Maybe I should give it a chance."

"Seriously?"

"Yes, I didn't realize how much Allen loved me until tonight. He drove all the way from Cottonvale to bring me a box of Valentine candy. After he arrived, I told him I wouldn't marry him—"

Maggie threw her hands in the air. "Well, Hallelujah, you've seen the light. I was beginning to worry about you, Liz. I really was. Now that he's out of the way, I can relax."

"You didn't let me finish. I told him I wouldn't marry him, and I was afraid he would try to pressure me, but he didn't. Then I learned how much he really loves me. No man has ever loved me the way Allen does."

"That's because you've never given anyone but Carter and Mick a chance to love you and they were both jerks"

Liz rolled her eyes. "You mean Mack."

"Whatever. I always get it wrong."

"But I haven't finished my story. Allen has purchased the perfect building for me to start up my own bakery. I can't tell you what a surprise it was. I couldn't have chosen a better location."

"You're selling your soul for a bakery? I'm shocked, Liz."

"Maggie, you only see what you want to see. Why don't you let me explain?"

"Go ahead. Whatever makes you feel less guilty."

"See, what I'm talking about? You jump to conclusions without knowing the details. You have no idea the lengths this sweet man has gone to, to help me. It's made me realize how much he really loves me. He's agreed to keep the title until I pay him back, in full. He knows how much it means to me to do this on my own. Therefore, I won't be able to open until I get the money to buy it from him, but at least I know that he won't allow anyone else to buy it out from under me. Even if it takes a year or longer, just knowing that one day it will be mine is enough for me."

Maggie groaned, then went into the bathroom to get her gown. There was no use trying to talk Liz out of something that would never take place, anyway. She wasn't thinking straight. Sunday, she'd meet Doyle and after the two of them became acquainted, Liz would forget all about the realtor. Maggie wanted to tell her, but then Liz would refuse to go Sunday if she knew what was up.

"Maggie, I want to go home."

Maggie's throat felt as if she'd swallowed a coconut. She wrapped her arms around her middle. "Oh, Liz, we can't leave yet. Not before Sunday."

Maggie, I'm glad you're having fun, but I have a confession to make."

"Oh, my. This sounds serious."

"I let you believe I stayed in the room all night while you were at the banquet."

"You didn't?"

"No. I went to the Cupid's Ball."

"That's wonderful, hon. I'm glad. So how was it?"

Liz gave a dismissive shrug. "Okay, if you like that sort of thing."

"You don't sound very enthusiastic. Didn't you have fun?"

"I suppose." She had no desire to discuss the horrible night. The quicker she could erase it from her mind, the happier she'd be.

"I don't understand, Liz. Why did you feel the need to hide it from me?"

"Because I knew you wouldn't have approved. I went there to

meet Mack."

"Liz! For crying out loud. Not that louse who broke your heart. Did he do it again, sugar?"

Her lip quivered, and she broke out into full-blown sobs.

Maggie wrapped her arms around her and gently rocked back and forth on the bed, as if she were a child. "Don't cry, precious. He's not worth it. Some men delight in being heartbreakers and I think he's one of them. But Liz, I've found someone that I know will love you like you need to be loved, and I know you'll love him, too."

Liz pulled away. "No, Maggie. No. No. No. I don't want you finding me anyone. Do you understand?"

"Okay, sugar. Whatever you say." Maggie hadn't meant to mention it, but it slipped out. She clamped her lips together to keep from saying anything more.

CHAPTER 38

Liz had cried herself to sleep, but she awoke hungry, and Maggie was nowhere to be found. She brushed through her hair and grabbed her bag. Traipsing downstairs, she stopped and picked up an apple from the snack table and walked out on the porch. Maggie sat in a rocker, chatting with a young couple with a beautiful baby.

"There she is now," Maggie said. "Liz, have you met the Brooks?"

"No, I don't think so. I'm Liz Blackstone."

"Todd and Becka," the young man replied, nodding toward his wife who was holding the infant.

"Precious baby."

"Thanks. We think so."

"I suppose you're here for Homecoming, also?"

Todd nodded. "It's my tenth reunion. Becka's from Montgomery."

"Did you ride on your class float at the Parade, Thursday?"

"No, I preferred to stay here with Becka and the baby and

watch the procession."

Maggie stood. "Liz, I don't mean to interrupt, but you and I should start making plans for dinner, so you can get back in time for the Homecoming game."

"I'm not going to the game, Maggie, but I'll take you to dinner."

Maggie's shoulders slumped. "Why don't you go to the ballgame, honey? I would go with you, but I've made other plans."

Liz bit the inside of her cheek. "I've had all the excitement I can stand for one day." She turned to the couple. "I suppose you two are going."

He reached for his wife's hand. "No, Becka doesn't want to take the baby, and I don't want to leave her here alone."

Becka's eyes pleaded. "Todd, you've hardly had a chance to be with any of your classmates. Honey, please go. I'm just afraid the noise will be too much for the baby's tiny ears, but we'll be fine. I promise."

Liz said, "I have a great idea. Since I'm not going, why don't you both go, and let me babysit?"

"No. No, we couldn't." Becka gushed, "But how sweet of you to suggest it."

"I mean it. Please. I have no plans, and I'd enjoy watching him . . . or is he a her?" Liz snickered.

"No, you guessed right the first time. His name is Duncan."

"Okay, then you two make your plans, because Duncan and I have a date tonight, don't we sweetheart." She reached for the baby, and he immediately smiled and cooed. "Aww, look! I think he likes me, already."

Becka looked at Todd, who nodded approvingly. "Are you sure about this, Liz?"

"Of course, I am. Just knock on our door when you're ready to leave. We're upstairs in the first room on the right at the top of the stairs. Which room is yours?"

"We're in the Miss Pitty-Pat's Room, the third door on the right. It's a beautiful room with an antique crib. We love it."

Maggie said, "Then y'all are in the room next to Jim."

"I wouldn't know. I haven't met the people next to us and they probably aren't eager to meet us, since Duncan woke up at three o'clock crying and it took forever for me to get him back to sleep again."

Liz said, "Leave me his schedule, and I promise we'll be fine. What time would you like to leave?"

"The game doesn't start until seven-thirty, so we won't need to leave before seven-fifteen."

"Perfect. It'll give Maggie and me plenty of time to go enjoy a leisurely dinner."

CHAPTER 39

Todd and Becka brought the baby upstairs and handed him and his diaper bag to Liz. He looked precious in his little yellow onesie. He was such a beautiful baby with a headful of dark hair, and big blue eyes. Liz had a warm and fuzzy feeling watching Duncan giggle when she kitchy-kitchy-cooed. The way he so readily took to her, led her to believe she had a natural mother's instinct. What would her baby have looked like, if Carter had agreed to start a family?

"You're so kind to want to do this for us," Becka said, handing her the key to their room. "His diapers are in the diaper bag, and when he gets sleepy, you can put him in his crib. I just fed him, so he shouldn't need another bottle. We'll come back as soon as the game ends."

Liz held the cuddly baby and shook her head. "No way. I want you to enjoy the party afterward. We'll be fine. I promise."

Becka's nose crinkled. "That may be too much for you."

"Come on, honey," Todd prodded. "She wouldn't volunteer if

she didn't know what she's doing. It's almost time for the tip-off."

Becka blotted the infant's mouth with the corner of the burp cloth then kissed him on the cheek. "Thanks again, Liz. I hope he doesn't give you much trouble."

"Get going, you two. How much trouble can a tiny baby be?"

Todd grabbed his wife's hand. "Sweetheart, I think that's our cue to get away, before she answers her own question."

Liz held the sweet, cooing baby and waved at Todd and Becka as they scampered down the stairs, giggling. What an uplifting feeling to know such a simple act of kindness helped make a young couple's night so special.

Maggie gave a faint whistle and said, "You're brave, honey. I know nothing about caring for an infant, and to be left in charge would scare me to death. But I admire you. That was thoughtful and they seemed very appreciative."

"I had nothing better to do and I'm actually looking forward to spending some time with this cute little fellow. Aww, look at him, Maggie. Isn't he precious?" Liz bounced him on her knee. "I'll put Duncan in his crib in a few minutes and get some reading done while you're out. He's probably getting sleepy."

Liz looked at the clock and groaned. Maggie had left shortly after Todd and Becka—Only fifteen minutes ago, yet it seemed like hours—or days—or even weeks. The baby started crying the minute everyone left, and he hadn't let up.

Where are you, Maggie? I need help! Maggie didn't have any more experience with babies than she did, but together they might be able to figure out what to do with the little screamer. She'd walked the floor with him until her arms ached. She trudged out on the porch, hoping the change of scenery might help him relax. The night air cooled her perspiring forehead. Liz was glad the porch light wasn't burning. Maybe she could lure him to sleep in the swing.

She eased down on the slats, gently rocking back and forth. The motion seemed to calm him, temporarily, but Liz moaned loudly when he started bawling again. She bounced him on her knees the way she'd seen other women do, yet nothing worked longer than a few seconds at the time. Maybe she wasn't doing it right. Perhaps the pace was too slow. Holding her hands underneath his arms, she increased the rhythm, yet he continued to scream.

Mack sat in a wicker rocker on the other side of the porch. He squinted in the darkness. *It's her! She has a baby?* In all the time they'd spent together, she hadn't bothered to mention it. His pulse raced. *Allen Albertson?* Of course. Now, it all made sense. He recalled Red saying, "Liz and I have a little something that will hold us together like glue." Mack assumed he was just blabbering, but he was speaking of the baby. Liz and Red. Ugh. How could he have been so blind? Mack couldn't feel sorry for Liz if she had no better judgment than to fall for that womanizer. But the baby was a different story. Poor little innocent tyke couldn't help who his parents were. Mack had a hard time sitting there listening to the tormenting cries. It was evident the baby was in pain. Why didn't she do something, instead of bouncing him up and down. If she didn't stop churning him, he'd soon turn to butter. Liz no longer mattered but the poor kid needed someone to save him. When he could stand it no longer, his deep voice pierced the darkness. "Colic?"

Squinting her eyes, she saw the outline of a figure sitting in a wicker rocker on the opposite end of the porch. Had he been there all the time? It almost sounded like . . . no, it couldn't be. "Excuse me? What did you say?"

"Sounds like your little one has colic."

Though hid in the dark shadows, Mack Mackenzie's voice was unmistakable. Liz cringed. She had enough problems without having to deal with both Duncan and Mack.

"Boy or girl?" He asked.

"Yes!" Liz couldn't concentrate on what he was saying. She could only think of what he hadn't said—sixteen years ago when he dumped her with no explanation. How gullible she'd been for allowing him to do it again. No more! What was he doing at the B&B?

Mack raised his voice. "Excuse me? Did you just say 'yes'?"

"I did. Are you unable to compute an affirmative response?"

"Not at all. You're saying the baby is either a boy or a girl. I have no problem computing your answer, since most of the kids I've known have been one or the other. I'm not surprised to learn the tyke falls into one of the two categories."

Liz winced. So, she wasn't paying attention. No need for his sarcasm. She cleared her throat. "His name's Duncan."

"Nice name."

"Thanks." She swallowed hard. *Did I say thanks, as if I named him?* He made her nervous. Why didn't he go away and leave her alone?

"How old is he?"

She drew a deep breath and answered bluntly. "Two months, I think. I don't remember."

"You don't know?"

"Not exactly. What difference does it make?" Suddenly, the infant stiffened, drew his head back and let out a blood-curdling scream.

Mack's voice sounded gruff. "Pardon me for asking."

Liz whimpered. "I'm sorry. I'm tired and I'm scared. I don't know what's wrong with him. He's been screaming like this, nonstop, for almost an hour. I don't know what to do."

"Are you sure it's not colic?"

"Oh, I hope not." She paused. She'd rather die than admit she had no idea what he was talking about. But what if the baby needed immediate medical attention? "Do you really think he might have—colic?" She held her breath, waiting for his answer.

"That's my guess, but then I have no way of knowing."

Her heart raced. "Do you think I should take him to the ER?"

"Well, I doubt he needs professional medical help but I'm not sure about you. My unprofessional opinion is that little Duncan has a bubble. Why not see if that's his problem?"

Liz had rather stick pins under her fingernails than to ask, but she had no other choice. "A bauble? Oh, no! Would you mind?" She quickly perused the buttons on her shirt to make sure there were none missing. If he swallowed a bauble, it was not on her watch.

"Would I mind what?"

Why was he making this so hard? He could see she needed help. "Could you check him for me? To be honest, I'm exhausted." She let out a long breath.

"Liz, are you alright?" His voice took on a sympathetic tone.

She flinched at hearing him call her by name. "Of course, I'm alright," she shrieked. "Duncan is the one with the problem."

Mack made no apparent effort to hide his annoyance. "I suppose you've already tried burping him?"

"Burping him?"

"You sound like you've never burped him before. Sheesh! No wonder the little fellow is in pain."

"Don't sit there scolding me. Do something. Can you help me, or not?"

She heard the rocker squeak when he stood.

"I'll try," he said. "Do you mind sharing the swing?"

Without answering, she slid over.

Mack reached for the baby and cradled him in his arms. "Hey big guy. What's the problem?" His voice was low and soothing.

With his right hand, he gently rubbed the baby's stomach. "Oh, my. Your little tummy feels awfully tight. Let's see if we can't do something about that." Lifting Duncan to his shoulder, Liz watched in amazement.

Mack patted the baby on the back as the swing rocked slowly back and forth. Seconds later, Duncan let out a giant burp. "Atta boy!" Mack said.

Liz's heart was touched as she watched Mack lovingly caress the tiny infant, as if rewarding him for burping. Duncan immediately stopped crying. Mack continued to hold him on his shoulder, gently caressing the tiny face against his own.

"Ah . . . that's much better," Mack responded. "The poor kid was in agony. He's as limp as a dishrag now. I can't see his face. Can you tell if he's asleep?"

Liz nodded. Though embarrassed, she had no regrets. Mack appeared to be comfortable around kids and had known exactly what to do.

He stood. "Would you like for me to put him in his crib for you?"

She gave an emphatic nod. The last thing she wanted was for him to hand the baby back to her. "Would you mind?" Though she'd never admit it, she needed Mack to stick around. What if the little fellow should wake up? Hating Mack could come later, but at the moment it wasn't an option.

"Lead the way and we'll follow," he whispered.

Liz unlocked Todd and Becka's door, and motioned him in.

Mack was tiptoeing across the room, when he suddenly stumbled on a pair of men's cowboy boots.

Liz gasped. "Ooh, sorry," she whispered, while picking up the boots to set them out of the way. Relieved that the jolt failed to awaken the baby, a soft whistle escaped from her lips.

Mack glanced at the boots, then carefully laid Duncan in the crib and covered him with a blanket. Then turning to Liz, he said, "I'm puzzled. Why didn't you tell me?"

She bristled, expecting him to reprimand her for not knowing how to care for a baby. "Mack Mackenzie, don't get the idea I'm somehow beholden to you just because you put Duncan to sleep. I was quite capable of doing it myself."

His eyes went hot. "Yeah, right. I saw how well you were doing. I can't believe. . ." He stopped. "Forget it. I don't even want to think about it. I must've been stupid."

"I can vouch for that." How dare he criticize her? Wasn't it a known fact that babies come with instructions? How could she possibly know about babies' baubles and burps when she'd never given birth?

Mack bolted out the door, slamming it loudly.

Liz's face burned. "Ooh! He did that on purpose." Her tense muscles relaxed when Duncan continued to sleep through the noise.

Thirty minutes after Mack stormed out of the room, Liz heard chatter in the hallway. Recognizing Todd's voice, she tiptoed across the room and unlocked the door.

Becka looked at the sleeping baby in the crib and cooed. "Oh, doesn't he look peaceful?"

Todd said, "I told you there was no need to leave early. I knew Liz could handle him."

Becky wrapped her arms around Liz. "Thank you so much. We had a wonderful time. You must have a real knack with children. I'll bet Duncan enjoyed getting attention from someone besides his Mommy and Daddy for a change."

Liz feigned a smile. "I'm glad you had a good time."

"Did he give you any trouble?" Todd asked.

"After he burped, he was fine."

"Oh, I should've told you. He has a tendency to get acid reflux. But I'm glad you knew what to do. I suppose Maggie kept you company while we were gone?"

"No, she took a stroll downtown shortly after you left. I'm sure she's in our room sound asleep by now. I think I'm ready to go upstairs and do the same. Goodnight."

"Goodnight, and thanks again." Todd whispered, when Duncan squirmed in his crib.

CHAPTER 40

Sunday morning, Maggie shook Liz at six o'clock. "Wake up, sleepy head."

"Sheesh, Maggie, it's not even good daylight. Why so early?"

"Haven't you heard? The early bird gets the worm. I've already laid out your clothes. Come on. Wake up."

Maggie could hardly contain her excitement. In some ways the past three days had gone quickly and in other ways it seemed forever. The time spent with Jim seemed to have flown by. However, Maggie had worried that her plan to set Liz up with Doyle could fail. First there was the fear of Liz running into Mick, allowing him to worm his way back into her life. That fear was dispelled when Maggie discovered the two had already had an encounter, and as much as she hated to see Liz heartbroken, she couldn't help believing it worked for her good. Liz had carried a torch for the two-timing Romeo for years. Maybe now, she'd get him out of her mind, freeing her to find happiness with Doyle.

But there was the realtor. Maggie couldn't deny that if Liz

hadn't found Doyle, she would've encouraged her to marry Mr. Albertson, who could offer her financial security. She didn't know much about Doyle's financial status—actually, she knew nothing at all—but what she did know, she liked. He would offer her love. Maggie had been blessed to have both wealth and love. And if she had to trade one in and keep the other, there was no contest. Love would win every time. Robert was on her mind most of her waking hours, but her thoughts were on how much he loved her and never on how much money he accumulated.

****

Liz sucked in an amazing aroma coming from downstairs and stretched. "Ah, I smell sausage. Doesn't it smell delicious?"

"It smells wonderful, but honey, you know I can't eat sausage."

"Since when?"

"It's been fairly recent—a new allergy."

"That's too bad. But Catherine said she always makes cheese omelets on Sunday."

Maggie groaned. "Yuck."

"What do you mean, yuck. You can eat an omelet."

Maggie shook her head. "Cheese bloats me."

"Well, there are grapefruit, oranges, apples and bananas in the wire basket next to the coffee pot. I'm sure Catherine wouldn't mind fixing you a nice fruit plate."

"Grapefruit sounds wonderful."

"Great."

"But I can't."

"What do you mean, you can't?"

"The doctor warned me against eating grapefruit."

"I told you that you should change doctors. I've never heard of grapefruit hurting anyone."

"It interferes with my meds. I love a good fruit salad, and I don't reckon there's anything I enjoy more than a crisp, juicy apple but I've recently had to quit eating them."

"Why?"

She placed her hand on her heart and shuddered. "Worse thing in the world for indigestion."

"Maggie, how is it that you could tolerate anything the first of the week, but suddenly you've become immune to everything?"

"It's not so unusual hon. It's age-related. One day, you're fine. The next day, all these strange ailments attack you like a pack of wild dogs. It's best not to fight it, but to retreat."

"What about a bowl of cereal?"

"I can tolerate cereal, but only if it has bananas in it, and unfortunately, bananas are no longer included in my diet."

"Since when? You eat them in cereal almost every morning, along with a couple of my muffins."

"You're right. And much to my regret, my potassium has skyrocketed. High potassium can affect your heart, and that's a fact." She placed her forefinger against her cheek. "Oh, I know something I can eat. I can't imagine why I didn't think of it sooner."

"Good. I was beginning to worry. I'll hurry and dress and we'll go downstairs." Liz reached in a drawer and pulled out a gray sweat suit.

Maggie grabbed it and stuffed it back in the drawer. "I told you I've already laid out your clothes." She handed Liz a pink sweater and a new pair of jeans. "Wear this, honey. Pink looks good on you."

"Maggie, the sweater is beautiful, and I thank you for it—but we're leaving today. I can wear something a little—"

"Sloppy? Is that the word you're searching for?"

"No. Actually the word 'comfortable' came to mind."

"Humor me, Liz. You know I want you to take an interest in your appearance." Maggie picked up a scrunchy from the dresser and tossed it in the trash can. "And comb your hair, please," she said, thrusting a brush into her hands.

Liz begrudgingly ran it through her long dark hair, making no attempt to hide her annoyance.

Maggie reached up and brushed a wisp of hair away from her face. "There. That's better. You look beautiful."

"Thank you, but we're only going downstairs. There'll be no one down there who cares what I wear to breakfast."

"Downstairs? No, honey. You must've misunderstood. I'd like one of those chili dogs at that little place we went to the other night. Now, that's something I could eat. I need the protein, and it was loaded with good, healthy protein."

"For breakfast?"

"Yep, it's the best thing for me. You don't want me to get sick, do you?"

Liz had known Maggie long enough to know she was as stubborn as a mule. If she made up her mind, nothing or no one would ever change it. She might as well take her to Heartie's.

Liz pouted all the way. She'd been thinking about the omelet ever since Catherine mentioned it. Why did she allow Maggie to talk her into coming to Hearties? Who books a room at a Bed & Breakfast and instead of eating breakfast there, goes to a hot dog joint?

Maggie clasped her hands under her chin. "I'm so excited, I can hardly wait. I know you were looking forward to an omelet, but this will be our last opportunity to enjoy one of Heartie's delicious hot dogs. It'll be the perfect send-off meal, don't you agree?"

Liz refused to answer such a stupid question. If she were lucky, the diner would be closed. Her hopes soared when she drove up and there were no cars to be seen. Employing her most sympathetic tone, she whimpered, "What a bummer, Maggie. Looks as if they're not open." She glanced in the rear-view mirror, then shifted in reverse.

"Oh dear. This can't be happening." Maggie pressed her hands to the sides of her head. "They can't be closed." There was a definite sound of panic in her voice.

"I'm sorry you're disappointed, Maggie. Really, I am, but we'll go back to the B&B and I'm sure Catherine will be happy to accommodate you with something your stomach can tolerate."

Maggie leaned forward, her eyes squinting. "Hold on, Liz. Stop!"

"What's wrong?"

"Pull back up. I want to go check the door. Someone must be in there. I saw a car parked in back, when you turned the corner." She was opening her door before Liz could come to a full stop.

Liz strummed her fingers on the steering wheel, while watching Maggie sprint toward the locked door, then turning, she lumbered back toward the car. Seeing the forlorn look on Maggie's face caused Liz to question why an omelet had been more important to her than her best friend's simple request. Overwhelmed with guilt, she was almost sorry the diner was closed. Almost.

The only possible reason Maggie had wanted her to come back for her Homecoming was a desire to see her have a good time, yet Liz had done nothing but gripe. Her chin quivered. Maggie even pretended to enjoy spending time with a complete stranger, in order to free Liz to have fun with her friends. There was nothing Maggie wouldn't do for her—yet all she asked was one last opportunity to eat at a local diner. Liz's throat tightened. How could she be so heartless?

Maggie had almost reached the car when the door to the diner opened, and a man yelled, "Come on in, we're open."

Liz groaned. If only he'd waited one more minute before opening that door, Maggie would've been in the car, and she'd be sitting down to a delicious omelet served on a linen cloth with lovely China. All the guilt that overwhelmed her moments ago had been quickly replaced with an enormous regret for not having left sooner.

The owner welcomed them and apologized for the room being so cold. "I always turn the heater down before I leave at night, but it'll only take a few minutes for it to warm up." He handed them menus and explained the cook was running a little late but had called and was on his way. "Have a seat, anywhere, folks."

Liz rolled her eyes at the absurdity of the obvious. She plopped down in the nearest booth. Maggie kept walking toward the back of the room. Motioning with her head, she said, "Yoo-hoo, let's sit closer to the back, Elizabeth. It's much warmer over here."

Liz cocked her head. "Did you just call me Elizabeth?"

"I believe I did. I think it's a lovely name. Very regal. Don't you like for people to know you have such a beautiful name?"

Liz stalked over to where Maggie was standing and slid into the booth, while making a point to search the empty room with her eyes. Then, with a sweep of her hand, she said, "I assume you're referring to all these people who are here to eat a nourishing breakfast?" She threw up her hand in a mock wave. "Good morning, everyone. What a lovely day. May I suggest the chili dog?"

288

CHAPTER 41

Liz was upset, but Maggie finally had her where she wanted her. Now, to get her in a better mood.

"Honey, I know you think I was being ornery by insisting we come here, but you were sweet to agree."

Liz rubbed her arms. "It's freezing in here. I thought he said it wouldn't take long to warm up."

"Oh dear, you *are* perturbed. I'm just an old lady, hon, and sometimes we old folks have a tendency to worry too much about what can kill us. But you're right, that was selfish for me to think of myself. We'll go, and I'll eat grapefruit. At my age, I won't live long, anyway."

"No one has accused you of being selfish, Maggie, but I will admit I'm having a difficult time figuring you out."

"You have a right to be angry, Liz. You wanted an omelet."

"Maggie, forget it. We're here."

"Fine. If you insist, dear." Maggie bit the inside of her cheek to keep from smiling. The only thing Maggie hadn't counted on was Liz plopping down in the seat with her back facing the front door. Liz needed to be sitting on the opposite side of the booth, facing the front, so when Doyle walked in, she'd be the first person he saw. He'd immediately recognize her from her picture. His eyes would light up and Cupid would take it from there.

Maggie stood. "Honey, why don't we switch places?"

Liz shook her head. "I'm fine."

"But sitting on this side, you'll be able to see people as they come through the door. I don't know anyone from Heartsboro. You might recognize a few faces."

"I said I'm fine, Maggie."

The owner walked over and handed them menus. "Our breakfast special is the egg and wiener casserole."

Liz said, "What's in it?"

He looked bewildered. "Uh, that would be a scrambled egg with chopped wieners and ketchup. We serve hot dogs for breakfast, also, but most folks come for the wiener casserole."

Liz murmured something under her breath and handed him her menu.

He leaned down. "I'm sorry? What was that."

"I'd like a cup of coffee. I'm not a big hot dog fan, so would it be possible for the cook to make me a grilled cheese sandwich?"

"Not a problem, miss."

Maggie's eyes squinted as she perused the menu. Then, pursing her lips she said, "I know I shouldn't."

"What are you talking about, Maggie. You shouldn't do what?"

"Order the grilled cheese."

Liz's eyes widened. "You're right. You shouldn't, because you said—"

"I know what I said, but now that I think about it, maybe it isn't cheese that bloats me—I think it's onions. I haven't felt right since eating onions on my chili dog Wednesday night. But what's a chili dog without onions?" She handed her menu to the Heartie's owner. "I think I'll take a grilled cheese sandwich, also, please, and a cup of hot coffee."

Liz fumed. "We could've stayed at the B&B and had a delicious cheese omelet."

Maggie leaned over and whispered. "Stop frowning, Liz. The wrinkles on your forehead make you look older." Glancing at her hands under the table, she discretely checked her watch. Six-fifty. The timing was perfect. Her heart fluttered with excitement.

When the server brought their order, Maggie looked up and was pleasantly surprised to see Jim walking in the door. "Don't look now, Liz," she whispered, "but the man I told you I've been seeing is coming into the diner with his son." She jerked off her glasses and tucked them in her pocket.

"They aren't coming over here, I hope. Maggie, you've acted very strange. I thought something fishy was going on. Please tell me you didn't invite him to have breakfast with us. I'm in no mood to meet anyone."

"Honestly, Liz, I had no idea they'd be having breakfast here."

Jim lingered at the front and appeared to be searching for someone. She assumed he was looking for a waiter to seat them. Maggie squinted, then quickly grabbed her glasses. *It's . . . It's Doyle. He looks just like his picture. It can't be—Jim's son?* Her breath came out in such fast spurts, she feared she'd hyperventilate.

Liz lowered her head and whispered. "Please stop staring. I don't want him coming to our table."

The owner walked out of the kitchen with two grilled cheese sandwiches. He waved to Jim and his son. "Welcome to Heartie's Diner. Take a seat, anywhere and I'll be with you shortly."

Jim mentioned he had a son, but never would she have guessed it to be Doyle. A horrifying thought flitted through her head. Doyle mentioned in the letters that he and his father were close. Did he read her letters to him? What would Jim think if he should discover it was her and not Liz, writing those mushy letters to his son. What seemed perfectly logical before, was now making her sick. The letter that frightened her most was the one where she talked about wanting to walk barefoot on the beach, their toes squishing in the sand.

She was suddenly torn between staying or leaving. Concluding it was more important for Liz to meet Doyle, than it was to save her own self-respect, she sucked in a heavy breath and braced for the consequences.

Doyle didn't look too cheerful, but she could understand he'd be nervous, meeting Liz face-to-face for the first time. He stalked over and took a seat near the front of the diner, leaving his dad standing there.

Maggie surmised he chose to sit near the door, to watch out the window for Liz to walk in. It was then that Jim saw her and waved.

Doyle didn't look too cheerful, but she was sure he was nervous.

His lumbago appeared to be bothering him more this morning, as he limped over to Maggie's table. "Good morning, ladies," he said rubbing his chin, his eyes still searching the room.

Maggie's voice quaked. "Jim, this is Liz, the adopted daughter I told you about."

CHAPTER 42

Jim stroked his chin. "Liz, is it? I suppose that's short for Elizabeth? Land sakes, if you ain't pretty as a picture." His heart hammered. Was it possible? Elizabeth was Maggie's daughter? It was her, all right. He had trouble catching his breath. What if Maggie were to discover that he wrote all those mushy letters? Would she think he was a dirty old man? It was too late to worry.

"Would you ladies mind if my son and I share your booth— after all, I feel as if Maggie and I are old friends."

Jim hobbled halfway across the floor, then with a sweeping motion of his hand, he beckoned his son. "Over here, Doyle. I have someone I'd like you to meet."

Liz whispered through clenched teeth. "This day keeps getting worse."

Maggie's pulse hadn't slowed since the two walked in. She whispered, "Liz, there's something I probably should've told you. I meant well, but I'm afraid I didn't think—"

One would've thought Doyle was the one suffering from lumbago, the way he ambled slowly back to the table with his father's arm resting—or pushing—on his back.

"Doyle, I'd like to introduce you to my friends, Maggie and Elizabeth. Do you ladies mind if we join you?"

Maggie slid over and Jim sat down.

Liz kept her head lowered. Without looking up but feeling his presence, Liz grudgingly slid over to make room for the man's son on the seat beside her. When he remained standing, she was glad. She slowly lifted her head to scrutinize the intruders. Her face distorted. She shrieked. "Mack?" Then turning to Maggie, she said, "What's going on?"

Maggie said, "You're mistaken dear, this is Doyle. Jim's son."

"No, Maggie. This is Mick, Mark, Mack, Muck, choose whichever name you will. I have a few choice ones for him."

Mack stood, legs apart with his thumbs stuck in his jeans pocket. His face glowed red. "Well, well. Liz Farley. Fancy meeting you here—Pop, I'm afraid I can't stay. Ladies—excuse me."

Caught off guard by his son's rudeness, Jim pointed first to Doyle, then to Liz. "You two know one another?"

Doyle blurted, "I know her as well as I want to know her, so come on, Dad. It's time to go."

"But son, what's the hurry? Let's eat first."

"Suddenly, I feel full. Up to my neck. The thought of eating a hot dog for breakfast didn't sit well when you insisted, and it's suddenly become nauseating." He turned around and stormed out of the diner.

Liz jumped up from the table with tears pouring down her cheeks. "Maggie, I'll be waiting in the car." The door slammed behind her.

Maggie and Jim exchanged glances.

Maggie's eyes welled with tears. "Oh, Jim, I've done a terrible thing. I don't blame her for being furious. I'm so ashamed. I should've minded my own business. Poor Liz. She's traumatized and I can only imagine what you'll think of me when you hear what an awful, unforgivable thing I've done. She'll never forgive me when she learns I'm behind this debacle."

He shook his head. "No, Maggie. I think I know what's going on here, and it has nothing to do with you. Trust me, it's all my fault. I'm embarrassed to admit what an idiot I've been."

Jim followed Maggie out the door and they both went to their respective automobiles.

Liz sat in the car, sulking. Maggie held her tongue on the way back to the B&B, convinced Liz wasn't ready to hear the truth.

Maggie winced when she heard Doyle slam the door next to their room. How was she to know he was the louse who broke Liz's heart.

Liz fell across the bed squalling. Maggie wanted to confess her terrible blunder and plead for forgiveness but the chance of Liz ever forgiving her was nil. The safest thing would be to make herself scarce until Liz had time to calm down. She pulled a handkerchief from her drawer and walked out on the porch.

Her bottom lip quivered, when she noticed Jim sitting in the swing. He patted the seat next to him, inviting her to sit. A lump formed in her throat, seeing the sheer pain etched on his face. For several minutes, they gently rocked back and forth in silence.

When Maggie felt she could get the words out without blubbering, she said, "Liz is devastated and it's all my fault." The tears she'd fought to hold back, flooded down her cheeks.

Jim wrapped his arm around her. "I can't let you take the blame. There's no way you could've had anything to do with what happened today."

"But I did. Without Liz's knowledge, I registered her with an online dating service, and apparently your son signed up with the same service.

Jim said, "Her hair was a tad shorter and a wee bit lighter in the picture."

"You're right. I think it was. So, you saw the picture?"

He chuckled. "I saw it, alright. Frankly, as pretty as she was in the picture, it didn't do her justice. She's even prettier in person."

"But I'm sure Liz was shocked to see Doyle standing there because she had no idea that I had arranged for them to meet at Heartie's this morning. It's also easy to understand why he was so upset. I'm sure he was expecting a warmer reception than the icy one he received."

Jim's lip curled. "It's all coming together."

"I meant no harm, Jim. I'm just a nosey old neighbor who

doesn't know when to mind my own business. Liz didn't write the letters to your son. I did, and I signed her name. But was it so wrong for me to want Liz to find someone to love? I won't be around forever, and I wanted her to find someone that would love her as I do. Doyle's emails were so sweet, I thought he'd be perfect for her. I had no idea that he was the guy who broke her heart years ago."

"Maggie, are you telling me that you not only signed Elizabeth up with the dating service, but it was you writing the emails and not her?"

Maggie covered her face with her hands and sobbed. "Yes, it was a stupid thing to do. Oh, Jim, she'll never forgive me."

Jim gently placed his arm around her and patted her shoulder. "Don't you fret your pretty little head over this, because I have a confession to make. Doyle didn't write those emails. I did."

Maggie's eyes widened. "You? No. I know what you're doing, Jim. You're trying to make me feel like it wasn't all my fault, but you would never have done such a dumb thing."

"I think you give me too much credit, my little honey bun. How would you like to take a stroll down the beach with me, with our bare feet squishing in the sand?" Jim cocked his head and grinned, as he searched her face for a reaction.

She cupped her hands over her mouth and let out a squeal. "Jim Mackenzie. Why you old Romeo." Maggie laughed as tears streamed down her cheeks. "Well, I must admit, you're a real romantic cuss. I enjoyed every email and could hardly wait for the next one."

"Thank you, Maggie. Yours were very sweet. They touched me right here." Jim grabbed his heart, then slumped over.

"Jim?" Maggie giggled. "Stop teasing. Jim." Her pulse raced. "JIM?" Maggie screamed. "Help! Someone call 911. Please, hurry."

Catherine heard the screams and quickly made the call. She ran upstairs and beat on the doors to both Liz and Mack's rooms. "Come quickly, I'm afraid Mr. Mackenzie may be having a heart attack."

CHAPTER 43

Liz and Mack darted out of their respective rooms at the same time and the EMT pulled up within minutes. Jim was placed on a stretcher and whisked away, with sirens blaring. Mack jumped in his car and yelled to Liz and Maggie, "Don't just stand there. Get in if you're going."

Liz slid into the back seat, and Maggie sat in the front.

"You were with him. What happened?" Mack asked accusingly.

"It's my fault. All my fault," Maggie sobbed.

"Stop freaking out, lady and just tell me what happened."

In between sobs, she said, "I've ruined everyone's life. And now, I may have taken Jim's life from him."

Mack stomped the accelerator to the floor. "For crying out loud, what did you do to him?"

Liz bristled. "Don't scream at her! Can't you see she's upset?"

"Yeah? You think I'm not? My dad may be dying, and she's sitting here screaming she may've killed him. You think I don't have a right to find out what she did?"

"She didn't do anything to him. Just drive and watch where you're going, okay? You almost ran into that truck."

Liz reached her hand over the seat and patted Maggie on the shoulder. "Try to calm down, Maggie, before you have a heart attack, yourself. I don't know what happened, but I know you well enough to know you could never ruin anyone's life. So, take a deep breath and try to explain what happened to Mr. Mackenzie."

She nodded. "Jim and I were sitting on the porch, and he was trying to comfort me. He put his arm around me and pulled me close. He's such a sweet man. He was telling me how much he liked my emails, and I was telling him I enjoyed his."

Mack shot her a sharp glance. "Emails? You're trying to tell me my daddy's been emailing someone?"

"Me."

He raised his voice. "In your dreams, old woman. That's absurd."

Liz had never wanted to slap a man before now, but he had no right to talk so harshly to poor Maggie. "Mack, why can't you be civil? I thought you wanted to hear what happened. Let her talk, but one more hateful outburst from you, and you may never know." She patted Maggie on the shoulder. "Go ahead, Maggie. You won't be interrupted again."

She glanced over at Mack. "Well, Jim looked at me and my heart melted when he said, 'Your emails were very sweet. They got me right here,' and then he grabbed his heart. Naturally, since he'd just said, 'right here,' I thought he was cutting up when he grabbed at his heart. He's such a tease. But then—then." Maggie sobbed. "Oh, m' goodness, it was awful. He just slumped over. I called him but he didn't answer. I thought he was gone." Maggie stopped, drew in a breath and blurted out, "I think I love that man."

Liz bit her lip. "Maggie, you're upset. You don't know what you're saying."

Mack muttered, "I think I'm gonna puke."

Maggie said, "I know exactly what I'm saying, Liz. I don't want to lose him now that I've found him. Where's that hospital? We've got to hurry. How much further?"

Mack pulled into the parking lot and pointed. "We're here." When he couldn't find a parking place, he drove up to the ER door and jumped out.

They ran inside and Mack hurried to the information desk, "My Dad—Jim Mackenzie—brought in with a heart attack. Where is he?"

"He's being taken care of, sir, have a seat and the doctor will talk with you shortly."

"I don't want to sit down, lady. I want to see my father."

"I'm sorry sir, but you'll have to wait for the doctor to finish examining the patient. It'll only take a few minutes."

Mack paced the floor for forty-five grueling minutes before the doctor came out.

"Are you Mr. Mackenzie's son?"

"I am, how is he doc?"

"We're running tests. I'll know after I've had an opportunity to see the results. There's coffee in the pot in the waiting room."

"I don't want coffee, I want to see my dad."

"I can only allow one at the time to go back." He looked at Maggie. "I gather you're Mrs. Mackenzie?"

Mack said, "My mother is dead."

"I'm sorry." He laid his hand on Maggie's shoulder. "Is your name Maggie?"

"Yes." She lowered her head and swiped at a tear. "Yes, I'm Maggie."

"Then you're the one he's asking for. I'm sorry, I assumed you were his wife, the way he was pleading with me to find you. His room is the third one on the right."

Maggie's lip trembled. "I can't. I'm not family. His son needs to be with him," she said softly. "You go on in and see your daddy."

Mack's voice lowered. "No. He's calling for you."

Liz sat on one side of the emergency room and Mack sat on the other. She wrung her hands and mumbled, "I'm so sorry, Mack. I'm praying for your dad."

"Thanks." They simultaneously glanced at the clock on the wall.

An hour and fifteen minutes later, Mack growled, "Pop's a sick man. Why is that woman staying in there so long?"

Liz could keep quiet no longer "You heard her. She's in love with your father, and from what she's told me, I suspect he feels the same toward her, so why don't you calm down and stop referring to her as that woman. Her name is Maggie, and she's probably the best medicine for him right now."

"My dad, in love?" Mack guffawed. "You don't know him. He's still in love with my mama. Always has been, always will be."

"I believe Maggie says your mother died five years ago. Is that right?"

"What's that got to do with anything? You bury people. You don't bury love. Love lives forever." His face was red. "But then you wouldn't understand the concept."

"Oh, so when did you become an expert on love?"

Before Mack could answer, Maggie appeared in the hallway and motioned for them to follow her into Jim's room.

Mack's face wrenched, seeing his father lying there, looking like a corpse. Slowly, he walked over, bent down and placed a kiss on the elderly man's forehead. "Pop? Can you hear me?"

Jim appeared oblivious to the world around him, as he lay there with his eyes tightly closed. Occasionally, he'd moan. Mack looked over at Maggie, who dabbed at her eyes, her face revealing her pain. She whispered, "He looks awful, doesn't he? He's white as a ghost."

Mack nodded, as tears streamed down his cheeks. "Pop," he whispered. "I'm so sorry. I shouldn't have yelled at you. You did nothing wrong. It's just . . . I . . . I wasn't expecting to run into . . . well, what I'm trying to say is, please forgive me for taking out my frustrations on you. I didn't mean to hurt you. I know you meant no harm, and if you love this lady, then I can . . . I will accept it."

Jim's eyes slowly opened, halfway. "Doyle," he whispered. "Is that you, son?"

Mack leaned over and laid his hand gently on his father's forehead. "Yes, Pop. It's me. What do you need?"

Jim moaned.

Mack grimaced. "Hold on, dad. I'll go tell the nurse to give you some pain medicine."

Maggie shook her head, cupped her hand around her mouth and whispered. "Unfortunately, the doctor has given him all he can take. It should take effect any minute, now. We can only hope that he wakes back up, afterward, but if there's anything you wish to tell you father, now would be the time."

Jim said, "Doyle?" His arms flailed in the air. "Where's my boy? Where's my Doyle?"

Mack squeezed his hand. "I haven't gone anywhere, Pop. I'm right here."

"I'm glad, son. You're a good boy, Doyle. You've always made me and your mama proud. Where is your mama? Why ain't she here?" His voice rose in a panic. "Thelma? Thelma! Where are you, Thelma?"

Mack's voice cracked. "Mama couldn't come, Pop. She's in Heaven. You try to rest."

"You say she can't come? Then maybe I should go to her. I'll miss you, Doyle, but there's just one thing I want to ask you to do for me before I leave here."

Mack wiped the tears trailing down his cheek. "No, Pop. Don't say that . . . you're not going. Not yet. You'll be fine and I promise I don't intend to spend as much time at work as I've done lately. I'm gonna take good care of you. You'll see."

"You're a good boy, son, but I've been a burden long enough. But if I could ask just one request before—" He let out another moan. "Forget it. I'm sure you're eager to get back to work."

"No, I meant it Pop. You've been right all along. I've poured too much of my life into my work. That's going to change. What is it you want me to do? Just name it. Anything."

"Do you mean it, Doyle. I was hoping I could count on you. Please, take . . ." his face distorted in obvious pain. "Take Elizabeth to . . . to lunch at The Old Mill Restaurant."

Mack turned and whispered. "I think the medicine is beginning to work. He's out of his head."

Jim said, "I heard that, Doyle. I didn't figure you'd have time."

Mack flinched. "Of course, I have time, Pop."

"Then it's settled. I want you to order her a steak dinner, in memory of your sweet mama. That was Thelma's favorite place to eat. The last thing I promised her was that I'd try to find you a good woman. I feel she's looking down from heaven, God bless her, and I want her to see I tried my best, even though it didn't work out." Jim squeezed Mack's hand. "Promise me, son. Promise?"

"But Pop, I don't think Liz—what I mean is, it wouldn't be fair for us to insist. I'm the last person in the world she'd want to share a meal with."

Jim moaned loudly. "Oh, Maggie. Would you get me a sip of water, please? I'm dye . . . dye . . . dying. Of thirst."

"Sure, Jim." Maggie snubbed and wiped her eyes. She held the glass and put the straw to his lips.

Jim took a swallow and gurgled. Mack grabbed a pan and held it close. Jim motioned for Maggie that he'd had enough water. His lips quivered. "I asked my boy for one last favor, and he can't even do that for me. Where did I go wrong in raising him, Maggie? What's Thelma gonna think? I didn't do the one thing she asked of me on her dying bed."

Mack drew a deep breath. "Okay, okay, Pop. Don't get so worked up. I'll take her to The Old Mill, but if she doesn't want to go, I can't make her. Besides, I'm not sure they serve lunch."

Maggie spoke up quickly. "Oh, she'll go. I'm sure of it. Liz would never deny a sick man his wish, and I happen to know The Old Mill is open for lunch. My friend Merle called last night and invited me to have lunch with her there today, but I told her we were leaving. Of course, that was before—" Maggie dabbed her eyes with a handkerchief.

Jim closed his eyes as his face twisted into a painful-looking frown.

Maggie's lip quivered. "God bless him, I believe he's at peace with the world, now. . . it was important to him to say what was on his heart."

"Are you saying he's gone? Pop? Pop?" Mack's eyes muddled with tears.

Maggie tiptoed to the other side of the bed and put her arm around him. "I believe he's resting. . .. the medicine, you know. But did you notice how pleased he looked when you agreed to grant him his wish. You're a good son."

"But . . ." Mack threw up his hands and stomped toward the door. He looked at Liz and barked. "Are you going or not?"

She threw her bag over her shoulder and grunted. "I think that was the plan, although it wasn't *my* plan."

CHAPTER 44

Mack and Liz stalked out of Jim's room and headed toward the hospital parking lot. With his hands crammed in his pockets, Mack took long strides, while Liz ambled slowly, managing to stay two paces behind.

He did nothing to hide his impatience as he held the car door open, waiting for her to get in.

She muttered an insincere 'thank you,' through clenched teeth. They both remained tight lipped on the way to the restaurant. Liz didn't care if she never spoke to him again. So, he knows how to burp a baby. Big deal. Her lip trembled as she recalled how gentle he'd been with little Duncan. The image of him holding the infant on his shoulder, tenderly caressing him with his big strong hands, brought an annoying lump to her throat. Her eyes clouded. She blinked hard to keep the tears from falling.

Liz was surprised to see The Old Mill still in operation. Not that she'd ever eaten in the restaurant, but she'd often ridden to the adjacent store with her Pawpaw, to buy their cornmeal. She wondered if the Wheeler family still owned it and if they continued to grind meal. Mack would probably know, but she'd die before she'd ask. It was obvious by the number of cars out front that it was still a favorite place to eat.

It looked more like a large barn than a steak restaurant. Built of hewn lumber with a tin roof, the rough, rugged appearance had a homey feel. Maybe it was because it made her think of a much larger version of Memaw and Pawpaw's tiny house on Gilmore Street. Even the inside with plank floors and tongue-and-groove ceiling brought back memories. Some good. Some not so good. The smell of fresh baked bread reminded her of the many times she watched Memaw kneading dough and the way the kitchen smelled when the rolls were taken from the oven. It seemed with every memory she had of her grandmother, she was wearing a faded blue dress and an apron she made from a flour sack.

Liz and Mack took a seat in the entry way. waiting for the hostess to seat them. Liz glanced down at an odd substance on Mack's slacks. He apparently had rubbed up against something, but it was none of her business, so she wouldn't bother to mention it. The hostess returned and asked, "Would you like a booth or a table?"

Mack stared straight ahead as if he were mute. She could play this game also.

The hostess repeated her question. Annoyed at Mack for not answering, Liz mumbled, "Booth, please." The hostess led them to a booth in the far corner of the restaurant. Now, that she'd broken her vow of silence she might as well ask the question that was bugging her. "What's all over your pants?"

Without bothering to look, he snapped, "What does it look like?"

"Like you fell into a flour bin."

He looked down and shrieked. "Man! Where did this come from?" He brushed his pants leg and white dust flew everywhere.

Mack picked up the menu, and without lifting his eyes, mumbled, "What d'ya want?"

"Why ask me? Your dad told you what to order."

"You don't have to eat it. Get whatever you want. Doesn't matter to me."

"Steak is good. I wouldn't want something to happen to your dad and you have to live the remainder of your life knowing his last wish didn't matter to you."

"Fine." He shoved the menus into the server's hands. "Two steak dinners, and two sweet, iced teas."

Liz had never felt so embarrassed. She picked up her napkin and placed it in her lap. "That was very rude," she whispered.

"What?"

"The way you shoved the menus at the server and barked an order. Did you never learn the magic words, please and thank you? She's probably had a very long morning and is exhausted. The baby could've cried all night, keeping her awake and the last thing she needed was a grumpy customer treating her with disrespect."

"Excuse me, Miss Manners. I'll try to do better. And as for the baby, he probably just needed burping, but I've known mothers who were so consumed with their own selfish desires they never took time to understand the needs of their own flesh and blood."

"You are such a snob."

Mack drummed his fingers loudly on the table—a habit Liz found most annoying. His eyes darted everywhere, except at the person seated across the table from him.

She picked up a saltine from a basket and nibbled. A chill run down her spine. Despite her misery, holding on to the bitterness was her way of wanting to punish Mack for the pain he'd caused her—yet she had a peculiar feeling she was the only one receiving the punishment. They were stuck here together. Why not try being civil? "Mack, you know better than anyone, how long I've dreamed of opening a bakery."

"I guess." He took a sip of iced tea.

When he didn't appear at all interested, she wanted to suck the words back into her mouth.

He glared. "So, are you saying you've bought a building?"

"No, but it's finally about to happen. It's in the works."

"Let me guess. The Lunch Counter."

"How did you know?"

"Because I heard Allen telling you all about it."

"Well, I was hoping you'd be happy for me."

"Maybe I could be if it wasn't a big fat lie."

"Why are you doing this, Mack?"

"Because I happen to own the building and the last person in the world I'd sell it to is Red Albertson. But I have more important things on my mind tonight than that lying scoundrel. Pop could be dead before we finish eating. I shouldn't have come."

Liz blotted her tear ducts with her finger when the server brought out their food. Though the steak looked great, she wasn't sure she could eat a bite.

Mack bowed his head and mumbled, "Oh, Lord, please don't take him from me—I have to make things right between us."

Liz's throat constricted. She'd heard two conflicting stories. Who to believe? Allen or Mack? She glanced across the table. Mack was hurting. Hurting bad. She had a strong urge to get up and put her arms around him to offer comfort. Was she crazy? After the way she'd just finished reprimanding him, any attempts she made to console him now would be construed as fake.

CHAPTER 45

Maggie stood beside Jim's bed and gave him a playful nudge. "You bad, bad boy, don't you feel sneaky, sending the kids away like that? You had your eyes closed, but I wish you could've seen Doyle's face when you moaned. I had to think fast when he said he was going to ask the nurse to bring you something for pain."

A deep laugh rose from the pit of Jim's belly. "I've never had so much fun in all my life. How did I do, my little Magpie?"

"You were so good, you almost fooled me. We may need to consider taking our show on the road. With an act like ours, we could be the next George Burns and Gracie Allen. You're a riot, Jim Mackenzie, and that talc did the trick. I Suwannee, if you didn't look like death warmed over." She could hardly get the words out for laughing so hard. "And all that moaning was pitiful. It's a good thing the doctor didn't walk in. He would've had the coroner on the way."

Maggie took a wet cloth and wiped the powder from Jim's face. The door swung open, and a nurse came in reminding them they were in a hospital and needed to keep the laughter down. "Please be a little more considerate. There are sick people on this hall, and a few patients have already complained about the noise coming from this room."

Maggie apologized and promised they'd abide by her wishes.

After the nurse walked out, Jim said, "You were brilliant Maggie. I didn't think I'd be able to get Doyle to take her to lunch, but when you told me to convince him I was dying, I knew it would work. He couldn't deny his old man a last request."

"Jim, I've laughed so much, my side hurts."

"Maggie, come here. Hold my hand. There's something I've got to tell you, and this can't wait."

The urgency in his voice frightened her, though she was determined not to let it show. "Hey, you might have fooled Doyle with that sad story about having no time left, but I'm on to you, you old coot."

"Hear me out, darlin'. I ain't fooling, this time." His eyes welled with tears.

"I'm listening, Jim. What's on your mind?"

"When I was lying flat on my back on the stretcher, my body being poked and prodded with all those confounded gadgets, and me wondering if I was gonna die, all I could think of was, 'Lord, please let me stay a little while longer.' It was then I realized I'd fallen in love with you, my little Magpie. I knew it was real, because ever since Thelma died, I've begged God to take me home, too. I didn't think I could live without her."

Maggie patted him gently on the arm. "Don't try to talk too much, sweetheart. I'm afraid it's not good for you. After all, you did have a slight heart attack and need to take care of yourself."

"No, let me get this out, Maggie. The doc told me this little episode I had with the ol' ticker ain't gonna kill me, but I believe if I keep these feelings bottled up much longer, my heart may bust wide open. I won't be able to rest 'til I get it off my chest."

Maggie touched his lips with her fingertips. "Take it easy, Jim. I know exactly what you're trying to say, but you don't have to say another word dear. I feel it too," She plumped his pillow and pulled the light thermal blanket up to his chest. "Just lay here and relax and don't let yourself get all riled up. I plan to take very good care of you, now that I've found you."

Jim reached out and took Maggie by the hand, then gave it a squeeze. "I thought when I was writing those love letters, I was writing 'em for Doyle. This morning, I realized it all started that way, but the more we went back and forth, the more I realized I was writing them for myself. I didn't need to steal words from King Solomon, they were flowing from my heart faster than my fingers could find the keys. I fell in love with the one who was writing back to me. Ain't no way to explain this so you'll understand, since I've had a dickens-of-a-time trying to understand it myself, but I'm gonna say it anyway. I didn't fall in love with the girl in the picture, but it was the woman I saw in my mind that I fell in love with. Your emails made me feel alive again.

Even my buddy George said, 'Jim, you're forgetting she's not writing to you, but she's writing to your son.' Made me mad as a hornet at the time—not because he was wrong—but because he was right. At times, I did want to forget the emails were to Doyle, because I wanted to believe such a sweet, caring woman could feel that way about me. I read your emails over. I was glad I'd found someone so wonderful for Doyle—but I longed to hear those sweet words said to me. And to tell the truth, it scared me, Maggie."

"Why did it scare you?"

"Don't you see? I couldn't understand what was happening to me. After Thelma died, I thought I could never love another woman again. Didn't want to love nobody else. Then out of the blue, I began to fall for someone I didn't think really existed outside the confounds of my mind."

Maggie caressed his cheek with the back of her hand. "Shh! Shh! You're getting riled up, Jim. Please try to relax."

"You've gotta understand."

"I do, Jim. Trust me, I understand perfectly."

"Do you, honey bun? After your Robert died, did you just wanna curl up and die, too, because you didn't think you could go on without him?"

Her chin quivered. "That's exactly how I felt. I didn't want to wake up in the mornings to an empty bed."

His voice rose with emotion. "Yep, that was one of the hardest things for me, too. Before I'd go to sleep at night and the first thing I'd do when I'd wake up every morning was to plead with God for that Heavenly Homecoming. But little did I know; He had another

317

Homecoming for me to experience first—and what a Homecoming this has turned out to be for me."

Maggie squeezed his hand. "And I thought I was coming here for Liz's sake. I wanted her to find love. I never thought love would find me."

"You really do understand. I began to fantasize as I pictured this lovely, mature lady writing back to me. The lady I visualized was exactly like you, Maggie. I saw you with my heart before I ever saw you with my eyes."

"Oh, Jim, that's so beautiful. You're even more romantic than your son was." She winked, then planted a kiss on his forehead and chuckled. "Of course, the longer he wrote, the better he got at saying sweet nothings."

"Well, we should let those kids read the e-mails and see what they said to one another. They may be surprised at how romantic they can be." Jim's laughter filled the room.

Maggie covered her giggle with her hand. "I'm sure Doyle will be shocked to find out he had to look up in the Bible for tips on how to compose a love letter. The email that threw me though, was when you said Liz had bird eyes. I kept looking at her eyes, and thinking, 'they aren't tiny and close together—she has big, beautiful green eyes, perfectly set. But I knew you were searching for words, and I was thrilled to know you went to King Solomon for inspiration."

"Well, I'll admit Solomon stumped me when it came to describing bird eyes. But my little Magpie, your eyes are small, and they're beautifully spaced close together, so it's plain to see why Solomon fell in love with a woman with bird eyes."

"Jim, I have a confession to make. It's true Liz's teeth are all there, but I can't say the same for mine." Maggie reached up and tugged on a partial plate.

"That's alright, honey bun. You've got those round pomegranate cheeks and a mighty fine neck. Two outta three ain't bad."

"You're a riot, Jim Mackenzie. A regular riot. But I need to slip out dear, and let you get some rest."

"Please don't leave me, sugar. I promise to rest, if you'll sit over there in the chair. I want to see you when I open my eyes."

Maggie was glad he'd asked. She didn't want to leave. She bent over and planted a kiss on his forehead. "You close your eyes, darlin', and I promise to be here when you wake up."

CHAPTER 46

After a long, awkward silence, Mack laid his fork down and wrung his hands. "Liz," he whispered. She looked up and he saw the moisture welled in her eyes. Was she feeling what he was feeling?

"Liz," he began again. His throat closed. Where were the words he wanted to say to her? He was angry, but he wasn't angry with her for what happened to his dad, or for her not knowing Red was a jerk. She wasn't the only good woman Red had ever fooled. He was angry with himself for letting her walk away from him at the Cupid's Ball. Why couldn't he tell her? Letting her slip away from him over such a silly argument was worse than stupid. And over Bonnie Bloodworth, for crying out loud, when Bonnie meant absolutely nothing to him, and Liz meant everything. But he'd blown it and this time he was afraid it was forever.

"What, Mack?"

He shrugged. "Forget it. It wasn't important." What was the point? She'd never forgive him for the angry words spoken, and he couldn't blame her. But she had some explaining to do, too. Why had she not told him about Duncan instead of keeping him hidden away in her room? He was a precious kid. If he had a son—

His lips tightened. He supposed the neighbor who accompanied Liz to Heartsboro was the baby's nanny. Liz had plenty of opportunity to tell him she had a kid. Never would he have imagined that she would be one to hide her own child, regardless of the circumstances surrounding his birth. What kind of mother would do that? Mack's emotions spun from one extreme to the other. He loved her passionately; yet, at the same time, he resented her with equal fervor for not being honest with him about the baby.

Liz had always been able to read Mack's emotions, and she felt confident she wasn't misreading him now. He was in love with her, just as she was in love with him. She saw it in his eyes, the way he looked at her. It was in his voice, the way it quaked when he said her name. The tilt of his head, the same way he did years ago when they sat in the booth at Hearties, and he gave her a promise ring. Her stomach knotted, recalling the letter he sent from college. Wasn't it time to forgive? She had no idea what he might've been going through at the time he mailed it. Was it exam week? Was he about to lose his scholarship? He obviously regretted it, and hadn't she made her share of mistakes? Though she was hurt at the Cupid's Ball, was it really his fault? It was a set-up and now that she had time to think about it, she knew it. Mack was not Bonnie Jo Bloodworth's perfect love. He was hers. Always had been. It was evident he knew it, just as she'd known all along.

The waiter brought the ticket and after Mack paid the bill, they walked out of the restaurant and headed back to the hospital. The tension between them had definitely eased, and the ride seemed much shorter on the way back than it did on the way to the restaurant. Mack was quiet, but he had a lot on his mind. She could only imagine his remorse at the harsh words he must've spoken to his father after that surprise encounter at breakfast. Now, that he could be losing his dad, it was understandable that the misspoken words would be haunting him. Liz understood because she'd come down hard on Maggie, also, but Maggie could take it. It wasn't the first time Liz had blown her off, and wouldn't likely be the last, but then Maggie wasn't the one dying.

The doctor met them in the hall. "Your dad did have a slight heart attack, Mr. Mackenzie, but it appears there's no damage. He's in excellent physical condition for a man his age. I'll keep him overnight for observation, but you can take him home in the morning."

"You're discharging him, so soon?" Mack's brows shot to his hairline.

The doctor stiffened. "I thought you'd be pleased to know he's doing so good. He tells me he lives with you. I know you enjoy his company. He's a delight with such a great sense of humor. He's kept the nurses in stitches."

"But Doc, I don't get it. I was with him less than an hour ago, and he looked horrible. He could hardly talk."

The doctor rubbed his hand over the back of his neck. "I don't know which room you were in, sir, but Mr. James Mackenzie and his lady friend were laughing so hard while you were gone, the nurse had to go in and quiet them down."

It took a few seconds for Mack to compose his thoughts. He turned to Liz. "Are you thinking what I'm thinking?"

Her face split into a craggy smile. "I think I'm following you."

Mack opened the door to his dad's room, and followed Liz in. They glared at Jim. Then at Maggie—then at Liz.

"Pop, you look as if you've made an incredible recovery."

Jim glanced at Maggie and winked. "Now that you mention it, I reckon I am feeling a mite better. Did you two kids enjoy your lunch?"

Mack looked at Liz. "It was good." He eased up to the edge of his dad's bed. "Hmm . . . you even have your color back. Amazing. Don't you find it amazing, Liz?"

She feigned a look of disbelief. "Simply amazing." Liz picked up a small container from off the bedside table. She sprinkled the contents on the back of her hand. "Look, Mack. Powder. This looks exactly like the substance on your jeans."

He nodded. "Looks the same, alright, but it would be impossible for it to be the same thing, since I didn't go near that table."

Liz chewed on her bottom lip. "No, you didn't. But you did lay your hand on your dear, dying daddy's forehead. Poor man was as pale as—"

Mack finished it for her. "As pale as white talcum powder? I smell a conspiracy, and somebody better start talking."

Maggie and Jim exchanged glances, then exploded in laughter. Maggie said, "I confess. We're guilty, but Jim and I know something that you and Liz don't know."

"I'm listening."

"We both felt guilty and blamed ourselves for what happened at the diner this morning."

Mack stood looking stoic with his arms crossed over his broad chest.

Maggie glanced back at Jim for approval, and he nodded. "After we both insisted it was our fault, we realized we couldn't both be responsible. Or could we? Before we admitted to you kids what we'd done, we needed time alone to sort it all out. That's why we pulled that little ruse." She squeezed Jim's hand and giggled. "For weeks, I've been sending emails to a handsome guy I met on the internet, but I was signing them Elizabeth. The handsome guy in the picture signed his name, 'Doyle.' After things went awry at the diner, Jim and I talked and discovered he was Doyle and I was Elizabeth."

Mack's jaw seemed to have come unhinged. "I can't believe what I'm hearing."

Maggie said, "Don't be too hard on us, Mack. We both meant well. Your dad wanted to find you a wife, and I wanted to find Liz a husband. If you want to blame us for something, then blame us for wanting the two of you to be happy. We finally pieced our stories together and discovered the break-up years ago was not the fault of either of you. Mack, she never loved Carter the way she loved you. Liz was devastated, when she received your letter."

Mack grunted. Was this supposed to be a joke? *She* was devastated? What did she expect him to do, after getting the note from her boyfriend? Show up at the wedding with a wedding present? His jaw jutted forward. "Doesn't matter, now."

Liz's face turned red. "He's right. It doesn't matter."

Mack felt sick on his stomach. And to think he almost made a dope of himself when he came close to pouring his heart out at the restaurant. His lip quivered as their gaze locked. He wanted to hurt her the way she hurt him. He blurted, "I could forgive a woman for dumping me, but never for trying to hide her own child. Where's Duncan, anyway? When did you plan to tell me, you had a kid? I would never have known if I hadn't happened to be on the porch when you snuck him out there, thinking you were alone."

Maggie giggled, though Liz didn't find it humorous.

"What? You thought Duncan was *my* baby?"

"Are you saying he isn't?"

"That's exactly what I'm saying." Liz's mouth gaped open. "You didn't think . . . oh m'goodness, that's too funny."

"Go ahead. Make fun of me. There's nothing you can do anymore to hurt me, Liz. I made up my mind years ago not to let another woman jerk me around the way you did but I almost broke that promise. I hope you and your fiancé, Mr. Allen Albertson will be very happy."

"He's not my fiancé, Mack. He means nothing to me."

"Really? You seriously expect me to believe that?" Mack pressed his lips into a long tight line and shook his finger at Liz. "Then whose boots did I stumble over when I laid Duncan in his crib?"

"Oh, Mack, I was babysitting so Duncan's mommy and daddy could attend the ballgame. The boots belonged to Duncan's father. Allen is no longer my realtor."

"Are you saying you aren't marrying him?"

"Of course not. I heard two conflicting stories about the Lunch Counter building. Your side and Allen's side. I knew which one I wanted to believe."

"Wanted to believe? But you still don't trust me, do you?"

"Mack, I was hurt by you, sixteen years ago. I agree it will only pour fuel on the fire to rehash the past, and I can't promise you that I can get it out of my mind. It's all I've thought about for sixteen years. I wish I could forget."

"I hurt *you*? What about what you did to me, Liz?" He shoved his palm forward. "No. Don't answer. We both know what you did."

Maggie stuck her fingers in her mouth and let out a shrill whistle. The room came to attention. "Would you two hush for a minute, long enough for Jim and me to tell what we know? It'll answer a lot of questions for you both." Her expression was tender as she reached for Jim's hand. "After Jim and I put our stories together, we discovered there was more to the breakup than either of you know. I explained to Jim that Mack dumped you. But he said it was the other way around. As it turns out, neither of you dumped the other. It was Carter Blackstone who maliciously drove a wedge between you."

Liz's palm shot forward. "Maggie, don't. I know how you feel about Carter, so—"

"Liz, hear me out. Jim says Carter wrote Mack that you were no longer wearing his ring. He asked whether to send it to Mack's home address or to the dorm. He counted on Mack reacting as he did."

Liz's eyes widened. "Is that . . . is it true?"

Mack nodded. "Of course, it's true. That's why I wrote saying you could do *whatever* with the ring. I didn't want it."

"Oh, Mack, I didn't take off the ring until after I received your curt letter. I was crushed. I couldn't believe you could send such a cruel note with no explanation."

Mack said, "Pop remembered it exactly the way it was. You can't imagine how I felt when the guy wrote that you two were dating."

"Oh, Mack, Carter lied. I didn't date him for months after the breakup. I was deeply hurt, and he appeared genuinely sympathetic. He kept pursuing me, although he knew I was still in love with you."

Liz felt as if a huge boulder was lifted from her chest. The intensely heated words spoken earlier seemed to have evaporated into thin air. All the bitterness and anger she held toward Mack had disappeared. There was so much she wanted to say, but if she opened her mouth, sixteen years of heartache would gush out in sobs.

Maggie chimed in. "So now that you two have the whole story, I think it's high time to kiss and make up. It's obvious you're both still very much in love. Jim and I went to a lot of trouble to get you to this point."

Liz crossed her arms over her chest. "Hold on. There is one more thing I need you to clear up for me, Mack. You don't have to answer if you don't want to. But I've wondered how you could possibly know so much about babies if you've never had one."

His eyes twinkled. "That's easy to answer. I worked in the church nursery for five years, where I acquired my Burp master's degree." He held her in his unwavering gaze. "I've spent a lifetime trying to forget you, Liz, and now I feel like such an idiot for wasting sixteen years—all because I didn't give you the option to explain."

Liz reached out and grasped his arm. "It's not your fault, Mack. I'm so sorry. Carter was a manipulator. I should've known he was behind the whole thing. If only I had written you back—"

"But we didn't know. However, thanks to Pop and Maggie we've been handed a second chance at love. I say we waste no time getting started." Then, placing his hands on either side of her face, he tilted his head and kissed her tenderly. "We can't change the past, Liz, but we have a wonderful future to look forward to. You're gonna open a bakery, and I'll be eating pecan pie every day for the rest of my life, just as you once promised. How much better can it get?"

The laughter in the room overtook the tears rolling down their cheeks. Mack walked over and threw his arm around his father's shoulder. "I don't know how you did it, Pop, but you did great. Of course, Mama would've recognized Liz's picture right away. She was always very fond of Liz."

"I can't take credit, son. The Good Lord had a hand in this from the beginning. Now, you kids scat. You have a lot of courting to catch up on, and I don't want you wasting time, sitting in a hospital room. So, shoo. Besides, Maggie and I have some courting of our own to do. I have a strong feeling the love dust is about to fall. You understand about the love dust, don't you Elizabeth? It's in the Bible, you know. Talks about it in the book of Ephesians, Chapter five, verse two."

Mack popped his hand to his forehead. "Dad, please don't start that again. We've had this conversation before. It's best not to share your thoughts. The men in the green coats may come haul you off before you have time to finish."

Liz said, "Wait, Mack. He has my curiosity up. Mr. Jim, you say there's a scripture that talks about something called love dust?"

He gave a thumb's up. "Yep." He reached over and lifted a Bible from the bedside table and patted the front cover with his hand. "It's in here, all right. Plain as day. But now, it's real important that you understand the law behind it in order to experience it."

Mack walked away with his head down and clasped his hands together behind his neck.

Liz said, "And what law would that be, Mr. Jim?"

"Well, according to the Good Book, you must first, walk in love." He nodded as if agreeing with his own statement. "That's it. That's the law. Then Bam! It happens."

Liz said, "It? What do you mean? What happens?"

"I'm saying that's when the Love Dust falls."

Mack looked at Liz and shook his head. "Liz, Pop is misquoting a verse but trying to convince him he's wrong is a waste of breath."

Jim's brow shot up. "I know what I'm talking about, son. The Bible says it plain and simple. Christ has love dust, and He wants us to have it, too."

Mack cleared his throat. "But Pop, the Bible doesn't say, 'Christ has love dust.' It says, 'Walk in love, as Christ also hath loved us.'"

Jim's eyes widened. "Well, I'll be. You finally said it."

"No, I didn't, Pop. I was quoting from the Bible."

"Of course, you were, and you were right. Like you said, Christ has love dust." A broad smile stretched across Jim's leathery face as he motioned for Maggie. "Come over here and stand by me, my little Magpie and wait for it. It's coming. I feel it." His eyes muddled with happy tears. "There's no doubt about it, it's on the way." He suddenly broke out in explosive laughter and held out his hands, as if he were catching something falling from above. "Hold your hands up, darlin'. Don't you see it? Love Dust, straight from Heaven," he gasped. "It's so strong in this room, I can feel it, taste it, smell it, hear it and see it."

Tears trailed down Maggie's face. She rubbed her cheek, then looked at her hand.

Jim's lip quivered. "You feel it too, don't you, my little Magpie?"

"I do, Jim! I do feel it." She held her head back and opened her mouth. "I can see it, feel it and taste it. How sweet it is. You're right, Jim. It's real and it's falling all over this room."

Liz twirled around in circles with both hands lifted in the air. She squealed, "Oh m'goodness, Mack. Your dad is right. It's falling, and it's fresh."

Jim's face lit up. "You do see it, don't you, Elizabeth."

Mack said, "Pop, she—"

Liz touched his lips to silence him. Then holding her palm in the air, while Mack watched, she slowly brought her hand down and licked the tip of her fingers. "Hmm . . ."

Mack's eyes squinted. "What are you doing?"

"Shh! I'm thinking."

The room grew silent.

She gnawed on her fist. Seconds later, she squealed. "I think I've got it. I know what to do with it."

Mack's jaw dropped. "Have you all gone nuts?"

Liz said, "If I were to combine a couple of cups of sugar, a half-cup of light corn syrup, a half-cup of water and a tad of salt and cook it to a hard-boil stage, then slowly pour it over a couple of stiff egg whites—"

Where was she going with this? Without making a sound, Mack, Jim and Maggie waited in eager anticipation for her to finish her thought.

Liz raised her finger in the air. "Then if I added a teaspoon of vanilla and a heaping Tablespoonful of Love Dust and beat for say, about four or five minutes, I think I'd have a winning icing recipe for our wedding cake."

Mack lifted both hands, palms up and looked toward the ceiling, then licked his lips. His face split into a craggy smile. "Well, I'll be dog. It's Love Dust. Who woulda thought it?"

On a cold February day in a hospital room in the little town with a big heart, two hearts mended while two hearts blended . . . on the day the love dust fell.

www.ingramcontent.com/pod-product-compliance
Lightning Source LLC
Chambersburg PA
CBHW020400260626
47156CB00007B/2190